CAMPARI
for
BREAKFAST

Sara Crowe

BLACK SWAN

TRANSWORLD PUBLISHERS
61–63 Uxbridge Road, London W5 5SA
www.transworldbooks.co.uk

Transworld is part of the Penguin Random House group of companies whose
addresses can be found at global.penguinrandomhouse.com

Penguin
Random House
UK

First published in Great Britain in 2014 by Doubleday
an imprint of Transworld Publishers
Black Swan edition published 2015

A CIP catalogue record for this book
is available from the British Library.

ISBN 9780552779647

Typeset in Berkeley by Kestrel Data, Exeter, Devon.
Printed and bound by CPI Group (UK) Ltd, Croydon, CR0 4YY.

Pengiun Random House is committed to a sustainable
future for our business, our readers and our planet. This book
is made from Forest Stewardship Council® certified paper.

MIX
Paper from
responsible sources
FSC® C016897

1 3 5 7 9 10 8 6 4 2

© Nikki Holland

Sara Crowe is best known as an actress. She has appeared on television, stage and film, including the iconic *Four Weddings and a Funeral*. She has won the Olivier Award for Best Supporting Actress, the Variety Club Best Actress Award and the London Critics Circle Theatre Award for Most Promising Newcomer. Sarah's West End appearances include *Private Lives, Calendar Girls* and *Hay Fever*. She has also toured with *Acorn Antiques: the Musical*, and appeared in *The City Madam* for the Royal Shakespeare Company.

Campari for Breakfast is Sara's first novel, inspired by a crumbling old house and a love of English eccentricity. She began writing as a child and has also written comedy sketches for television and stand-up. But in the tradition of late developers, she recently re-opened the notebooks of yesteryear and some of the characters climbed out.

DISCARDED

www.transworldbooks.co.uk

For Allen and for Neta

The Commonplace Book:

The Commonplace Book was not only a diary, but a scrapbook and book of wisdom. It was often given to encourage learning and interests in children. A most personal journal in which quotes and comments are collected along with cuttings, letters, recipes.

Essentially one's own book of life.

Giovanni Rucellai was an Italian poet from the olden days. He described his Commonplace as 'a salad of many herbs'.

The Commonplace Book of Coral Garden: Volume 5
Green Place, 3 June 1986

Newspaper Cutting, 'Births, Marriages and Deaths', *Egham Echo*, May 20th 1986:

Evelyn William Garden 1898–1986
Survived by his daughters Coral Elizabeth Garden and Buddleia
Rose Bowl

We do not expect our deaths, though they are inevitable. Had he known he would die on Tuesday, I'm sure he'd have cleared things on Sunday, just as you would if you had a meeting to prepare for.

He left me instructions to destroy his papers. But as my shredder only takes one page at a time, Buddleia came to help me with a bonfire in the garden. It had a sad flame that hissed quietly, its smoke hung in the sunbeams. Beams that prevailed against the odds on that unsteady morning. We each managed our side, in case the wind should catch it. Four score years' worth of papers; the towering blaze of his life.

I prodded gently at piles of old cards, Easter rabbits, Christmas angels, a dental appointment slip from the back of a diary, receipts and vouchers. And then, through the heat and haze, I noticed Buddleia pick up an envelope. It had fallen away from the other documents in the thick of the pyre and lay at the edge of the bonfire on a bed of last autumn's leaves. Perhaps providence made it suggest itself and curiosity made her retrieve it – because there shrouded in the remains of a plain envelope we discovered the truth.

The Commonplace Book of Coral Garden: Volume 5
Green Place, December 1986

Copy of letter:

> Green Place
> Clockhouse Lane
> Egham

Dear Nicholas,

I'm writing to tell you that it would give me great pleasure to have Sue to stay with me at Green Place. I know that these are trying times for you both and I humbly offer such support as I am able.

My companion has a daughter who is with us in the holidays, so you may reassure Sue that she would not always be surrounded by the elderly.

I would be delighted to offer her an allowance of £50 per month for such modest needs as she may require. I am sure she would be like a sunbeam around the house, as I hope I may be to her.

My heart is with you at this dark time.

Yours truly,

Coral

Sue

Sunday 4ᵗʰ January 1987

IT WAS EASY persuading Dad to let me leave. In my heart I'd hoped he would object, but since it would give him more time alone with Ivana, he didn't. Persuading myself was easy too. Stay in Titford or go to Egham? Most of my friends are having gap years picking strawberries, living in communes, whereas I want to go straight into life with no gap, and earn good money doing it. And so Titford holds nothing for a girl of my ambition any more.

It's an understandable and terrible fact that Dad's taste has deserted him since we lost mum. I think he just got so lonely that anybody would do. He met Ivana at Titford golf club. She was playing a round with his boss and Dad was to take them to dinner. She'd really been after the boss, but settled for Dad's attentions because the boss was a terrible lecture. I don't know much about her, other than she comes from somewhere in Denmark. She just appeared out of nowhere like bad wind.

The only things I have to show for my life so far are a love of words and some interesting relatives, and mum always drilled me to make the best of what I've got. So in the end my decision has absolutely nothing to do with Dad or Ivana. Ultimately I think Green Place will be a good place to write.

Aunt Coral is my mother's sister, though they are twenty-four years apart (my mother was a late addition) and this is what makes Aunt Coral a lot more like my nana than my aunt. She's the sort of person who likes elderly singers in long gowns and floral teapots, so it was with a box of specialist teabags and a bunch of early daffodils that I arrived on her step at the start of the week. I was surprised when she opened the door, I'd forgotten how small she is and how clever, but she's sociably skilled and made me feel at my ease pretty fast.

My first impressions of Green Place were actually second impressions because I had been taken there as a child to visit the various relatives, although we hadn't been recently due to my Grandfather's turbulant Will. It's a grade two listed building, so big it has to be split into sections like countries within a continent. The West Wing is the only part of the house that's heated, so I have to wear my coat in the rest of the house as if I am going outside. I could fit my house in Titford four hundred times into Aunt Coral's; I never noticed how small it really was until now.

You approach off the B4532, Clockhouse Lane, and then towards the bottom you turn right between two brick pillars with lions on the top. The right hand lion is headless, just a body with chipped mossy paws, but the left hand one is intact and looks somewhat smug. Then a long drive bends this way and that for almost a mile, and after the second bend, Green Place comes into view. It hits you like a dream, like a beautiful private Palace, and you get the feeling that it isn't really 1987 any more once you get to the top.

Glorious gardens flow up in graceful tears from Clockhouse Lane, and crumbling paths lead to sunlawns, framed by flowerbeds that need freeing from the thorns. An old Croquet Hut houses the mallets and hoops that have once seen busier times. There are orchards, rockeries and rose trails, a swing seat, and a house full of chairs. The back faces of the building command the rippling hills, and birds hover on distant currants like little specks of dust on the wind.

To the rear of the house off the kitchen there's a magnificent sweeping terrace, with a private pool at the heart, where Delia, Aunt Coral's companion, goes swimming every day, despite it being January. She is a hearty, bohemiam sort of woman, and often swims in the nudey. Her skin tone is peachy and fragrant, like a Victorian soap ad, and her hair looks freshly brunette, though her complexion appears born fair. Two forlorn, round eyes dominate an equally round face, under a holy page boy hair cut that requires daily tucking under.

Aunt Coral on the other hand is quite different. When she's in her swimsuit she cuts a neat little figure, but is quite self-conscious at the poolside and walks backwards along the terrace if she knows someone is behind her, especially her lodger Admiral Little, who is the apple of her eye.

The first time the Admiral stayed at Green Place was during a blizzard. He'd answered an ad that Aunt Coral had placed in *The Lady* magazine three months after Grandfather died, which said 'rooms require modest updating, would suit outdoors enthusiast. Two energetic ladies also in residence within the house.'

They weren't prepared for him to stay overnight, but he had to, because he couldn't get back down the drive. So they decided to put him to bed in the East Wing as a precaution, for they weren't sure what to do with a *man* in the house when they hadn't yet seen his references. (They knew he would never be able to find his way back to the West Wing once he was in the East.)

The East Wing is a kin to the Arctic, even with a blow heater, blankets and whisky, but lucky for them the Admiral is a Naval man, and prefers the great outdoors, so he ended up taking the rooms and sparing their lady blushes.

I had to follow directions to get to his suite. You have to go up to the landing, turn left off the hall, right past the nursery, then left again into the East Wing, first right, and then follow the plates. The celebration pieces depict the royals in front of various sunsets, and act as a guide along the wall in case the Admiral loses his way.

When you eventually get to his suite, it's a bit like a gentleman's club, with a bed of Napoleon and a collection of Toby Jugs which belonged to Aunt Coral's father. It's definitely worth the journey, if only to view the antiques.

Unbeknownst to the Admiral, Aunt C hides behind the curtains in the mornings, watching in secret as he drives off in his car on errands.

'Oh Sue,' she confides, 'I'm not dead yet.'

The interesting thing about the Admiral is that he is remarkably slow on the uptake and totally blind to Aunt Coral's feelings for him. She could walk past him with no top on and he wouldn't even drop his pipe.

Aunt Coral's favourite daily custom is to have a drink with her tenants before dinner, (especially the Admiral). In winter they sit in the drawing room, where the early evening light is so nice. Conversations are punctuated by the Westminster chimes of the mantle clock: it has a deep tick and whir, and a sixteen-ding chime that's followed by the count of the hour.

Dinner is quite a big business and is normally prepared by Mrs Bunion. She is cleaner, cook and housekeeper at Green Place and comes several days a week. Her tasks are many and varied, and include some light gardening and fisselling. She is also required to perform the duty of 'Bat Patrol', for Green Place houses many bats. Mrs Bunion finishes her work just before dinnertime, when she will leave something tasty on the stove, and then her finale job is to go and ring the dinner gong. The Ad and the ladies then come down and congregate for a drink before dinner. It's a thousand miles from Titford, the microwave, and Dad and Ivana.

Mrs Bunion comes from a poor family. When she was young she was sent to Egham on an apprenticeship. She learnt her many culinary skills at the hands of a cruel Head Chef at Egham Grammar School, and feels she landed on her feet the day she answered Aunt Coral's call. She makes all the Green Place food from scratch, even the bread, and every dessert comes with custard.

It's all right for the oldies, they can eat all the full fat foods and then take heart pills, but for me it isn't so easy and I am struggling to control my wasteline. Unfortunately nothing makes Aunt Coral happier than watching me eat, and nothing makes me happier either. For don't the Chinese say 'when there is sadness in your heart, you should feed your stomach'?

My new bedroom, the Grey Room, is in the West Wing, above the ladies' bedrooms. It is a small attic room facing the pool, that was used for staff in the olden days. Late at night I conjure the faces of long-dead inhabitants out of the shadows. If I were a more nervy type I would certainly give myself the willies.

But the most unsettling thing about bedtime at Green Place is that Delia curses in her sleep. Sometimes she sounds like she'd like to give you twenty lashes with her bath cap, and I have to reassure myself.

Aunt Coral loves to tell you how her life was incomplete before she met Delia, which is why, after a few trial holidays together, she offered her bargain board to come and live here. Delia, like me, hasn't got much money, but she's an excellent and loving companion to Aunt Coral even if she does say 'fuck' in her sleep. They compliment each other perfectly: Aunt Coral is a traditionalist, a pragmatist, an hundred per cent Nana, whereas Delia is joyous and o'reverand and brings Aunt Coral to life. They're both very interested in me and are always asking about my writing.

In spite of appearances, and her big house, I think Aunt Coral must be a little straps for cash, hence her taking in lodgers. And now she has to give me an allowance as well, but I think the Admiral at least pays a hefty rent, which must be where it comes from.

It's cold and stormy tonight, as is January's way, so I've wrapped myself in old blankets, and I'm listening to the rain hit the pool cover. Here in the stillness of the Grey Room, I'm flooded with memories of mum. I can't believe she's not here any more, my mind just can't absorb it. It would make more sense to me to find her hiding in a bandstand than to accept that she is gone.

Her Christian name was Buddleia, after the plant famous for attracting butterflies, but she preferred to be called Blue, as Buddleia is easily mispronounced. You say, 'Bud-lee-a', as in 'bud', the flower, 'lee', the calm side of a ship, followed by an 'a'. She said that blue was the colour of the flowers, although I used to argue they were purple. We had agreed to differ on that some time before the end.

The long drive running up from Clockhouse Lane happened to be lined with buddleia. Their scent is woodier than the lilac and not so sweet, just as she wasn't sweet but intense. She met Dad on a plane in the sixties – he was a passenger, she was a stewardess, and almost nine months later they had me, after a shot gun wedding.

I think Mum was rebelling from glamour names in calling me Sue. I think she'd have preferred to come from a line of Sues, Janes and Sarahs, and not from Corals and Cameos. But she had a way of saying it, that still made it sound like a glamour name: 'Soo', she said, as though it was the name of a quiet Chinese Princess.

The first time I went on a plane with her, I was four, and anxious when I couldn't pop my ears. We'd been on a chocolate buying mission to Holland, because she still got the cheap air fares. I remember I'd been crying because my ears were so uncomfortable, so she gave me some tiny chocolate clogs from a packet to chew on. But I put the clogs in my ears.

Yet she was my chief supporter and defender of all my deficiencies, explaining to Mrs Hughson from the maths department at school, 'Sue is not daft, but talk of algebra and her mind goes the other way.' She persuaded Mrs Hughson that she just didn't understand *who I was*, and that the minute she did, a whole new world would appear.

Once at school sports day, I must have been about 7, I was running in the ninety metres and I was a hot tip to win. I was warming up at the start line, all wound up and nervous, and I spotted mum standing by the sideline in front of the crowds watching. I got off to a flying start, leaving everyone well behind me, but trying to run past mum had a peculiar effect on my emotions and for some reason, instead of finishing the race I ran into her arms instead. I was very embarrassed afterwards. The crowds snickered and one Dad said I was a bird brain.

But mum said 'If I were running, and I saw you standing there, I'd have done exactly the same thing. How canny of you to know, it's not about winning – it's about loving.' She managed to make the silliest thing I'd ever done sound profound.

She was also crafty, and replied to the notes I left for the fairies without my ever finding out. I still check under the watering can – or at least, I did.

And she was chaotic, at a loss in the kitchen, and was always being given joke cookbooks for awful chefs and hapless mums, including one called *This is a Spoon*. So she tended to keep things simple, such as floppy sandwiches presented in a rush to my lunch box. She wasn't a technical sort of mother, she was more a magician.

To have been the object of her love is the most beautiful thing I have known. Of course I took it for granted. I had no idea it would fade away.

She often used to say to me, 'You are a joy and a care.'

'Why a care?' I would ask.

'In case I should lose you,' she'd say. She was born serious.

When people ask me if I'm OK, I say I am, but how could I be? I have seen my dead mother in a box; my live mother has vanished. But one has to lie, to make others feel comfy. One has to join in the conspiracy. It's a curious phenomena, the unmentionable, and knowing about it makes me feel twice my age.

I can't tell you how much it hurts sometimes, how tired I get of being strong, and what a relief it is to say I am devastated, if only to a piece of paper. But we are so British about these things in Britain, we try so hard to hold it all in. It makes me laugh sometimes, because when else is it OK to cry? I believe the Italians have it right. I've heard that at funerals they even have official criers to help lead the wailing.

When I struggle under clouds like this and I'm full of hopeless longing, what saves me is my writing. I can think about something different and I don't have to be Sue Bowl for a while.

The Nun's Bonnet Never Sees Daylight

A SKETCH
By Sue Bowl

It was a navy bonnet with a cherry motif on the top resembling a school badge. She put it on the top shelf as a reminder of her old life.

Her room was like all the others, bed, book and candle. She had three habits, one in the wash, one in the cupboard and one to wear.

'Fedora! You are always late!' called Mother, 'Why is your head in the clouds?'

'I am with Jesus, Mother,' said Fedora.

'Then you have no excuses,' Mother said, scurrying off to Maxims.

Fedora glanced up at the bonnet she had arrived in, now in the shadowy recess on her top shelf. The old days were gone for ever, and the new days were yet to be born.

After dinner this evening I was relaxing with my new housemates, the fire was trying to get up and the Admiral was enjoying his pipe, when Aunt Coral was taken by one of her searing insights, which often take place at this sort of time, subsequent to a gin.

'I think, Sue, that you come from a bygone age, that you don't belong to your own generation,' she said. 'You remind me of a time of seasonal strawberries, a time when briefs were large—'

'And kept locked,' added Delia.

My cheeks let me down with a small blush. It is irritating to think they're so sure that I'm some sort of sexual novice. I have actually had many experiences of desire in my mind and I am easily arouselled by the poets. And back at home I have come close to kissing at least once. So Ivana may proclaim that I am very innocent for a girl of my age, (as if she would know anything about being innocent), but it is not strictly the case. I just don't like to go on about it.

'Oh I have my methods,' I said, trying to move them off the topic of briefs with an enigmatic answer, while the blush possessed my face.

'Is it love that you like to write about?' asked Delia.

I thought my answer would have thrown them off the scent of briefs, but Delia had managed to pick it up again.

'Oh no, not really love,' I said, 'I've got a book of writing exercises. It's nothing really, it's just for fun.'

'For example?' she said.

'Well . . .' I went on, with the blush raging across my chest. 'Well, say you have a list of belongings in your packing . . .'

'In your packing?' said Aunt Coral.

'The premise is an imaginary holiday,' I explained, 'and you have a list of activities you want to do when you get there, and you have to try and put unusual ones together. For example, if you've got "book", "pen" and "flip flops" in your packing, and "surfing", "dancing" and "skipping" in your activities, you could make up sentences like: "She was surfing through the book", or "Cara's flip flops were skipping beneath her", or "My pen danced down the page.'"

'And who is Cara?' asked Aunt Coral.

'She's for example,' I said. I didn't want to tell her that Cara was the name I have chosen for the heroine of a story which I have yet to put down on the page.

'Ah ha! So I might say that my feet danced into my flip flops, or the books skipped off the shelf? It's a beginner's book then is it?' asked Aunt Coral.

You can imagine that this revelation quite took my breath away.

Then she rushed off to her study to fetch the manual she considers the world authority on creative writing, and so I have come up to bed with Mr Benjamin O'Carroll's *The Dorcas Tree* under my arm.

'Let's talk about it tomorrow morning after you've had a look,' Aunt Coral called after me. 'And it'd be nice to have a little talk, just the two of us,' she added, before returning to her tenants by the fire.

I feel so lucky to have landed in a house with a wordsmith. It is a world away from Titford where I suffered a major writer's setback on the day that Ivana had the misfortune to read one of my stories. No one was supposed to read them, and well she knew that, but she sneaked under my bed when I was doing my exams and found my secret papers. That was bad enough, but to make matters worse, she had the odacity to give me a review.

'A hoot!' she proclaimed. It was very undermining. I had tried to be maganimus and open my heart and forgive, but I was devastated that she'd read it and even more devastated that she thought it was a comedy when it was a drama set in an Elizabethan prison.

Writing is more important to me than anything, though I sometimes doubt anyone will want to read the musings of a seventeen-year-old from Titford.

As I lounge here in the Grey Room, writing up a small section of the story I'm working on, my mind wanders back to the earlier subject of locked briefs, which is a matter that gravely concerns me. Love is just such a private, impossible thing, I wonder how any of us are born.

Cara

A SKETCH
By Sue Bowl

Cara turned her face to the new dawn. Childhood lay behind her, just out of reach of her soft hand. What lay ahead was a world of men who would win her. Her eyes smarted with the tears of being torn from her mother. Yet her father, so cruel to send her away so young, had said nothing, just sharpened his knives on the plinny. Suddenly from the distant hills her dear black spaniel ran towards her.

'Keeper, you must go home,' cried Cara, her heart breaking with a cute despair.

She rested upon the rude ground, and from thence, her clogs skipped off her feet.

Friday 16 January

It was on Delia's advice that I put up this notice at the local post office offering my services as a babysitter which would A, ease me fiscally, and B, help me meet new people. She told me that her daughter, Loudolle, babysits in the holidays and makes decadent extra money. (Loudolle goes to a very expensive finishing school in Alpen, Colorado, which is curious, because I know Delia is a little straps.) So as soon as I had settled in, I put up the notice and signed up with a temp agency, Pronto, and within the week I was in a position. Life can be such a whirlwind – who'd have thought I'd have left Titford, moved house and got a job all within two weeks.

It's a morning job at a café, which I thought might be somewhat chique, so you can imagine when I first arrived at the 'Toastie' it was something of a disappointment. The setting is an urbane scene, with a tyre repair place over the road. It's a canteen style of a café and part of a small parade of shops that follow the curve of a five-exit roundabout just off the A30.

There was no formal interview, or panel, or very much pressure at all, but I did have to go and meet the owner Mrs Fry that same evening at her family's flat in Egham. She looked like she meant business and had precious little time for small talk, and she offered me the job on the spot, which felt a moment of sheer destiny. It had been worth every tortured minute I spent getting myself ready to look intelligent.

So although it may not be quite the most snazzy of restaurants, I must steel myself to do it as, fiscally speaking, I can't live on £12.50 a week, not if I want to be well-dressed. The job is 'Canteen Apprentice', for the pricley fee of £2 an hour, which at four hours a day, and three mornings a week, will beef up my allowance by £24 to just over the £36 mark. Not the big time, but if you include the perk of working at close quarters with a decadent number of handsome men, I would have done it for nothing!

Mrs Fry has three sons, who I met that first evening. Icarus is by far the best looking, and if he were to show me any interest at all, I predict that I'd fall! But Sandy and Joe are not bad either! And Mrs Fry also has a daughter, poor little Mary-Margaret, who is the spitting image of Mickey Rooney. Life can be most unfair.

Sandy, the eldest Fry, is on a visit from university, and Mary-Margaret, the youngest, still goes to school. Joe has just left like me, and Icarus is a part time biker. Both Joe and Icarus work in the Toastie. It's at moments like these when I wish I didn't waver in the column between slimmish and chubby.

I nearly forgot in all the excitement that it was my seventeenth birthday yesterday. Because in the secret back places of my mind I have been worrying about how I would feel on such a day in a world without mum. But it is not the Green Place way to let a birthday slip by unnoticed, and so with some discretion at tea time, Mrs Bunion provided a chocolate cake with candles and ice cream to follow. Then the ladies presented me with a writing folio as a gift for all my thoughts. The Admiral made a gift of himself and got changed into cavalry twill trousers to come down and join us for the cake.

And with the gift of my new job to boot, my mood is surprisingly upbeat. I can't wait to get to know the ropes. I start on Monday!

Wednesday 21 January

How time flies at the Toastie. I feel I have been there for years!

I work part time, Monday to Wednesday, starting at 7.00 in the morning and ending at 11.00, unless Mrs Fry needs an after-hours. There are five of us working on breakfasts: Mrs Fry calls out the orders and takes the money up at the front, Icarus grills bacon, eggs and tomatoes, Joe makes cappuchinos, and I am on the toaster. Mueslis, fruit, and serial orders have to be fitted in around the cooked breakfasts, which causes a little bit of chaos. Nina Scrafferton is the last of the personnel, and she is a full time girl. She has a hair style so short that everyone calls her Michael.

Mrs Fry describes herself as a laps catholic, but for someone with religion she works us very hard. She's what I term a jangler, she's all bunches of keys and bracelets. How I shudder at the sound of her tinkling – though luckily it means you can always hear her coming before she's actually there.

At 9.30am I come off the toaster and go into the kitchen and start buttering up the deliveries, overseen by Mrs Fry who pounces on me if I use too much butter. When they are ready, the baguettes, rolls and sandwiches are loaded on to the Toastie van to be delivered out to the Egham borders, and to hungry office workers who could hardly imagine the humble beginnings of their lunch.

This is what women like Ivana refer to as 'life experience', though she's never had any. I think of her dossing around Titford in her car shoes and it nearly makes me spit.

It has been Joe who has helped me the most during these first few days. If you burn a round of toast when you've got a big queue of customers, the knock-on effect means that you fall behind with your orders and *that* means that pretty soon the breakfasting public will be getting cold toast, or toast that comes after they've finished eating. You can spend entire mornings behind with the toast, never managing to catch up the timing, trying to make sandwiches as well, jumping every time Mrs Fry calls your name. Joe has been very supportive, even putting the cappuchinos in jeopardy so that he could help me out.

Mrs Fry is not so patient and makes me go up to tables and apologise for late toast and docks the price off my wages. Nina Scrafferton told me that previous canteen apprentices have cracked.

Icarus hasn't said a word to me, but I have sensed him looking. He has a shocking pair of blue eyes that take in my every floor. The only thing he's said to me during this awful week is to ask if I like toast and I'm not sure if he was mocking me. Actually I adore toast and can eat six slices at a sitting, but I wasn't going to tell him that and shatter all his illusions. Nor did I want to speak against toast, because toast is his mother's livelihood. In fact I struggled to say anything at all, as his presence renders me speechless. He is dark and over six feet tall with long tousled hair, and much as I find tight trousers a bit obvious on a man, Icarus gets away with them.

Every morning around 11.00am there is a lull at Green Place when Aunt Coral and Delia are out shopping and the Admiral is at his club. So after my Toastie shift yesterday morning, I decided to get back into bed in the Grey Room and get cracking with Mr O'Carroll. In the very first chapter he suggests getting together in a writers group. It sounds like a much better way to progress into authorship as it's very hard to be your own editor, but being new to the area I don't know enough people to form a group.

On page 5 he says: 'Once you have got your group together and nominated a guru, you should try the following exercise: write a letter to yourself from a relative or friend, someone who owes you an apology. This is a healing exercise designed to aid you in any blocks. Then share and discuss your letters.' In the absence of a group I decided to do this on my own. Here it is:

Dear Sue

Forgive a very silly woman writing to you, but I only want to say
that I am so sorry I read your private story, and I am equally sorry
I misunderstood it. It's only because I am an idiot and I never had
any life experience. It was wrong of me to go under your bed and
into your private things. I am a stupid and ridiculous woman and I
ask for your forgiveness.

But I am the most sorry for being with your father. I understand that it is far too soon after your mother's death for me to be
carrying on with him and I apologise for this deeply. He is only
doing it because he is lonely. I have no excuse.

There was nothing going on before your mother died. You have
my solemn word.

Forgive me.

Ivana

*

Then I realised why the book suggests you work in a group as I spent the rest of the morning sobbing. Dad and Ivana's behaviour and their special relationship with the truth is like a thorn in my heart and it bleeds all the time. I don't know how I will ever know what was really going on between them and when it started. Nobody will tell me the truth.

I was still up in the Grey Room when I heard Aunt Coral and Delia get home. One of the problems with living in someone else's house is that you can't retreat in your bedroom all day, not if they know you're at home, so I dried my face and went downstairs.

They were in the kitchen unloading their bags and spotted my red eyes in a nanasecond. I think Aunt Coral was about ready to phone an ambulance. She dropped her shopping and swept me up.

'Oh dear! Delia, chocolate, quickly!'

There is nothing on earth so upsetting as kindness and it unlocked everything I was trying to hold on to: Mum, Dad, Ivana, toast, page 5, the letter.

'May I see the letter?' asked Aunt Coral, and in spite of being a very private person I didn't hesitate before I went to get it. My heart was crying out to unburden itself, even unto the elderly.

'Let's think about the positives first. You are a beautiful girl,' said Aunt Coral as she finished the letter, clearly launching a rescue mission.

'Beautiful girl, that's a positive,' said Delia.

'And Ivana is a woman in the last chance salon when it comes to affairs with men,' said Aunt Coral. 'She's a double divorcee and that can't be easy for her. Women like that can't help themselves but pounce on every man that arises.'

'And *you* should know,' said Delia, which I thought was a little unfair on Aunt Coral, although obviously given a green flag she would definitely pounce on the Admiral.

'What I am trying to say,' continued Aunt Coral unthwarted, 'is that one shouldn't marry too often or one will become known as a colourful character. But the other side of the coin is that everybody has a hungry heart.'

'You can't make me feel sorry for Ivana,' I said.

'No,' she said. 'But it may help if you try. You're very young, but old enough to know that life is cruel. As for your father, it's true a grieving man will long for a little comfort. We should have a nice talk about it later, quietly on our own,' she said, glowering at Delia who didn't know when to stop with her jokes.

I soaked her beige cardigan with my tears and emerged into the sunshine again. Aunt Coral is wise beyond her years.

'Now,' she said, 'you should absolutely not attempt to do this kind of emotional work on your own, and in the absence of a group, Delia and I will stand in for you. If you want to continue with the course that is.'

'I shall write a letter to myself from my ex-husband,' said Delia, 'and we can all have a jolly good laugh.'

'And I could advertise immediately in the post office for more members,' said Aunt Coral. They were chomping with the bit between their teeth and I was totally carried along. Soon they were steaming ahead debating what we would call it and where we would have it and when it would be and what snacks would be served. Anybody'd have thought that they didn't have much to do.

When the Admiral arrived home and came in to knock his pipe out in the kitchen, he got infected by the excitement too.

'Does your group admit gentlemen?' he asked.

The thought of doing emotional work in a group containing the Admiral was more than Aunt Coral could hold on to. 'Yes!' she exploded.

In my opinion Admiral Avery Little is a difficult man for Aunt Coral to have got eyes for. After dinner, when we go and relax in the drawing room, although the Ad is present, he never really joins in the conversation, but is king of his pipe and books. As a consequence he misses all the juicy bits we ladies talk about and only joins in when something really dull comes up, such as all the best parking spots in Egham. But to give him credit the Admiral didn't miss the fact that I'd been crying, and kindly offered to drop me at the Toastie next week so I don't have to get the bus.

The Commonplace Book of Coral Garden: Volume 1
Green Place, May 22 1929
(Seven years today)

Hickory dickory dock, this is seven o'clock. I am an early riser, a lark while the others are owls, so I am being trained to stay in my bed until 7 and have been given a clock for my birthday. I have learnt the time from the hickory mouse that runs around the clock face, before I had only the sound of Mother's passing slippers to tell me it was a polite time to get up. The long hand must be straight at the top and the short hand must be about where a mouse's nose would be if it were running away from the top. And then the second hand must be as one with the long hand and not a tick before.

Birthday news

Father called me into his study just before breakfast today. I was concerned that I might be in trouble, because he caught me up and about at a quarter to six. I knocked on his door, and the great handle turned. I was expecting a scolding, but he was there sweetly in his singlet and pyjamas and he presented me with this Commonplace Book. He has already put in some cuttings for me, which are about something called 'The British Empire'.

Mother bought me a sailor suit, the one on the dummy in Thomas Tyrelle. It is of a poplin of cornflower-blue, with salty white anchors on the pockets. This was in addition to a new frock and bloomers to wear when we're walking the dogs. She says Green Place girls are fashion plates even in ruftie tufties.

Nature news

There was a slow worm on the pipe outside my window earlier, but before I had time to draw it, Terry and Ross had a fight. Ross is jealous of Terry for many reasons, not least his shiny red coat. We have to paint Ross's bald bits with eczema cream, while lucky Terry gets to sleep in the laundry. I am sorry for Ross, because he's treated like a dog, while Terry is treated more like the third child. Mother and Father bought Terry from Red Setter Rescue, but Cameo and I found Ross straying and we begged for him to be given a home. Cameo is so affable, she has M and F round her finger, although she's only two! Even when I am just pushing her around the garden in her pram, I find her really good company.

Sue

WELL YOU SHOULD have seen their faces when I got out of the Bentley at the Toastie this morning! Mrs Fry's eyes bulged as though she had a condition.

'Pick you up at eleven Sue, I'm looking forward to Group!' yelled the Admiral as he bay parked.

'Thanks a lot,' I shouted.

'Avery Little helps!' he bellowed, calling out his motto.

So as I approached the toaster on my seventh day as canteen apprentice, I was relishing in the triumphs that had already featured that morning. I'd got out of a Bentley, I'd get back in one too and, though they were seniors, I now had a group. I went straight on to the toaster and of course Mrs Fry could not stop goggling at me.

'Who was that?' asked Joe, passing me a cappuchino with his signature chocolate twist.

'Was it your Grandpa?' asked Michael.

Icarus asked the same question, but silently and with nicer trousers.

'That? That's just the Admiral,' I said. Mrs Fry was straining.

I thought about asking Joe if he wanted to join the group, but though he is beyond a gentleman to me, I think he is still a bit young for that sort of thing. Actually we are the same age, but everyone knows how boys lag.

Poor Joe is a boy whose body doesn't belong to him. He is even taller than Icarus but not half as well-built. I could never see Joe in the same way I see Icarus, because, for someone like me who is quite strapping, Joe is the sort of boy I could injure, whereas Icarus is much more the type who will throw you on the floor and ravish you census without so much as batting an eye.

Friday 30 January

The Inaugural Egham Writing Group

Aunt Coral suggested that our newly formed writing group should meet, when availability allows, on select Fridays after dinner. I think it's a good idea, although the after-dinner slot has been worrying me, as it's a time when I am capable of little else than digestion and sleep. Aunt Coral also decided, after a great deal of thought, that we should meet in the conservatory, which has far-reaching views out over the pool and down to the Egham borders. So this evening, after another sumptuous Mrs Bunion dinner, Aunt Coral, Delia, the Admiral and I made our way to inaugurate.

Aunt Coral had freely offered herself as guru, which was a load off my mind because I thought I might have to. But everyone knows the best gurus in the world are the people who have lived.

'Good evening, Group,' said Aunt Coral.

'Good evening, Aunt Coral,' we chorused, (for everyone, even the Ad, had taken to calling her that. I'm guessing this has been my influence!). She stood framed by the conservatory windows, the lights coming on in the distant houses twinkling all around her. We sat round a wicker table and although Aunt Coral had supplied extra heating, I still felt the need of a hat.

'I've chosen for our inaugural agenda some warm-up exercises from Mr O'Carroll,' she said. 'It occurred to me in the light of Sue's distressing letter to herself from Ivana that we ought to leave the deeper work for a later session, and use tonight for fun and games.'

'But I want to write a letter to myself from my ex-husband,' said Delia.

'In our next session,' replied Aunt Coral firmly. 'So tonight on our agenda we have a two point plan: 1, Fun and Games with Dialogue. And 2, Fun and Games with your Secret Sweetheart.'

I typed out these headings on my typewriter.

'So,' she continued, referring to her notes from time to time, 'to kick off, it's fun and games with dialogue. This exercise is designed to help you learn how to make dialogue jump off the page. Often what makes a character really live is when you can speak its slang. This might relate to a stammer or tic, a dropped "H" or "G", or might involve low, every-day language that you think you ought not to repeat. So, I want you to imagine a character and write down a line or two of dialogue for them, and then we will share them.'

The rain hit the roof of the conservatory as the sound of creation began.

'Right,' said Aunt Coral as we finished, 'who'll begin? Delia?'

Delia stood up and read aloud. 'Goddamnit, Gedouda here,' she said.

'Good,' said Aunt Coral. 'But we need to know a bit more about who is speaking. Sue?'

'"Fuck me," said Fiona, "I ain't never bin so fuckin' tired in me 'ole fuckin' life,"' I said.

Aunt Coral couldn't say anything to my ingenuity at first. 'Good,' she said eventually. 'And Avery?'

'Yaroo!' shouted the Admiral.

Aunt Coral paused for a breath, and glanced at her notes, unsure momentarily of what to say. 'Well tried,' she finally managed, 'but per-haps a little derivative.'

At this point, I have to admit I wondered how much use the group was going to be to my progress, but I thought I'd give it another session. They were only doing it to help me after all, and a group of elderly bohemiams was better than no group at all.

'So,' continued Aunt Coral, 'let's get a little more involved now. I want you to think of your secret sweetheart—'

'What if you haven't got one?' said Delia.

'Then you can make one up. I want you to think of your secret sweetheart and jot down a few words about how you feel about them, and don't worry, I won't force you to read them aloud.'

Again the noise of creation filled the conservatory, as we wrote by the light of old fringe lamps, while outside the Egham borders lay beyond us in a mournful mist.

'Now,' said Aunt Coral when we'd finished, 'who would be willing to read aloud?'

She was looking expectantly at the Admiral, probably hoping that he'd written her an ode, but he and Delia had both fallen quiet and were looking at their shoes, so I stood up and offered mine:

'I haven't known you long my dear, hirsute, it makes no difference. Whenever you are near to me I smell the flowers along the way. I know I shouldn't tell you this, hirsute, I cannot hide it, for a glimpse of you will linger gentle on my mind all day.'

'Excellent Sue,' said Aunt Coral, 'really excellent, well done. Two questions though. One, obviously, who is your secret sweetheart? I'm sure we're all dying to know, and two, what do you mean by "hirsute"?'

'My secret sweetheart is just someone I made up,' I said, 'and what I mean by hirsute is "nevertheless", of course.'

'But hirsute doesn't mean nevertheless,' said Delia, 'it means hairy.'

My mind raced back to all the occasions when I had misused the word, with a terrifying awareness of my stupidity. But then it quickly seized on the positive thought that the group had set me to rights.

At the same time my head was also swimming with Icarus. I'd just said I'd made him up, when of course he is more than real. But now I was wondering: what if it was the other way round? What if what I made up became real? Now *that* would be interesting. I jotted down a private fantasy, while the Admiral and Delia offered their work. Here it is transcribed:

The Wounds of Love

By Sue Bowl

It was January the 27th and we were sitting
as usual in the drawing room after dinner,
when suddenly the Admiral came running into
the room.

'It's Icarus Fry. Come quickly!' he shouted.

'What has happened?' said Aunt Coral and
Delia as they ran into the hall.

'I knocked him off his bike,' said the
Admiral.

So we took Icarus up to a West Wing bedroom
and the Admiral went for the Doctor. It was
very late. Aunt Coral and Delia fell asleep
in their chairs immediately, with their heads
lolling. But I watched over Icarus as he lay
wounded and cradled him in my arms. I could
have stayed like that for ever, but he awoke
and became arouselled. Lost in the warmth of
my cleeverage, he began to gently stir. How I
wish that the Doctor had never come.

'Well, my secret sweetheart is Marlon Brando,' said Delia, bringing me
back to the present. 'You can't judge a book by its cover,' she said.

Much later on after Group I was laying in bed in the dark, making
figures out of the furniture, when I was startled by the familiar tap of
a sensitive hand at my door. Aunt Coral slipped into my room, tweed
skirt brushing against her good tights, making my bedcover erupt with
electric shocks as she sat on my bed with a crackle. She inspected my
face for signs of life, so I pretended to be asleep, which I do when I don't
feel like chatting. I had committed to the charade, so I couldn't change

my mind when, through my shuddering lashes, I noticed she was holding some papers and had on her special glasses which magnified her eyes like an owl's.

After a while she left me, closing the door behind her, in expert and silent control of its usual heavy clunk. I wonder what she wanted?

The Commonplace Book of Coral Garden: Volume 1
Green Place, Sept 29 1930
(Age eight)

Writing

I decided to start usimg Mother's old typewriter for my momthly mews letter to the relatives. The omly fly im the oimtmemt is that it has mo letter before M. Mother was mot calm about this and told me mot to write to Umcle Meal.

Pepsi

We went for a walk today, Cameo was in her pushchair and I was leading Terry and Ross. We went to Donal Brown's kiosk in the park and Mother bought us a can of Pepsi each, which we drank with two straws!

Housekeeping

Mrs Morris (our housekeeper) is going down the garden to be with the fairies according to Mother. This is because it so happens that at the present we have four maids working here, two upstairs and two down, and all four are called Mary. Mother is convinced that Mrs Morris chose them deliberately, that she only employs girls called Mary. But this is not true, they are known as Mary because Mother can't remember anyone's name.

Father

I was in the Drawing Room with Father as usual before bedtime, in the middle of doing my sums. He sets me work every night before bed, when I'd much rather be read *Winnie-the-Pooh*. Rare are the moments when he allows me to stray from the path of great learning. But tonight a poor blackbird crashed into the window, and so we abandoned mathematics and went to bury it, scooping it up from where it had fallen to the ground. Father offered some words of comfort, for I was more than a little distressed. He said I was to try not to worry because he felt certain that the bird had been so stunned that the last thing it would have remembered was flying.

When we had finished we had a little evening stroll around the grounds of Green Place. He told me what all the flowers are called and how the roses bloom one after another, so that there's always one that is out. He said that the Michaelmas Daisies are so called because they are in full swing on the feast of St Michael. He told me that badgers dig for bees' nests underground, and that squirrels catch fish from the pond. It is wonderful being with Father, even if he does turn life into lessons! I asked the name of the purple trees that line our borders and he says they are called buddleia. He said that they love to grow by the railways, where the speeding trains cast their seeds into the air, to be caught up on the wind and scattered afar.

Sue

FEBRUARY IS A MONTH that is all about the promise of the year to come, about the buds that haven't opened yet, poking their tiny shoots out of the ground.

At the Toastie, Joe and I are getting along, which is intriguing as I'd thought that I was going to get along with Nina Scrafferton, but it turns out she is a closed-in sort of a girl and not a 'woman's woman'. Perhaps she sees me as competition because she likes Icarus as well. You can tell because she simply thrives when he talks to her, and indulges all his jokes, then when he leaves the room it's as if she suddenly ceases to exist. I understand the syndrome because I feel it too. One look from Icarus can keep me thriving for days.

In an attempt to drum up business, we all came into work in fancy dress for Mrs Fry's birthday last week and she took a photo of the Toastie personnel and gave us all a copy. So I got my hands on a picture of Icarus, even if he was mostly obscured by his mother's horns. I put the photo up on the wall in the Grey Room, just level with my eye line as I was lying in bed, so Icarus's face would be the last thing I saw when I went to sleep at night and the first thing I saw in the morning. Aunt Coral raised an eyebrow at it, because the photo predominantly features Mrs Fry in a tarty costume, but if you look twice you can just see Icarus's right eye.

I have spent many an hour gazing in that eye and so it is a hundred per cent distressing when Icarus is offish with me at the café. He isn't a man of many words, but I'm afraid this only adds to his allure. I have been nearly a month at the Toastie and I can't tell if my feelings are reciprocal, but I live in all the agonies of hope that they are.

As I have said, Joe is the opposite of Icarus and always chats to me, as long as Mrs Fry isn't looking. For some reason unknown to herself she does not approve of her boys fraternising.

'What sort of things are you into?' Joe asked me one morning last week, while he was on the frother.

'I'm into writing,' I said.

'No way,' he said, 'because that coincides with me being into reading.' He is an interesting boy, but quite square and with a collection of earnest shirts.

After hours, I have been working hard on stories for my leading characters, the protagonists for my book: Cara, Pretafer, Fiona and Keeper. Cara is a skinny, simple farm girl and Pretafer is a beautiful seventeenth-century heiress and Cara's nemecyst. Fiona is Cara's servant friend, who is forced to dress in weeds, and Keeper is Cara's spaniel.

Wednesday 11 February

Something I so wanted to happen has finally happened. And something I didn't want to happen at all has also happened.

Today, being a Wednesday, was the last day of my week at the Toastie. It was getting on for 10.00am, and I was expecting to finish my work and go back to Green Place as usual, and settle down to some writing.

'Are your Mum and Dad coming down to visit you at all?' asked Joe as we toiled with the toast, the froth and the steam.

'No,' I said. 'Dad doesn't like to leave the house at Titford, and my Mum is . . . not alive any more.'

I deliberately didn't use the 'D' word – I don't like it much anyway, but also I knew it would come as a shock to a boy still blessed enough to have his mother just along the counter.

'I'm so sorry,' said Joe. 'Whe— when did she pass away?'

'September,' I said.

He squeezed my hand on top of the toaster. 'I lost my Dad when I was ten, I understand what you must be going through.'

'I'm so sorry,' I said, and then there was a pause. Joe seemed unsure what else to say.

'What happened?' he continued unexpectedly. 'Was she very ill?'

'No, she committed suicide,' I said.

Poor Joe was so shocked that for a minute every cappuchino went cold and every slice of toast went hard and everything was still.

In real life though, nothing ceases, except your loved one. You struggle on and nothing stops for a moment. Life inside you has changed for ever, but life outside goes on the same as before, and you have to go on living with that riddle every single day.

'Do you need to go home?' asked Joe then, looking grave.

'No I'm fine,' I said, 'but let's not talk about it now.'

He squeezed my hand again over the toaster and then changed his tack. 'Sandy's having a party on Saturday night,' he said. 'I was wondering if you fancied coming?'

'What a shame, I can't,' I said, 'my Dad is coming over.' Then I realised that I'd only just told him my dad didn't like leaving the house, but it was out of my mouth before my editor was on to it. I just knew I couldn't risk saying yes to Joe and possibly spoiling my chances with Icarus.

'Oh, right,' said Joe, and he smiled before getting badly distracted by some froth.

Back in Titford, if someone like Joe had asked me out I would have jumped at the chance, but Icarus has changed all that in just three and a half short weeks, and without barely a word. But, as they say in the classics, the language of love is speechless. How he can say so much to me, without saying anything at all, is a bewitching justaposition.

CAMPARI FOR BREAKFAST

It was therefore some sort of miracle when, half an hour later, as I was in the kitchen buttering up the bread as usual, Icarus walked up behind me and said: 'My brother Sandy is having a party on Saturday night, Sue, I was wondering if you fancied coming?' The temperature in the kitchen rocketed and my knees knocked together. I held on to the counter without turning to face him because of my runaway cheeks. It was the most he had ever said to me. More than a word, more than a sentence, and *so* much more than a question. This was life, and it *can* suddenly happen.

'I'd love to,' I said, perhaps too willingly.

'Great,' he said. 'See you Saturday, 6.30 till midnight,' and he handed me a napkin with the address of a bar on it, and within a nanasecond he was gone. It said: 'Saturday 14th Feb, Sandy's birthday at Christine's'. The 14th of Feb! That's Valentine's Day! Asking me out in the first place is a sure sign that Icarus likes me, but asking me out on *Valentine's Day*, is just *so bold*. I feel so giddy that I could run through a fountain with my clothes on!

As I walked home from the Toastie, every tree, every flower, even the seeds in the earth were singing my name. 'Sue Bowl,' they sang, 'Look there goes Sue', and all the builders wolf whistled. The February buds thrust their way up through the soil, threatening every minute to burst into flower under a sky as radiant as the sun. There was only one small problem. What would I say to Joe?

Back home I went straight to my wardrobe and flung open the door. Pinafores, pinafores, nothing but pinafores. It is just my luck to be in a pinafore phase with a date with Icarus Fry in the diary. I began to feel the strong temptation to blow all my savings on a devastating dress, but I lay on my bed in the Grey Room instead and gazed into his eye. I could have stayed like that for ever, but then I heard the Admiral calling me.

'Sue, Sue, it's your father on the phone.'

I ran down to the hall and took up the receiver, still in heavy thought about love's sudden beginnings. I could hear Ivana's heels in the background clacking on the floor, yet another in the catalogue of complaints I have against that awful woman.

'Hi darling.' Dad's voice was clear and familiar. 'How are you?'

'Great,' I said.

'Good, listen darling, Ivana and I are coming through on Saturday to take you out for dinner.'

In Keeper's Care

A SKETCH

By Sue Bowl

Cara fell to her knees and cradled her Keeper to her. He howled at the moon as she cried out in sorrow and steeped his damp fur with her tears.

'What is this whimsy!' she screamed with abominable confusion.

And though the night was dark and starless, Keeper kept the shadows at bay. Not afar off in the pantry below, the maid was still in labour.

'Fuck me!' said Fiona, 'I ain't never bin so fuckin' tired in me 'ole fuckin' life.'

Friday 13 February

I had a dream last night that made me red, for the dream starred Icarus Fry. After my concerns over the double booking, it was a relief to wake from a dream which I believe to be erotic. In my dream, I was sitting, almost lying, in a basket which was attached to the handlebars of Icarus's bicycle. We were freewheeling down a country road and for dream reasons, Icarus was dressed as a Frenchman, with berret and stripy T-shirt, and his bicycle had strings of onions around the frames of the wheels. We rolled at speed past dream pastures, sparkling brooks, random sheep, he with his legs out, abandoned from the pedals, and I delicately balanced across the basket, in a floaty dress with my legs off to the side, and light as a feather. But we whizzed down the lane so fast that we crash-landed in a heap in a meadow. Unfortunately at that point I woke up.

After recovering for some minutes I got myself dressed and went down to breakfast. When I had finished, Aunt Coral sent me up to her bathroom to fetch a cotton tip for her ear, I think in a helpful attempt to distract me from my worries about the double-booking. It was the first time that I had been in her suite alone and I couldn't help but have a little look. There were some specialist pieces of furniture in there, including a highboy and a lowboy. The highboy is a chest upon a chest, and the lowboy is Aunt C's dressing table. There's also a Robert Manwaring chair which is inlaid with her favourite satinwood. Aunt C told me he was a competitor of Mr Chippendale, and a fan of the *Five Orders of Architecture*. (NB, I looked this up, *The Five Orders of Architecture* is one of the most successful architectural text books of all time. It was written in 1562 by Giacomo Barozzi da Vignola who was an assistant to Michelangelo and was a surprising hit as it's full of drawings and doesn't contain any text.)

Her bed cover is of quilted pink satin with tassels of olive and gold, and over the beheaded hangs a monogrammed panel with the letters 'C E G' on it. The pillows have a monogram too, but bear the initials 'B R G' (Mum). It made me catch my breath, because of course she was not just my mother, Aunt Coral has lost a dear sister too. I tend to forget sometimes, because in life they were somewhat distant due to their ages. Aunt C had already left home by the time my mother was born.

There was an old wooden desk in the window, sewn with papers. A typewriter, with Mr O'Carroll's book open next to it, stood in the centre of the desk. The notes beside it were a mad dog's breakfast of changes and crossings out. I also saw a To Do list sitting on her diary which read:

> ## To Do List
> Make Will
> Insulate letter box
> Ring Dean Martin
> Phone books

I must admit that the thought of Aunt Coral dying caused me to waver in myself. She is my saviour and there is little on earth as magic as her devotion. She also makes me feel like the most fascinating person ever born – she even remarks on my handwriting, eulogising the way I form my 'y's and 'g's, noticing my specialist swish under the line and back up through the side of the letter to create my trademark Spanish ovals. By the time she finishes noticing things, I feel like a million dollars, as though I could build a career around my 'y's and 'g's alone.

To shake myself out of any morbid thoughts of the loss of her, I went into her bathroom to find her cotton buds. There's a commode in there made by the Brothers Adam for the Countess of Derby. It's not plumbed into the mains but does as well for a fancy flower pot. I opened up her font, (the name she uses for her cabinet), and there along with all the usual digestive aids and private creams you'd expect for a woman of her age, I discovered the secret to her dazzling hair in boxes of specialist hair colour. No. 353, Arctic Silver Vixen. On the box was a picture of a foxy old lady stopping traffic on her scooter. It was such an intimate insight into Aunt Coral's private thoughts that my heart broke for her. But unlike the lady on the box, whose hair was cut in a jazzy bob, Aunt Coral's lightning locks are tidied in a bun which is often held up by a pencil, because she is mostly at a loss for a hair grip.

When I delivered the cotton tip she was on her own in the conservatory revising for that evening's group.

'Thank you,' she said, as she relieved the pressure in her ear. She put the cotton tip in a clean tissue and clipped it inside her handbag, and ran her hands round the bottom of her chin as though she was stroking a beard. She seemed to want to express something, something that was visibly difficult, but before she could say anything we were interrupted by the arrival of group members. She took up her notes at once, her action one of the utter professional, but her expression was a hundred stories. I must remember to ask her what's on her mind.

Egham Hirsute Group
On passion

'In my opinion Cinderella is the greatest story ever told,' said Aunt Coral, once the entire group was finally sitting earlier on this evening. 'So in this meeting of the Egham Hirsute Group, Benjamin O'Carroll and I will begin by asking you to think about, A, Myth, and B, Genre.' (As you can see, we have settled on calling ourselves the 'Egham Hirsute Group'. It started as a joke, but it seems to be sticking!)

'How can a myth like Cinderella translate into the everyday?' continued Aunt Coral. 'And how do myths fit into genres? For example, Cinderella could be said to fit into the genre of romantic fiction.' She tapped a finger against her notes. 'We, as authors, should think carefully about genres. Although we must also remember that whatever our genre, whether we write thrillers or crime novels or travel books, the point is to write books that sell.'

'Or dirty books,' said Delia. 'Sex is the best seller of all time.'

The Admiral chuntered into his pipe.

'Yes, Avery, you may well laugh,' said Aunt C, 'but Delia's made an interesting point – sex *is* the best seller of all time.'

This was not good news for me being so out of the loop on it. It's a horrible truth, but I haven't even been *properly* kissed, as yet.

'But writing good books,' Aunt C continued, 'isn't all in the genre or even in the story. There are other factors.' She was in full swing, and I was furiously typing. 'I don't think Charlotte Brontë would have sold nearly so many books if on the back sleeve it had said she was born in Bognor. Not that she was born in Bognor, but what I mean is that a writer has to create for her or himself a character that's marketable too. A certain panache to attract the reader. So even at this early stage, it's worth considering what you might say about yourself, should you get that far.'

'Sue Bowl was born in Titford and studied under Benjamin O'Carroll in Egham,' I offered.

'That won't attract many readers,' said Delia, 'how about something snappier . . . how about Hampshire-born Sue?'

'Hampshire-born Sue' – I liked that. I could see myself in years to come, tending quietly a few pet sheep, wearing wellies, before returning to my typewriter by the Aga, with the hint of husbands in the photos on the wall, and a monogrammed table cloth, perfect for the writer of romantic fiction.

'Malaysian-born Delia Shoot,' said Delia, 'has been having sex every night for the past sixty two yea—'

'Good, good', said Aunt Coral, 'you're getting the idea.' But then suddenly she threw down her notes. 'Departing spontaneously from my plan, as Benjamin O'Carroll encourages gurus to do, why don't we use sex as our exercise for this session, and write a few lines inspired by our passions?'

I had the strong inkling that Aunt Coral was seizing the un-precedented opportunity to get the Admiral to do sex exercises, using the Egham Hirsute Group for her purpose. Clever girl.

Just then Mrs Bunion came into the conservatory with a tray of nibbles. 'I've put you up a tray, Miss Coral, would you like me to ring the gong before I go?'

A small bow followed her question. She's the only one who calls Aunt Coral, 'Miss Coral'. It's because she thinks it's the correct way to refer to the mistress in this size of a house. Though they have known each other since 1968, and Aunt Coral wouldn't mind being called Aunt Coral.

'Thank you, Pat, we'll have it on our knees,' said Aunt Coral. She is the only one who calls Mrs Bunion 'Pat'. As far as the rest of us are concerned, Mrs Bunion was born Mrs Bunion.

Mrs B laid out the nibbles on the table, and gave a finale bow as she closed the conservatory door behind her, taking great care to avoid the creaks. I wondered whether to own up to the fact that my ideas about passion were only imagined and how unqualified I was to write about it. Delia and the Admiral were both engrossed, but I felt like a fraud.

'Sue?' said Aunt Coral, with uncanny telepathy, 'Have you a problem?'

'I'm not very clued up on it,' I said.

The other members of the group stopped writing and stared, but Aunt Coral salvaged me.

'What about your imagination Sue? I'm sure you must have felt passion, if only the yearning.'

It is true I have been feeling the yearning over Icarus. Perhaps passion isn't just the end result and the communion of two people, but the bits before as well. I'd never thought of it like that. Aunt Coral was brilliant to see it.

'And,' she continued, 'I believe that imagination is actually far superior to real life, an opinion that I am sure Benjamin O'Carroll would concur with. Perhaps you might write to him direct and get his reassurance on the matter? For example, I have heard you describe the Pacific Ocean as blue and yet you've probably never seen it. It's the same thing with the intangible emotion: you know, even when you don't know.' She took a swig of her Bombay Sapphire.

I must admit she lost me a little, but maybe Mr O'Carroll's thoughts *would* be helpful, that is, if he ever corresponds with his fans.

Suddenly and without any warning the Admiral stood up and scraped back his chair and, without even being asked to, prepared to read aloud his passion. Aunt Coral had to really gather herself together because she was so shocked and delighted.

'On yearning,' he said, and took a deep breath. 'I stand at your gate and there do I wait, for the moment you bid me draw nearer. Oh! Come let me lead you through woods cool and shady, thou pearl amongst corals, thou dear tiny lady.'

Well! Aunt Coral nearly fell off her chair and her cheeks boiled, exactly as mine did when Icarus asked me out. But was his use of the word 'coral' deliberate? Or was it a cruel, cruel flewk? But Aunt Coral is only five foot two so, surely not.

Aunt C was for the first time ever rendered speechless. I thought she might even collapse. What a dark horse he is!

'That was beautiful, Avery,' said Delia, salvaging Aunt C. 'And here is mine, which I have been longing to do since our group's beginnings.' She cleared her throat and stood up, holding her handbag for security.

Dear Ralph,
You are such an outrageous bastard I don't know where to begin. From one end of the day to the other my rage knows no end. You loathsome wastrel, I rail against the injustices you have caused me to suffer.

Leaving me for a twenty-five-year-old is a kick in the teeth, but leaving me with insufficient funds is the meanest, lowest, dirtiest trick in the book. On the former it would be less of an insult if she were a raving beauty and not such a great lump. Obviously the fact that she is young makes you feel young too, but you look shameful next to her with your new tattoo and your cut-off jean trousers. You don't fool anybody you ugly, smelly, rancid old bastard.

You could make some amends by sending me more money, so that I can at least get my knees done and keep Loudolle in nice dresses.

Miserable conceited wretch that you are, I hate you with all my heart.

D.

Delia was shaking when she had finished and Aunt Coral had to step in.

'There is real passion in Delia's letter, and it is so much better out than in,' she said, as she offered Delia some humus and carrots for comfort.

'I'm fine thank you,' she said. 'In fact I feel much better.'

Once again shock and silence rained on the Egham Hirsutists, so we all leapt into the humus as it seemed the natural thing to do.

Then I decided to read out my assignment, even if it did sound stupid. After all, I was amongst friends, two of whom had already exposed themselves.

```
They met at four and went to the hotel.
He ordered champagne and they had sex for
thirty-six hours and then went shopping. He
took her relentlessly, telling her off on the
floor. She had always wanted a dress in a
box and he gave it to her, though it was a
terrible price, and then they went back to
the hotel and ordered more champagne from
the room people and had sex again without
stopping.
    It was in parting that the pain of being
without him even for a single instant got to
her, and they had to have sex one more time.
```

What was it with the silences at our group this evening? If I hadn't known Aunt Coral better I'd have sworn she was crying. Obviously my writing had affected her. It was a huge compliment. That's why I want to do it.

'Excellent Sue, really excellent,' she said. 'Well done, and so full of longing, oh, how they go hand in hand, the yearning and the passion, it's practically mathematical. Sometimes as writers we must share the things we'd rather imagine in private. Excellent, really excellent, well done.'

I knew her praise was a little biast, though my piece was not without punch.

'What about yours?' asked Delia.

'Gurus don't do the exercises but oversee them and make remarks,' Aunt C said, her eyes full of warning.

'But I saw you writing—'

'Right, I think that's enough for this evening, I'm sure we've all got a thousand things to do. If anyone would like to join me in the drawing room later, Pat has laid a fire, excuse me I must go and telephone Dean Martin.'

We all filtered out of the conservatory and off to our respective rooms, all contained in that gargantuan house, with so much yearning beneath its bludgeoning roof. So it seems that it never stops, it would appear that you never grow out of it. Oh, love, love, I am so ready to know you. Come to my aid and let me live in your sunshine.

Saturday 14 Feb (St. Valentine's Day!)
3.45pm

Mum and I always sent Valentines to each other, in case we didn't get any. I've never had one from anyone else. (Although one year I received two. That was the year she eventually confessed she got carried away.)

I have spent hours going over and over my plans for tonight, and today has seemed to last weeks. Funny how being in love can alter your time frame.

In order to escape dinner early enough to have any kind of quality time with Icarus, I have persuaded Dad and Ivana to book the dinner table much earlier than they wanted, at five o'clock. They couldn't re-arrange coming for another night because they are flying to Venice early tomorrow morning. So Aunt C suggested that I tell them that I had a 'prior engagement', which they eventually accepted after a telephone battle.

This is the plan of action which Aunt Coral has cooked up: the Admiral will collect me from the restaurant at 6.30pm prompt, and then take me on to the party for 7.00pm. This will give me approximately three hours with Icarus for the loving. Meanwhile Aunt Coral will entertain Dad and Ivana back at Green Place. Then the Admiral will pick me up again at 10.00, leaving time for cognacs with everyone in the drawing room at 10.30 before Dad and Ivana leave for their flight. On paper at least it looks fluid.

I've been so worried about my wardrobe that at one point I nearly decided not to go. I considered spending decadent sums of money on a fabulous new dress, but Aunt Coral urged me not to.

'Young men are piglets and you should find out if he's worth it before you spend your pennies,' she said.

Icarus Fry a piglet? As if she's any kind of judge, for heaven's sake – she fancies the Admiral!

In the end I decided on my most devastating pinafore with a pair of Aunt Coral's jazzy high heels, though I've had to leave wet potatoes in them all night, which Aunt C told me would stretch them. Delia has helped me with my hair and face. I just hope Icarus will see through the packaging.

Sunday 15 Feb
Morning

At four o'clock yesterday, I went down to the drawing room for an apairoteef with the others. I couldn't decide which feeling was worse, the thought of seeing Dad and Ivana again, or my nerves about how I would come across to Icarus. How I would look, how I would walk, how I would sound, whether I'd be sweating, all the things a girl considers when faced with a potential future husband.

I kept thinking about how my mum would have been so good at all this. Her absence was galloping. She used to send me to school with an embarrassing ribbon in my hair, but I never took it off after she'd gone, because she put it there. It was the mark of her. It was the same yesterday evening with Delia's coiffure. She had put my hair in hot curlers and combed it out to look poof, signing it with her friendship. Normally I have just my home bob that I've had since I was young. I keep meaning to grow it into glamour locks, but it gets hot on the back of my neck. I don't normally do much to it, Aunt C says it dries like I've just been swimming, and so to be honest Delia's styling was somewhat bigger than I enjoy.

As I entered the drawing room, it was like a beautiful dream. The Admiral stood up and the ladies caught their breath.

'Oh Sue!' said Aunt Coral, and she rushed to the side board to fetch her camera.

'You're a knockout,' said Delia.

'A smasher,' said the Admiral and he went to the bar and fixed me a Pimm's.

Funny how two old ladies and an old boy can make you feel great, much more than anyone in youth can, although I am not so unwordy as to not know that Aunt Coral thinking I look pretty and Icarus thinking I do are subtly different matters. And this was no childish party, this was a big late night adult party with boys and a bar. This was what all the poets went on about. Oh, love, love.

The only thing I still hadn't resolved when I left the house was what I would say to Joe, but I decided to cross that bridge when I came to it.

At 4.45 when the Admiral took me into Egham it was already dark. The trees whisked past the Bentley window so dark and glossy. The sky was damp, but I could smell the summer coming, and in the magical twilight the early stars were just showing off in the gathering evening sky.

I looked across at the Admiral and for a strange second I thought he was Mum. She wore gloves with a hole in the back of the hand for driving, with a clicking button. She would glance over her shoulder and smile at me, like a beautiful face from a woman's calendar.

The Admiral dropped me bang on time and then went on to his club, yelling 'Avery Little helps!' out the window. He doesn't miss a chance for his motto.

At 5.23 I was still waiting for Dad and Ivana to arrive. The maître d' had brought me some bread and I'd nearly eaten the whole basket when they finally turned up. Ivana minced over, as croquettish as the day is long, and Dad followed behind and we all had the soup.

As I was rushing my soup so as to be ready to leave on time, I noticed that Ivana had white gloves on. In fact her whole get-up was a total decision on white lace. Now, she is well known in Titford for her stupid fashion choices, but I did think it odd that she hadn't taken off her gloves to eat her soup, and her hands slithered over her spoon.

'Why is she wearing gloves?' I asked Dad when she went off to the toilet.

'I'm glad you asked darling,' he said. 'We wanted you to be the first to know . . . Ivana and I are engaged.'

Just like that he said it, in the same way you might say 'pass the vinegar'.

'But I don't understand,' I said, 'what's that got to do with her gloves?'

'There's a ring under those darling, but she's sensitive to your feelings, so she wanted to hide it.'

Ivana came back from the loo and Dad nodded to her in their hideous love language, and she took off her gloves and demonstrated a diamond ring on her courtship finger.

'Ta da!' she said, waggling it.

I wanted to snap it off, but I couldn't because we were in a restaurant.

'Excuse me,' I said. But it wasn't my voice, it was the voice of politeness, allowing me to continue to function in society.

'Excuse me,' I said again. And I went into the loos where I exploded. I held on to a basin and then through a rampage of tears the memories came flooding back.

I remembered Dad and Ivana's first few visits to the cinema together last summer, which they claimed was because they were both Film Noir enthusiasts. (But my mother liked Film Noir too!)

I knew that mum knew that Dad was seeing a lot of Ivana, but she never let on if she *knew*. But on the very day she died, Dad and Ivana were at a 'conference' together, though Ivana was nothing to do with the firm and didn't speak very much English. Shortly before they got back, Mum walked into the library in Titford to the back section on the poets, and, having at some point swallowed her pills, she lay down on the floor to sleep. The librarian found her and the doctors were called, but they were too late. And she didn't leave us a note to explain.

My mind can sweep me back in a flash to that awful day in Titford, and to that police car outside our house, and the grim expression on the officers' faces inside . . .

But I wasn't back in Titford, I was in the restaurant toilet in Egham, and the feel of the cold ceramic basin brought me back to the present, and I had to reassemble myself. I don't remember the exact details of events as they continued to unfold after that, but somehow I went back to the table, and at some point the Admiral came to fetch me. And Dad and Ivana went on with their meal as if everything was all right.

How angry I am with them for getting engaged. How angry I am that they are together at all. Words fail. It is despicable, dreadful, disloyal, dire, disgusting, wicked, wrong. My poor mother, driven to her desperate action by Dad's infidelity, and now her memory trashed, as though she never existed.

If it hadn't been for the fact that Icarus was waiting for me I would certainly have gone home. But as I said before, I have realised that life goes on and Sandy's party was waiting for me. It was at a trendy café called Christine's, a big place and full of bikers because Sandy is in a gang. The Admiral offered to walk in with me, but I knew that would be embarrassing, so I walked in on my own and awaited at the bar. There was no sign of Icarus.

After a short time Joe bounced out of the shadows and came up to the bar with his wallet. 'You decided to come!' he said, breathless from disco dancing.

'Two drinks please,' he said to the barman.

'What kind of drinks?' came the reply.

'We'll have two wines,' said Joe, after looking at me in the manner of a gallant cowboy growing concerned. Then he moved me off into the body of the room and we sat at a table and shouted.

'Are you all right?' he asked.

'Don't I look it?' I said.

'You look lovely . . . but pale.'

There was a pause, then: 'What's your favourite film?' he said, out of all congruaty.

'E.T.,' I replied shakily.

'No way,' he said, 'I had to have the day off school after I saw that.'

Then the DJ started playing 'Walk Like an Egyptian' by The Bangles and Joe did a little Egyptian dance in his chair, with his arms above his head, and swivelled his eyes like the singer. But I felt too sad to join in, and so he stopped and grew embarrassed.

'Um, just tell me if you're not all right Sue and we'll go somewhere quieter,' said Joe.

I looked in my hand mirror and realised that I looked like nothing on earth. My make-up was smudged, my hair was matted, and the shock of Dad and Ivana seemed to have actually altered my temperature.

'Where's Icarus?' I asked him, and once again it wasn't my voice, my voice was somewhere in hiding.

'Icarus?' said Joe. 'I don't think he's coming.'

I stared at him with no breath.

'He's going out with Michael you see and they've had some sort of bust-up.'

'But he—' and without tactics in place for Joe's feelings, the truth came out. 'But he asked me to meet him here,' I said. 'He never cancelled me.'

'Oh dear, I'm sorry,' said Joe, although truthfully, he did not look that sorry. 'Would you like to dance?'

So there I was, dancing with Joe, and Icarus nowhere. All the hope and expectation of earlier was gone, and nothing was left. A vision of the back sleeve of my first book floated down to me out of the darkness. As Joe danced wildly about, I saw it clearly. It read:

'Her mother gone, her heart broken, her life in taters. What next for Hampshire-born Sue?'

Then, just as I was about to ask Joe if he would take me home I spotted Icarus on the far side of the floor. He was smooching a girl with long-or-burn hair.

'That's not Michael,' I said. And then the room began to spin as they walked over towards us, catching us up in their dazzle. He was beyond a man, and she – she was a nymph. I felt weak. Her hair shone, her shoulders shone, her shins shone. She looked like the fairies had been up all night buffing her. I could see my own reflection in the gleam of her chestnut hair.

'Hi Sue,' said Icarus 'this is—'

'Loudolle, Loudolle Shoot,' she said.

That's all I remember until early this morning, when I woke up in Aunt Coral's pink-tasselled bed, with an horrendous cold, having fainted at the party. Apparently Joe had called out Aunt Coral, and the Bentley had been used as an ambulance. Everyone was brilliant. Even Dad and Ivana hovered till this morning before they pushed off on holiday, but I didn't want to see them.

After breakfast I was transferred back here to the Grey Room and Aunt Coral placed a notepad and pen by my bed. There are flowers on the bedside table with a card by them which reads:

Get Well Sue
Love Joe

Aunt C told me that I was completely incoherent, and not only that: in a frenzy of fever I'd torn up the photo of the Toastie personnel which is the setting for Icarus's eye. The remains are now sewn with used Kleenex under my bed. It is over.

I must have fallen back to sleep for the last couple of hours because I woke up again at lunchtime. I was just turning my damp pillow when I heard a voice outside my door.

'Shall I take it in mom, or leave it here?' It sounded like an American.

As the door opened I pretended to sleep, but I watched as someone came in with a tray. It was the nymph girl from the party. I hadn't put two and two together until just now. It was Delia's daughter with the fancy name. This was Loudolle, come from Alpen. Even in her lounge wear she looked amazing. With no make-up she was camera ready. But there were a couple of strands of her hair out of place, just entussled enough to look human.

She put the tray by my bed and then began a decisive snoop in my things, opening up my draws and fisselling, with a disdainful glance at my clothes. Then she stooped to look under my bed where the torn-up photo lay scattered among wet tissues. My heart was pounding, for I had not yet checked to see if Icarus's eye was intact. She rifled through the fragments, making scuffling noises under my bed, before getting up and slinking out of my room.

As soon as she'd gone I plucked up the torn remnants, and found that Icarus's eye had now become separated from everything else in the picture. I tried briefly to reinstate the eye in situ with the rest of the remains of the staff, before giving up and putting his lone eye under my pillow for safety. I couldn't quite throw it away.

For some reason it didn't seem odd that the nymph girl had frisked me, and I felt this in all six senses.

When the sun has gone and the night has come and the cold bites you and the rain wets you, you must stay still till it passes. I feel as though I am in a great earthen plot full of weeds and flowers together, but the weeds are choking out the flowers, strangling all their sweetness, and everything hurts.

Susan Bowl
Egham Hirsute Group
Green Place
Egham
Surrey

Sun 15 Feb 1987

Dear Mr O'Carroll

I hope you don't mind me writing to you, but I am currently working through the coursework in your brilliant book *The Dorcas Tree*, and I wondered if you could help me with something important.

I have just lived through a great personal trauma and am desperate to hang on to the one thing I have left, which is my writing. The persisiant question that has been bothering me is thus: is it better for the fledgling writer to write from experience or from the imagination?

Until recently I have known little of romantic entanglements, but I now have had the misfortune to know more than was called for about heartbreak. However this 'life experience' has not affected my writing in a positive way as indicated by the poets and I would be introverted to know your response as I am more than confused and blocked.

You have many fans in Egham.

I look forward very much to your reply, when you are not overwhelmed by letters.

Yours truly

Susan Bowl

It's been a week since that night, the dashing of hopes and dreams. Each day I have been aware of nothing but feeling cold, and the smell of eggs from breakfast. But Aunt Coral has just told me something that has totally shocked me out of my sickbed.

At about four o'clock she tiptoed into my room, clutching an armful of papers and her Commonplace. I remember thinking it was an odd time for nostalgia as she put a cold hand on my forehead.

'You'll live,' she said, before regret ran across her face, because jokes like that are no longer appropriate. 'How are you feeling?'

'I'm much better, ready to get back in the saddle,' I said.

'Good,' she said, 'do you feel up to us having a chat?'

'Why?' I said, because really I'd have preferred to return to convalessing.

'We need to have a chat. I keep trying to find a moment,' she said.

'Of course,' I said, 'sorry.'

'Sue, there's something I want to tell you. I don't want you to hear this from anybody else. I want you to hear this from me. I don't know if your mother told you . . .' She was unable to continue for a moment. She laid down the papers, one of which I could see she had written up with a few helpful prompts.

'This will be a bit of a shock and I haven't been sure how to tell you. I haven't been sure if your mother told you before she died . . .'

'What? Told me what?' I said.

'I don't know how to begin,' she said, 'but I am not your mother's sister.'

'You're not my mother's sister? Who on earth are you then?'

'I am your great-aunt. And Cameo was your nana.'

'I'm sorry, I don't quite understand. I thought Nana Pearl was my nana – wasn't she?'

'No, I thought she was, but no. You see, Pearl was not your mother's mother as we have always thought,' she continued. 'She was actually her grand-nana. Your real nana was my sister Cameo and Cameo was your mother's mother.'

'But my mother was definitely my mother?' I said, finding it hard to follow.

'Yes, yes your mother was definitely your mother . . . Look, when my father died, your mother came to help me sort out his things and we had a bonfire to burn down his papers. It was while we were doing this that your mother found her birth certificate.'

'And it said that Cameo was my mother's mother and not my Nana Pearl?'

'That's right,' said Aunt Coral. 'It was a terrible shock'.

'You didn't know?'

'We didn't know, and Buddleia was naturally very upset.'

She continued, now unprompted, with a random confusion of memories.

'Of course, looking back there were lots of things that didn't make sense, but it happened just after the war you see, and you were just so glad to be alive then, you didn't ask too many questions, especially if you had no reason not to believe what you'd been told.'

I looked out the window at a stray star which had forgotten itself in the daylight; it had an attitude of faint amusement at what it saw as a pin-prick story.

'But if Cameo was my mother's mother, then who was my mother's father?'

'His name was Major Jack Laine,' said Aunt Coral, as though she'd just said his name was dog poo. 'He abandoned Cameo and the baby.'

She put on her close-work glasses and unfolded the birth certificate for me, trying to be reassuring, but her gaze was anything but. 'I'm so sorry I didn't know,' she said.

'You mean you didn't *notice* that your mother wasn't pregnant with my mother, and that Cameo *was*?' I said.

'I was away at college; I wasn't around to actually *see*.'

'You didn't go home for nine months?'

'No, I *did*—' She hesitated, as though someone had pressed her pause button, but I think it was only because she couldn't believe it herself.

'You see Nana Pearl had three miscarriages after having Cameo, so Buddleia seemed like a miracle because we thought she couldn't have any more. And that winter was the coldest I can remember, everyone was very wrapped up. I only made it home once – there were no trains because there was no coal. I was told that Mother hadn't known that she was pregnant. She was also prone to be stout. And then of course after Buddleia was born, she took her away to Australia. I didn't quite understand why at the time, but now I think she was taking Buddleia away from the curiosity of the neighbours.'

I already knew that Grand Nana Pearl had left England after the war, taking mum 'on a sabbatical' to the Bush, and found she preferred a tea chest, billy can and camp fire to a dining room, chair and fine china.

'But why did they pretend? It just seems bonkers,' I said.

'They were Victorians, respectability was everything. Marriage for a girl was the tops. It wouldn't have been possible for Cameo with an illegitimate child. It wouldn't have been accepted. It's ironic that they went to all that trouble, when Cameo—' She stopped for an involuntary moment.

'When Cameo?'

'When Cameo didn't make it,' she said, almost too choked to speak.

She was trying to put all her pieces together just as much as I was. I had the feeling I should not ask further about Cameo just then.

'But the worst of it is Buddleia *didn't believe* that I didn't know Cameo's secret,' she said, 'and some of her last words to me were unkind . . .'

'At least you *have* some last words,' I said. 'I have nothing.'

'Actually . . . you do have something.' And then she opened out a piece of paper. I froze in horror to think she'd been withholding it. 'Buddleia sent me *this*.'

'Oh God,' I said. I sat up in bed, my limbs without oomph, and read the letter in hunger, searching the next line for clues before I'd finished the one I was on.

June 12 1986

Dear Coral,

I just wanted to let you know where I have got to with things, which isn't terribly far. The record books at St Catherine's House are lodged in colour-coded sections within the building. Green for marriages, red for births and black for deaths. I have only found two Major Jack Laines, but one of them is deceased, and the other one is classified as 'an idiot'. However there may be hundreds of other Major Laines out there who are still alive and unmarried, and who obviously weren't born majors.

And so I am none the wiser as to who I am. The only one, it seems.

Buddleia

'But this doesn't tell us anything. This is a scrap of research about her real Dad. It isn't a farewell, or an explanation of why she did what she did.'

'But I think it is,' said Aunt Coral. Her eyes were welling with the small filmy tears of a lady, though she fought them back.

'Just imagine finding that your whole childhood has been a lie, that no one was who they said they were. Finding out your father is not your father, and that your *real* father, who you never knew, may be deceased or an idiot. I think it may be what drove her over the edge. And she died thinking that I knew the truth and didn't tell her. But I *didn't* know. It so presses on me.'

'I understand, it's called unfinished business,' I said.

Then the pressure of holding in her emotions overcame her and she had to let go of her real tears, not her socially comfortable tears, but big painful tears that weren't manageable. I had never till today seen Aunt Coral in such great distress.

'I don't understand why they kept it from me,' she said, 'but I suppose there comes a time with such secrets when it's too late to tell the truth.'

'So Major Laine, wherever he is, he's my . . .'

'He's your Grandfather,' said Aunt Coral.

'But do you think he *knew* he was Mum's Father?' I said. 'Do you think there's a chance that he didn't? Is there a law that says that fathers must be told?'

'They're all good questions, Sue, and the answer is I don't know, but I rather assume he did know if Cameo named him so on the birth certificate. It was too late to retrieve anything else from the fire, otherwise there may have been correspondence in there that could have told us. Anyway, the upshot is, I have taken up the cudgels, and short of tracing every Laine in the country and asking if they're a Major, I have started to comb through the phone books. There's a Jeremy Laine on the borders, he's a TV producer I think, and a Dave Laine out at Buswater. But I feel they are coincidental, so I'm going to place an ad in the *Echo* and see if that prompts someone to get in touch.'

'I still don't understand why Grampa Evelyn kept the certificate if he wanted it to be secret?'

'Probably just in case. He must have had his reasons, though now we will never know them. No, I'm afraid that now this is the only record that I have of the past.' She was referring to her Commonplace.

Then she pulled her threads back together, opened my window for fresh air and smoothed my appalling hair. She was back to being the strong one.

But it still doesn't make sense to me of Mum's decision to die, and most pertinently, of why she didn't tell me, but Aunt Coral is convinced that we need look no further for a motive.

The Commonplace Book of Coral Garden: Volume 5

Newspaper cutting, 'Personal Column', *Egham Echo*, 23 Feb 1987:

> Miss Coral Garden of Green Place, Clockhouse Lane, Egham, wishes to contact a Major Jack Laine, who was known to the Garden family c.1947. All information welcome. Contact C. Garden at above address, tel. 69950.

The Commonplace Book of Coral Garden: Volume 1
Green Place, Christmas 1932
(Age ten)

News

Cameo has had a terrible accident. She fell three feet and a ski pole went through her eye. Mother cannot stop weeping. She gave Cameo a doll's house for Christmas to help aid in her recovery. It is along the lines of the one made for Queen Mary, which set the doll's house world alight, boasting Louis chairs, Chippendales, and working electric lights.

The surgeons have been measuring the risks of brain damage if they proceed with more surgery, and she is still in great pain. She may end up wearing a false eye. She had to have a big bald patch shaved off the front of her scalp, which she found so thoroughly demoralising, that I shaved a patch of my hair off too for support. Mother offered to do it as well, at which point Father was not very calm. He said it would not be appropriate for a lady.

Cameo is just so stoic, and delights in wearing her sunglasses, joking when she goes upstairs to bed that she's just off for twenty winks. She has done an amazing drawing of a cat that lives in the dustbin. Here we call him Guido, but next door he is called something else. No one could believe the artist was a little injured girl of five. We are all very proud.

But I'm in the dog house over the doll's house. I didn't intend any harm. I merely wanted to see how the lights worked, so on Boxing Day I stripped them all out. I didn't get the chance to put it back together again before Mother came in and found me. Cameo was understanding, but to be quite honest she couldn't *see* what I'd done. Mother's rage was as bad as when I bent the cutlery to make up a tool kit.

As penance I had to clean out the flies from Father's collection of

Toby Jugs. He's very passionate about his Jugs, and boasts a Martha Gunn and a Thin Man among his twenty-five pieces, dating from 1760! The original Toby Jugs were modelled on a notorious drinker of the time, Henry Elwes, also known as Toby Fillpot, so sometimes the Jugs are called Fillpots too. Father's in love with this period in history and knows all the old songs. While I cleaned them he taught me the words of 'Oh Good Ale thou art my darling', which I can't get off the brain. But anyway that means he can't be that angry with me about the doll's house, which is a relief. To be shut out of his study is the worst penance I know.

Best Christmas Present

New doll named Karis who says 'Mama'. Her voice is created by a balloon and two ceramic bars in her torso, which, when squeezed, press on the balloon, forcing the air out and into the sound of 'Mama'. A slight reshaping and weighting of the bars makes the air come out sounding like 'pee pee'. I'm going to re-set it for Cameo because it makes her laugh so much.

Local news

Aurthur Longquist, a diminutive local boy, has chanced upon a supply of Liptons and has taken to the marketing and sale of the bags from the premises of his bicycle. Naturally we bought some, in the knowledge of his family's need. But the irony is not wasted on me, as Father owns half of Ceylon, and that tea probably travelled here on one of our ships. We also turn a blind eye to Longquist door-stepping some of our milk. Father says in whatever way, we must do what we can for the poor, and it will save him from waiting in line for the government hand outs. I suspect Aurthur thinks that being privileged also means we can't count.

Sue

I RECOVERED ENOUGH to go back to the Toastie on Monday, but what I didn't know was that while I was ill Loudolle had been standing in for me, and it turns out that with Loudolle on the toaster there had been a steady swell in the gentlemen breakfasting. And as a good salary is Loudolle's raisin d'être, and increased turnover at the Toastie is Mrs Fry's, I was immediately consigned to the back kitchen for the remainder of the holidays.

Mrs Fry positively fawns over Loudolle, and says she is a little gold-mind. And wherever Loudolle goes, Icarus's eyes follow. But it is a small comfort for me to know that at least *I* have his eye under my pillow.

I have also realised why Delia is so straps for cash – because Loudolle goes to a finishing school in Alpen. She's developed an American accent, which considering she grew up in Ealing and spent one term at college, is really silly. I've known people who spend *years* abroad and still sound as English as Billy O. Everything about Loudolle involves a finish, even her name – after all she was born a Lucinda. By the time she has finished finishing there'll be nothing left of the original.

The reshuffle at the Toastie, and the solitary hours that have become mine in the back kitchen, have allowed me too much time to reflect on the loss of mum. As I stood and buttered an army of sandwiches this morning, I recollected the moment it happened.

I was with some friends at the bus stop at the time Mum died, we were watching the rollerskating. The funny thing was that I did have a strange feeling, for I suddenly craved, for no good reason, a particular kind of sugar that Mum liked, which was out of all congruaty. By the time I got back home from the bus stop and Dad got back from his 'conference' with Ivana, the police were at our house.

The GP, Doctor Louden, asked if there were any other suicides in the family, as if it were somehow hereditary and not an act of despair. I explained that it was a freak act of despair, but the Doctor said that sometimes suicide's not an act of despair, sometimes it's an act of revenge.

'Sue,' said Joe's voice suddenly. 'Let me help you.'

He put his arm round my shoulder, and gently offered his hanky, because although my hands were still moving over the bread, I hadn't noticed I had sodden the sandwiches. I had forgotten I was in the Toastie at all. I had regressed to an earlier time.

Joe's just been such a nice guy to me, helping me re-butter and distracting Mrs Fry, and I felt so grateful that I asked him to come to Green Place for a bite this afternoon after his shift.

As soon as I got back home, in an unexpected move, I went straight up to my room and transferred Icarus's eye from my pillow to my sock drawer, which felt like progress emotionally.

When Aunt Coral and Delia came back from shopping I told them Joe was coming over, which sent them both into a spin. They dashed to get doilies and put them on the table and selected some crisps and, after lengthy talks, Delia went to bake brownies. Before Joe arrived at 4.00pm they both went to their rooms and changed, Aunt Coral into a chiff-en-chiff dress and Delia into a kaftan. Their combined scent was of roses, lilacs and musk all mixed together in a blooming fusion. You could have smelt them in Addlestone – it wasn't so much a waft as a punch in the face.

'He's not my boyfriend,' I tried to tell them, a pro-po their great efforts. But it didn't make any difference. A young man coming to the house was all the excuse they needed to turn up the volume.

When Joe arrived he had changed too, into a specialist floral shirt and turn-ups. This was spiralling from a casual on-the-cuff arrangement to a formal date with clean clothes. I took him into the conservatory and Aunt Coral kept coming in to check the temperature, trailing clouds of scent behind her. Even her shadow smelled nice.

'Come and join us in the drawing room soon,' she said, imposing her utmost knowing on me.

'She's your Nana?' asked Joe.

'No, she's my Aunt,' I said. 'Actually, Great Aunt. My mother's mother's sister.'

All was peaceful in the conservatory, apart from the sounds from outside of the Admiral hacking at the rampage of climbing ivy. It was just between daylight and twilight because the days are battling to be longer. We sat in awkward silence for a while and talk was hard to find. Then as so often happens in such circumstances we both started speaking together.

'I'm glad you're better, Sue,' said Joe, 'from your cold.'

'Would you like a crisp?' I said.

Then I salvaged. 'Yes, I have been practically living in a pot of medicinal honey.'

'Then I wouldn't mind being a bee,' he replied, which provoked us into more silence.

'What an amazing house,' he said into the emptiness of the conservatory. But I couldn't find my patter.

'Yes,' I said, before I dried up again.

'We don't have to talk about it, not if you don't want to,' said Joe.

But I felt like I owed him an explanation for the morning's sand-wiches. 'My Dad is marrying his girlfriend,' I said, 'but my Mum hasn't even been gone a year.'

Joe was quiet again, neither of us knew what to say, and then he shook his head and just said my name: 'Sue'.

There was something about the way he said it that held the meaning of who I was to him, and who I was to him was someone to be cherished. I noticed that I liked that. It was all rather adult.

He patted my hand on the seat of my chair, and of course at that precise moment, with perfection timing, Aunt Coral burst in with the brownies. She just couldn't help herself, or Delia either, and next minute they had both joined us in the conservatory, because they couldn't wait for us to join them in the drawing room. I almost guessed what was coming next, because I was getting used to the way they operate under high excitement levels.

'We thought we'd hold Group this evening. We were wondering if your young man would join us?'

Egham Hirsute Group
Wordplay

Our Favourite Words:

Concierge			Waltzing	
Freshen	Aunt Coral's		Thumping	The Admiral's
Paisley			Spooning	
Tribal			Nemesis	
Crisps	Delia's		Delicious	Joe's
Gown			Lavender	
Knarl			Burger	Icarus
Princess	Mine			
Confetti			Socialite	
			Shimmering	Loudolle
			Chambray	

First we discussed our favourite words and then Aunt Coral set us to incorporate them into a short poem. She had promised to keep off emotional work to prevent embarrassment.

'Has anyone seen Loudolle?' said Delia, 'she was supposed to be home for tea.'

Joe looked apprehensive. 'She went to have tea with my brother I think,' he said. It didn't wash well with me.

I still didn't know how she happened to be at Sandy's party. They aren't the sort of family Loudolle would normally be interested in mingling in.

'Right,' said Aunt Coral, 'without further ado, I'd like you to get into twos, and using the favourite words of your partner, I'd like you to write short poems for each other.'

She was, as ever, being cunning in her lesson plans, which usually led us head-long into romance. I was just wondering what I could do with Joe's words, when the Egham Hirsute Group as I had known it ceased to exist, because Loudolle walked in with Icarus.

'Sorry we're late mom,' she said, 'what are you guys doing?'

'We're having Group,' said Delia. 'Would you like to join in?'

'Cool,' said Loudolle. 'It won't take long will it?'

Is there to be nowhere sacred any more? She is everywhere; my home, my work, my love life, and now at my core at Group.

Aunt Coral did her best to be polite and recapped the plan for them. I was working with Joe, Delia had the Admiral, and of course Loudolle had Icarus.

'But Icarus can only think of one word,' Loudolle said, after we'd been working for a few minutes, 'and that is *burger*.'

'Then that is your challenge,' said Aunt Coral, putting the cat among the pigeons. She was clearly demonstrating her displeasure at the way Loudolle had swalked into our session. Though curiously, even though Icarus was as handsome as I'd known him, I thought that Loudolle had drawn the short straw. It gave me an awful relief in finding a little fault with him.

As we set about our wordplay there was a terrible amount of tension in the room. Delia obviously had issue with Aunt Coral for giving Loudolle such a difficult task and there were unspoken opinions between them. Loudolle was giving me bad eyes too and kept on stroking Icarus's knee under the table. The only ones not engaged in silent squabbles were the Admiral and Joe, who were both quietly getting on with their poems. The Admiral's hands were stained green with ivy, and he was sweating. Aunt Coral sat in the window, with all the blossoms outside now just in vision after the Admiral's ivy cutbacks.

The poetry exercise did not turn out to be a success as neither Icarus nor Loudolle could manage it. Although I wasn't very happy with mine, I read it out aloud for the group.

> The lavender steals against your gown so
> delicious,
>   But even so, I know, you are my nemecyst.

'You can't say "nemecyst"', said Loudolle, 'the word is "nemesis"'.

'But I mean "nemecyst", which is a cross between "nemesis", meaning "adversary", and "cyst", meaning "bag bursting with poisons",' I said. '"Nemecyst". I feel it adds meaning to the word. Not only an adversary, but an adversary bursting with poisons.'

'Don't be ridiculous,' said Loudolle, 'it makes it into complete nonsense.'

'I think Sue's right.' Joe tried to intervene. 'It adds depth to the existing meaning, it sort of . . . Sue-ifys it.'

'Sue-ifys it?' said Loudolle. 'Is that a new word as well?'

Joe hesitated to respond, he was a little out of his depth with such a rattlesnake. I was overwhelmed – it was valiant of him to stick up for me.

'Well, it's my choice of word, and I'm happy for it to be . . . Sue-ified,' he said.

Aunt Coral clapped her hands together to distract us like a geography teacher. The two visiting members obviously weren't up to it, so she turned us to other things with great largeness.

'This looks like a good moment to tell you that we have a long-term plan. I have entered the Egham Hirsute Group into a short story competition, which will be judged at the Ramblers' Association Gala in December.' There was an excited smatter of applause as she beamed out at us. 'Members are to enter individually, but there will also be group prizes, plus an overall individual winner and serious prize money. Entries are to be no more than six thousand words and are to begin with the phrase: "He, or She, awoke." All newcomers to EHG are of course welcome to enter, but this would involve a full commitment to the process.'

When she finished explaining the rules she sat down and sipped on her Sapphire. 'I think we should call it a night.'

Though she had cut the group short, I trusted Aunt Coral's instincts. Loudolle was causing ructions, Delia wasn't looking too happy and the Admiral needed a bath. All these things block creativity.

'Can I just read you my poem?' asked Joe, as I was showing him out after Group. I agreed, so we stepped back into the conservatory. He was so nervous he caught his shoe briefly on his turn-up.

'"I had rather sit with you on a knarl of oak, with only the leaves for confetti, than with the princess of all America upon her shimmering throne."'

'That's beautiful, Joe,' I said. But in truth, I felt somewhat embarrassed.

Here is the beginning of my entry for the Gala. I have chosen the seventeenth century as a setting because it is my personal favourite:

Brackencliffe

A SHORT STORY
By Sue Bowl

She awoke on the course ground, as it sprung back to life beneath the shimmering frost. Calling her Keeper to her, they set off together on foot. High, high she climbed, her skirts full of wind and Keeper gambling after, to yonder on the edge of the cliffs, where lay the gargantuan house. So this was Brackencliffe, the highest house on the ridge. And 'twas here she knew she'd find employ, here at the house of plenty.

As Cara peeped into the window, she spied the beautiful Pretafer Gibbon dancing, achingly pretty, yet shallow, held close in the arms of Van Day.

Knight Van Day lived but two stones by, so he was oftentimes suiting Pretafer. Rich and deadly and silent, but the publican says 'that don't mean ee don't ravish'.

The Commonplace Book of Coral Garden: Volume 1
Green Place, July 1933
(Age 11)

The London Aeroplane Club

Cameo and I have just returned from a school trip to see the latest in aviation.

'The Percival Gull' has folding wings and is believed to be the finest light aircraft invented. It has a landing speed of 40mph, three seats and delightful colours. It is fully equipped with a compass which makes flying in fog easier and safer, while its tremendous smooth landing promises only the most modest bounce.

Cameo is inspired and is considering life as a pilot. She intends to follow in the footsteps of Amy Johnson, who was the first woman to fly solo from England to Australia.

I myself, however, would prefer to remain firmly on the ground!

The weather report in the *Airfield News* said: 'Atlantic fronts will be grazing the coasts and flirting with the Home Counties.' Cameo was in fits all the way home.

The Garden

Mother and Father have instigated plans to update some of the flower beds. Many of the lavenders here are so old that their heads have gone white, like grey hair. And with unmistakeable loftiness Father prefers French lavender. So now we have white lavender to the left and French to the right, faded and vibrant opposites. A million pale butterflies flutter in the thick of the bushes, these ones are called cabbage whites. In her plot Mother has put a profusion of colours, and has forgotten the name of everything, but the effect is as lively and cheerful as she is.

I like all the scented things because I am very interested in making perfume. I love Sweet William, while Cameo loves the woody things, and all the herbs. In a dramatic moment she said she wished she could roll around in the mint, but Mother said that Green Place girls should stay upright (fat chance!).

Animals

Cameo has rescued another animal – an old horse she's christened Alto. He was abandoned between the train tracks and the sea, and had been grazing beside wet sand banks until the station master realised nobody owned him. When he finally discovered this, nobody would take poor Alto, so they were going to have to shoot him. That's when Cameo found out, and she's had him moved to our paddock. He's grazing there now, and seems to have not a care in the world. She's like the patron saint of elderly animals.

Sue

I got a letter today from Aileen Edgeley. Aileen is on a gap year in Australia picking strawberries. We were neighbours in Titford, and she was my first friend for life. Aileen and I used to spend all our time together. She was not only my neighbour, but my schoolmate and somewhat sister. She liked to dress up as the Queen and I liked to dress in rags and serve her Ribena, then we'd go behind the sofa and have Holy Communion. It was the best of times.

The Edgeleys were quite poor and Aileen used to shame her mother by sitting outside their house begging. I often used to see her because we were only two doors down. Someone would call Mrs Edgeley and say, 'Aileen's begging again', and Mrs Edgeley would rush outside and remove Aileen and her hat full of pennies.

Mr Edgeley is older than Mrs Edgeley, but as we grew up Mrs Edgeley ruled with a rod of fragility. All Aileen ever wanted was a dog but Mrs Edgeley wouldn't let her, and so for several years Aileen had a pet brick. We'd take that brick for a walk at the weekends if it was fine and my mother would put out a bowl for it. My Dad was very patient with Aileen and never got cross when we kept stopping to let it piddle.

In her letter Aileen told me the major news that her Dad has found a new ballroom partner. To explain why this is news: Mrs Edgeley is Mr Edgeley's second wife, but the second Mrs Edgeley can't dance. So Mum and Mr Edgeley were ballroom partners for quite a number of years. They danced at the Town Hall religiously. The dancing really made Mum thrive.

I wrote back and thanked her for letting me know. I do understand; even ballroom partners have to move on. I also told her the latest about Dad and Ivana, and how I've decided to excommunicate myself from them. I just don't want to hear, see or speak to them again, and I have written to Dad to say so. Aunt Coral agreed that I need time and space to sort through my feelings and that they must honour how I feel. That tiny lady is my rock.

Luckily my entry to the short story competition is really giving me a focus in these difficult times. I try and get a bit down each night, unless I am too tired from the Toastie. I have noticed that Cara and Pretafer seem to be reflections of myself and Loudolle. Fiona is perhaps a reflection of Michael, and Keeper is the dog of my dreams, (although Aunt Coral thinks he represents Joe!). Knight Van Day – no contest, I'd say he was probably Icarus. Now I understand what they mean when they say all writing is autobiographical.

It is a huge relief to know that Icarus and Loudolle have decided not to commit to Group, although Loudolle does want to enter the gala competition, as it would mean money if she won. It's bad enough suffering Loudolle at work and round the house, let alone in my cave. She has taken to swalking around the place in a silver bikini, making everyone feel inadequate. She is every inch the seedling love for a far-off film star.

Aunt Coral said in the drawing room one night over cognacs that, in her personal study of biology, 'If a finishing school girl walks round long enough in a bikini, it's only a matter of time before a boy will err.'

The Admiral is beside himself at the sight of Loudolle in her loveliness and keeps his whiskers in a heightened state of poof. He keeps rushing to his bathroom to freshen himself whenever Loudolle bathes in the blossoms. Aunt C may have said that it is perfectly right for young boys to err, because they have to or there is no chance for them to reform, but surely the Admiral should have really grown out of that sort of behaviour. It's not natural for a man of his age. He gets back to the conservatory very puffed after his trips to the bathroom and as a consequence of his infatuation, his short story is a lot of tosh about socialites. I feel sad to remember the 'pearl among corals' poem he wrote only a short time ago. I happen to know that Aunt C carries his piece of paper around with her in her handbag because I've seen her fisselling with it.

Interestingly, while Loudolle has managed to turn the Admiral's head, most surprisingly for the younger man, Joe is not for erring. Though she has tried and tried, in a succession of diminishing swimsuits, she simply cannot get Joe to err. Not for all the tea in china. He isn't a tea drinker.

Wednesday 18 March

Aunt Coral has presented me with a pink tasselled cover for my bed, just like her one, and she has also sewed me a monogram panel to put up on my wall with my letters, 'S. O. B.', on it. This has made me realise that I am becoming somewhat of her follower. Before I was a follower of Aunt Coral I was a follower of Mum, who led me in all her ways. I'm aware it is my habit, so I try not to lose myself to following, but it makes me feel like I belong, which is like air to me. Mum called it being like a sponge, but I call it being uncertain. Uncertain who I am, so I copy.

Being with Aunt Coral gives me a strong sense of identity, and I have discovered in her a sense of romance which I've wholeheartedly adopted. She affirms my mum's opinion that I might contain beauty and she who leads me to value the little things in life such as dressing up, conversation, bohemiamism, old tunes, butter curls and fine china. She has twelve pieces of everything, for who would give dinner for thirteen? But my gentleness I picked up from my mother – we are both paficists – and my pioneering spirit comes down from Mum's side too, such as travelling to Egham for my gap year. Funny how all the people you meet in your life all club together to inform you who you are. I feel particularly blessed to have had my mother and Aunt Coral put their stamp on me, informing me that I am a romantic bohemiam traveller.

But my writing is entirely my own, I didn't take it from anybody. It is just something I came into the world doing and I know I will leave that way too.

Friday 27 March

Today was like many another Friday: dinner, Group, cognacs, and bed. Mrs Bunion had gone for the weekend leaving a fragrant pie in the oven, Loudolle was out on the town with Icarus, Joe had left after Group, and the Admiral and Delia had gone off to bed. It was just beginning to get dark outside and I remember there was a strong smell of woodsmoke on the air. The last few logs of winter must have been burning across the borders. Everything was perfectly calm – calm before the storm, as they say.

The first hint of something wrong was when I couldn't find Aunt Coral when I went to say goodnight. Usually, before she turns in, Aunt Coral enjoys a bath with her candles. Her bathtub is something of a miracle in that she has no need of a plug, which she puts down to generations of mice who are now RIP in the pipe work. The bath holds its water for exactly forty-five minutes before draining, and then it takes a further forty-five minutes for the water to trickle out. But on this particular night I couldn't find her there, so I went upstairs, and from along the passage to her suite I could hear the sound of Nana Mouskouri singing. I tiptoed into her suite to wish her a goodnight. But as I went in I was mortified to see her sitting slumpen on her desk. She had a drink in front of her and was staring at an infestation of papers. On closer inspection I discovered they were bills. Electricity, council, credit card, plumber's letters, store cards, insurance, taxes.

Aunt Coral said nothing but totted up her drink as I sat down on the bed. Mrs Bunion had laid a small fire in the grate which was quietly fuming. On the surface it looked like Aunt Coral had got into fiscal difficulty. We sat there in silence for a while. When she eventually spoke, it all came tumbling out.

'I'm struggling Sue, I'm going under, I can't pay my bills. I've got through all of Father's money, all of it, and now all that's left is my guilt. It's all gone, gone, and I don't know how to get more of it.'

'You live in a very big house,' I said. 'You could take in more lodgers?'

'This house is not fit for paying guests, unless they're used to sleeping outside. And I've no capital left to restore it. Wildlife is getting in everywhere; the house is just too big. The Admiral's rent supports just the few rooms we use and my occasional trips to the food hall, but beyond that, Sue, if things get much tighter, I may even be forced to sell. We shall end up derelict, with weeds growing out of the doors. We shall be sold as an institution!'

I was speechless.

'If I sold I would have enough money to pay off my debts and buy a flat in Egham, but I love this house, I want to die here.'

I wished she wouldn't talk about dying like that, like it was such an easy thing to discuss.

'It's not just the bills,' she continued, with miserable tears breaking her cheeks. 'I owe thousands on my cards because I can't stop spending. It started when I lived alone with Father. There was only him and Mrs Bunion on weekdays, and I was lonely. Spending makes me feel alive. I even like the receipts. It's all gone though – gone on Harrods and holidays and handbags. Oh God, what have I done?'

She went to a large hanging on her wall and lifted it to expose acres of shoes and trinkets in shelving, not a surface clear of a bauble bought on her afternoons.

'We had no new shoes in the war, the military got all the leather, so I think I have been making up for it ever since,' she said.

Then she led me to a deep cupboard on the landing, where vacuum cleaners had taken a grip. There was one in every size, shape and colour, yet Green Place is the dustiest place on earth. Testament to Aunt Coral's true shopaholicalism: she'd much rather shop than clean.

Then she sank to the floor and sobbed and I had to perform a rescue.

'This needs action, Aunt Coral, and immediately,' I said. 'Let's look at the positives. How many people can say that they wish their house was smaller? You have a beautiful home, and you're not going to lose it. We've just got to exploit its potential.

'First of all, I will move out of the Grey Room and into the East Wing so you have a heated room to rent at once. Second, you will stop my allowance and I will see if I can become a full time girl. Third, if Delia's a true friend, she will move into the East Wing too – you could charge buckets for the Trout Suite. We won't mind camping in the East Wing if it means we can stay at Green Place. And fourth, if you do likewise that will instantly free up a third heated room to rent. All of that together should give you an income.

'Furthermore,' I added, emulating the way Aunt Coral rescues, 'give me your cards, I'm confiscating them. And *even* furthermore, you should arrange to auction your shoes. You could hold the sale here and invite all the ladies in Egham with size four feet.'

'You're a fine entrepreneur,' said Aunt Coral, pulling herself together and getting herself up again.

'You shall go gently into your old age, Aunt Coral, if I have anything to do with it.'

'You have cruel seventeen-year-old eyes,' she said.

I found it easy to be strong for her, but of course I am worried that Aunt Coral's spending threatens our whole way of life. If she had to sell Green Place, I'd probably have to go back to Titford, and that would be a fete worse than death. It's terribly shocking to realise that even Aunt Coral has a secret fault. I thought she was totally perfect until now. I suppose this makes her more human. I hope I don't have any secret faults, other than letting myself go – and I do let myself go when I'm writing, it's one of the reasons I'm enjoying living somewhere so remote.

Coral's Commonplace: Volume 2
Green Place, May 16 1934
(Age 12)

We were minded by Granny Morris last night, (Mrs Morris's mother), while Mother and Father went to the Savoy to see the Harry Roy Band. They were fortunate to get tickets. 'Live from the Ritz and Savoy Hotels!' I've never seen anything so glamorous. The HRB have been a complete sell-out since they were joined by Mr Al Bowlly.

Granny Morris also gives haircuts and Mother asked her to do mine only. Cameo's got a perfect pageboy at the moment, which is all Mother's own work. But Cameo hates to be left out of things, so Granny M pretended to cut hers as well. Before Cameo had the chance to examine the length of her hair too much, Granny M moved the subject along to her favourite topic, her widow's state pension, which includes in its weekly issue one packet of Woodbines. She told us that Woodbines were made famous by a Padre of the First World War, Woodbine Willie, who worked in the trenches, giving spiritual succour and cigarettes to soldiers in need. Later, we took it in turns to play Woodbine Willie and Granny M was the wounded soldiers. M and F returned to find we had not gone to bed.

Family news

Here is a copy of a letter that Cameo wrote to Aunt Fern (Mother's little sister). It was to thank her for her birthday present and I found it immensely shocking. I would never have got away with sending out such an abandoned letter, but Cameo is encouraged in pursuing an artistic nature, and her talent forgives all her trespasses.

Dear Aunt Fern,

Thank you very much for the birthday present, I can't remember what it was, but I can tell you how much I loved it.

Cameo X

She gets away with so much. Being the elder I fear the consequences of things more. Sometimes I wish I were the younger. It seems to be the easier choice. And yet I do understand it works the other way too, for example when M and F gave a dinner for the Aldermen and I was allowed to stay up late and Cameo wasn't. I found her at the top of the stairs with a tearstained face.

'Can I come down?' she said.

'No.'

'Why not?'

'Because you're seven,' I said.

Business news

Father is training me up to know the family business, so I am adding a business column to my Commonplace. He is switching from paddy to indigo because there are rumblings within his workers. This means he will major in tea, coffee, sugar, cinnamon and some rubber, which gives him a nice spread of crops. He has also signed a new deal to import more fruit from the Cape.

House news

We spent a large part of this afternoon at the worm graveyard. We wanted the full works for Zelda, and Rev Thomas obliged. We held the wake in the eastern tree house, but we had to cut it short because Ross got bitten by an adder. The vet said if it had been July he would not have survived, as adders' venom gets stronger as the summer progresses. Father says we are living in Tropical West Surrey, which has made Cameo scared to go for a walk unless she's wearing her waders. But adders are gentle and avoid human contact. The thing they will not tolerate is being nosed at by a dog. Ross is recuperating in the laundry, so perhaps it has all been worth it. Terry has been quite sniffy about it all, he doesn't like sharing his space.

At the end of the day I dressed Cameo up, head to toe in adder-proof costume, with winter socks and waders, and a little bell she could ring to alarm the snakes, and we went to the wood to pick bluebells before they all disappear. I needed Cameo's help, because I want to try to produce a fine woodland scent again. (I think I know what went wrong before, I shouldn't have added the yeast. Last year we had lined up thirty-two bottles in the laundry, filled with our chosen ingredients, forgetting that yeast rises when it is activated, and so we should not have closed the lids. It was very unfortunate, the entire batch exploded.)

However, it did lead us into the thought of trying our hands at making wine. Mother threatens she will open a vein if we do. But though she declares that my rose splash smells like urine, she is still loyal enough to wear it. So I have to improve or she'll smell, and we can't have that. Here is the recipe:

BLUEBELL CRUSH

6 large baskets of bluebells (crushed with large stone or bat)

1 Steep in kettle water at room temperature for no more than 2 hours
2 Sieve mixture, retaining the crush for compost
3 Add sugar (not yeast) and boil gently for 18 minutes
4 Cool the essence
5 Pour into dainty bottle
6 Add label

The bottles are at this moment in the laundry with the dogs. So far so good.

Sue

THE EAST WING at Green Place is now known as the Cobweb Kingdom. Until we all debunked into the dilapidated rooms there a week ago, the Admiral had the Kingdom to himself, with just the squirrels and birds for companions. We found most of the furniture there laying under sheeting like an army of unopened presents. A nest of tables here, a linen press there, the remainder of Aunt Coral's glory day airlooms shivering under thin cover. There is an old laundry in the basement where you can sometimes hear voices whispering at the sink. Ghosts of former residents I thought, but apparently it is an air lock.

There must have been hundreds of folk who have died at Green Place over time. My Great Great Great Grandmother Ellen bought the house in the 1840s, when Queen Annes were again in fashion, but there had previously been an even bigger house on the site, which was demolished long before the present house was built. So there have been lost souls wandering this site for at least three hundred years.

I sometimes wonder why Aunt Coral doesn't do more research into all of this, but I believe it would only fuel the imagination she is trying to control, leaving her prey to headless horsemen and maidens hanging from beams, in addition to the whisperers at the sink. She tries as hard as possible not to believe in ghosts. 'For what is a ghost?' she says. 'Only the shadow of your shadow.'

But getting back to the here and now, before I get the willies.

Underneath the laundry there's a cellar, with dusty rows of wine. Aunt C laid down a bottle for me when I was born, and is saving it for my eighteenth birthday. Down the way from the Admiral's quarters is a room which is always kept locked, and for which there is only one key, held by Aunt Coral in private. No one has been in there for years, not even Mrs Bunion on bat patrol. It is separated from the rest of the Wing by a dividing door and a long corridor, at the end of which are two steps up to the left, leading to the locked room, and two steps up to the right, leading to another bedroom, which is left open. These suites are known as Bluebell Left and Right, and Aunt Coral and Nana Cameo lived in them when they were children. Aunt C is evasive about the locked one, because she says it holds unhappy memoirs.

In the East–West reshuffle she gave Delia and Loudolle the most up-to-date suite, with its own bathroom with a *working* electric heater. This suite is called Snowdrop. She moved herself into a den type of room that used to be a study in its heyday, this room is called the Green Den. There isn't much room for her pink-tasselled bed, but the size of the room means that it is possible to heat with just one small bar heater, and Aunt Coral really suffers with the cold, being only five foot two and mostly of skin and bones.

I love my new room, which is right at the top of the East Wing and looks down the drive over the buddleia. It is separated from the other bedrooms by a small staircase, with some ominous treads and its own private corridor. This is called 'Pearl's Room', after Aunt Coral's mother, and is one of the largest rooms in the house. There is a painting of the desert on one wall, which Nana Pearl brought back from the Bush when she finally came back with Buddleia. Funny old Victorians, they really overdid things – Australia was a four-week voyage away back then!

There are two sets of grand doors which lead on to a balcony, but it's too dangerous to sit out on. A pity, because I saw myself having petty dejuner out there with Icarus after we'd lain in bed loving.

To warm the room I have two camping heaters, which make a sound like hot air balloons, but after they've got going do well enough if you stand right up close to them. I have just become used to wearing extra layers in bed and I think a lot about summer. I still have to walk over to the West Wing for my bath, as it is too cold to bathe in the East. This daily routine takes the best part of an hour, travelling down the dusty passages in my towels, gooney and coat. I've always wondered why the Admiral didn't wash very much.

We have cleaned out our vacant West Wing rooms and Aunt Coral has put up notices in the post office advertising for lodgers. Now all there is to do is to wait and see what happens.

The days seem to melt, like the secret journey of blossom petals on the spring trees. I work, I thrive, I fall to the ground and get blown in the house by the wind. There's barely a moment that isn't filled with the Toastie, or by writing, or by pottering around with my knickknacks. I've been through my chest of draws and put scented lining paper under my pants. I've hand-washed my thick winter hat and scarf, which are now drying on the bottom echelons of my washstand, and on my shelf I have created separate folders for each of my 'Brackencliffe' characters, into which I place inspirational notes. I don't know what it is about spring. It makes me want to fissel.

Dad didn't take the fact that I want to excommunicate him sitting down. He has written to ask me to think about it. He said that while he can understand my feelings about Mum, he needs to move on with his life in order to go on being alive. He also said that he and Ivana were considering having a baby because Ivana was in the last chance salon.

Moving on with his life I can understand, though it is fast, and having a baby is, I suppose, one in the eye for death, but being together before Mum died, driving her to despair – for that I can never forgive him.

According to Delia, widowers get into remarriages much quicker than widows do. But Mum's memory is not even misty. She is still receiving post.

I am currently going through a horrible phase with a nasty recurring dream in which I am hunting for mum's suicide note. In the dream I always seem to be looking in a stupid wrong place, like in the kitchen at the Toastie or in the swimming pool at Green Place, and although I know I am looking in a stupid wrong place, I look anyway in spite of myself. I don't find Mum's note, but I do find notes from other people written in other languages. It's like I've discovered the world suicide note bank, and though this upsets me, I still search through them all, hoping to find one from Mum, reading through all the despair and farewell, which is somehow understandable in any language, and then I wake up calling for my mother and Aunt Coral comes running.

At least I have a small silver lining, which is that Loudolle has gone back to Alpen. Before she left the Admiral had taken to watching her swim each morning, getting up at ungodly hours to catch the mermaid. He plucked up the courage to complement her on the last day of her holidays.

'Oh Loudolle, you were definitely hit with the pretty stick weren't you?' he said.

'Oh yes,' she replied, 'I was clobbered with it.'

She has *no* modesty. It is just simply *missing*. It's a wonder she can walk around without falling over under the weight of her great big head.

And although that day was a day of uncommon sunshine, a nasty wind got up and upset all the ground leaves, just as Loudolle has upset the entire household in one foul swoop. I dread what the devil her long summer holidays might bring.

Aunt Coral has been very strong about it all, and said that she understands the Admiral's behaviour because his urge to hear the birds once more was strong.

'How do you know?' I asked her.

'Because I'm canny,' she said. 'It's a curse.' She is convinced it was nothing more than a tender phase he was going through.

In fact it strikes me we have had a case of great opposites at Green Place this Easter. Loudolle beautiful on the outside, ugly on the in, everything she touches looks like she's advertising it. And Aunt Coral tired on the outside and lovely on the in. But what good is loveliness that can't be seen in the world of shallow old men?

I wish I were tall with slim knees and long hair like Loudolle. But being a large cup size means I must keep my hair short so that I don't disappear into my cleeverage. The Doctor says my knees are 'valgus', which makes them sound like they're brave, but I looked it up in the encyclopaedia and it means my knees are knocked. Joe has taken to calling me the knock-kneed novelist. I know he's only joking, but it's a bit of a sensitive issue. I wonder if Icarus has ever noticed my knees? I wonder how Icarus feels now that Loudolle has left, whether he'll pick back up with Michael again, or perhaps someone else . . . and I've put his eye back under my pillow. Maybe it's not over after all.

Monday May 4th

May is a month of bank holidays because of the work of John Lubbock. He was a Baron and a politician who campaigned for additional holidays and shorter working hours for the poor. I know this because I have been reading the encyclopaedia again in bed. I found a lovely thing he said about books: 'We may sit in our library and yet be in all quarters of the earth.' I'm going to put it on Aunt C's desk as a surprise and inspiration.

We didn't get many replies to our ads for lodgers in the end, so the Admiral offered two of his ex-navy friends suites in the West Wing, and they moved into Green Place at the end of last month. Admiral Gordon and Admiral Ted served with him on the SS *St Francis* when they were all young men. He knew that though they had been looking for accommodation in London, the opportunity to live in a catered mansion would be beyond their wildest dreams.

Admiral Gordon is a ginger man with a large stomach, and is a hearty outdoors sort of chap who slept up on deck when he was at sea. An expert in navigation, he has been blown away by Aunt C's marine timekeepers, which she was bequeathed from her Father's fleet. Over introductory cups of tea, Delia was trying to impress, and told Admiral Gordon that her Mother was a gypsy who cooked everything on one ring and served everything up with strong tea. I'm sure this is to exoticise herself; Aunt C says her mother came from Chiswick.

Admiral Ted is tall and swanaway, with a long tash that absorbs a lot of his dinner. He comes from a little place called Shooters Bottom, I wish he hadn't told me that. He's a helpful sort of chap, and interested in people's problems, and also a man of caution, who beeps his horn before the bends on the drive.

Although it feels like we now live with half the marines, the new Admirals have taken to life at Green Place like ducks to water. They pay their rent on time, help with the garden, wolf down the cuisine, and enjoy a game of bowels.

With three Admirals on site paying rent and being helpful, Aunt Coral should be able to start chipping away at some of her debts. She can also begin to get jobs ticked off her To Do list, such as the insulation of the letter box, and some sanding, drilling and planering, as well as cutting back the ground elder that is so rampant around the estate. Admiral Ted has already started on the latter, and dresses himself in full manly garb for the job, including a waterproof jerkin, trousers with patch pockets for his snippers, and traditional barbershop wellies which he prefers for country use.

The Grey Room has just gone to a Japanese gentleman on business, whose name is Mr Tsunawa. Aunt Coral promised him that the Grey Room is haunted to sell him the full English country house experience. This involves one of us going and clanking a chain outside his bedroom door late at night. It is a new way of life for us all, but we have quickly adjusted because we need to.

From the moment I discovered Aunt Coral sobbing on her bills I've made it my mission to help her, so I am in charge of cutbacks and debt management at Green Place. While the money from the lodgers keeps us all in food and heating, it doesn't do much else.

As well as leaving her the house, Aunt Coral's Father also left her his portfolio of shares. The shares are held in steel, coal, tin mines and Marks and Spencer's, and she also has a punt with some gold. In addition, Great Grandfather Evelyn left Aunt Coral all the remainder of his collections: tapestries, busts and sculptures, a rococo carving in the hall, and a valuable Dick Van Dyke that hails from his Genoese period.

Showing such favouritism to Aunt Coral and leaving very little to mum caused a great upset at the reading of his Will – though I suppose now we all know why. However my mother was not left without any-thing as when Nana Pearl died in 1955, she had requested that her bank accounts were formed into trusts entirely for Mum. There was enough to get a deposit, or do up a small house, and they were set up to become liquid on the 'second death' (that was Grampa Evelyn), so both Coral and Mum would inherit at the same time. But as Mum died so soon after Grampa Evelyn's death the trust money was frozen in probate, and it still hasn't come through yet due to the complicated nature of mum's death. By law my father has a claim to this as well as me, but at least the slow probate means that it's protected from him for now.

Anyway, it struck me that selling some shares would pay off a small amount of Aunt Coral's debts, but when I brought the matter up last week, she was adamant they remain as rainy day funds, in case she needs her hips done, or has some sort of medical emergency. She also argued that while the money was still in shares it is difficult for her to spend it, as converting shares involves a great deal of admin, and the reading of the *Financial Times*. I think she just likes to know they're still there.

However, I have also found out that the Bentley doesn't belong to the Admiral but is in fact Aunt Coral's. She just loved the idea of having a driver so much that she lent it to him and bought him a chauffeur's hat. In real life the Admiral only has a Rover, so driving a Bentley's a coo! But I think he's a very nice guy to go along with the hat.

So today I moved on to other tactics, and suggested that the sale of the Bentley would pay off some of her store cards, but she argued she has a very good reason to keep it. The reason is the Nanas. Though she is approximately over sixty-five herself, (which she smallens to sixty-three), Aunt Coral likes to help the aged, and once a week she goes to the home in Egham and takes three of the Nanas there out on a drive: Mrs Dryberry, Mrs Scott, and Mrs Viller. Because of their habitual clothing choices we call them Georgette, Print and Taffeta. They come for lunch once a week which they take on the terrace alf rescos. They share a lot of her interests, such as rambling and Nana Mouskouri. Apparently driving the Nanas gives Aunt C's life meaning. I also think that because they are so ancient, they make her feel young.

I worked and worked on her this morning as we sat out by the pool, trying to persuade her that the Nanas would just as soon be driven in the Rover as the Bentley, but she just doesn't know how to think like a parson. I realised that I would have to explore a more heavy approach.

'If you cut Mrs Bunion down to two days a week, you and Delia could clean for the other afternoons instead of shop,' I said. You can imagine what sort of a face this was met with.

'Pat's been with me for ever, I've known her for years, she's part of the building, and there's her family to consider.'

'We are all affected by your fiscal position, Aunt Coral, even Mrs Bunion, and there's no point in pretending otherwise. I'm sure she'll understand, you just need to talk to her about it.'

'I can't talk to Pat, she's the cleaner,' said Aunt Coral.

'But you just said that you've known her for years!'

'Exactly,' she said, implying she had just won the argument by re-acting as if I was agreeing with her. A clever trick of hers.

'Just tell her that you have to cut back for the restoration of the East Wing. You don't have to tell her about your shoes.'

There are going to have to be big changes at Green Place if we are going to make ends meet, but Aunt Coral seems to be in complete denial and preoccupied with other things.

'They didn't need to lie to me you know, I wouldn't have told anyone about Laine,' she said, revealing her hidden inner dialogue in an involuntary change of subject. (It seems a person can be talking about one thing and thinking about quite another.)

'Maybe they thought I couldn't be trusted not to run off and get pregnant myself. But the thing that hurts the most is that *Cameo* didn't tell me. I can at least understand that Mother and Father, however painfully, were trying to do their best, but Cameo had no reason on earth not to tell me the truth.'

'Weren't you very close?' I said.

'We were terribly close, always,' she said. 'She was a wonderful sister.'

And then as so often happens, the Admiral pulled up a chair, and Aunt Coral turned her attention to the come hither of her de collage. He himself had changed into a gaye cravat to come down to the pool side. It is difficult at times for us to talk at all, living in a public house.

Coral's Commonplace: Volume 2

Cuttings from the Willow Lodge School Reports, Autumn Term 1935:

Coral (age 13) is diligent, and blessed with a very good brain. She is hard working but is easily distracted by the workmen. If she learns to apply herself, she is certain to get into college. She is prone to display high spirits, and has been caught wearing drama department shoes.

Rev Harold Stubbs, Form Four

Cameo (age 8) considers it a waste of her time coming to school, and I consider it a waste of my time trying to teach her. She is disruptive, and makes frequent attempts to climb out of the window during maths.

She was given a new dolly for her birthday, which, in keeping with her family traditions for being called after jewellery, she has christened 'Bracelet'. I have confiscated the doll until she learns to remain in the class.

Priscilla Mooney, First Form

Sue

TODAY I INADVERTENTLY discovered the way to get Icarus's attention. The morning was breathtaking, one of those mornings when everyone is singing, and with Loudolle back at college I'd been reinstated on the toaster. Anyway, I had an accident with the frother which was turned the wrong way up and milk spurted out on my top. I had to borrow one of Michael's from her gym bag, which was a sort of a bra-cum-vest. I put a clean apron over the top of it but much of my cleeverage showed. Icarus couldn't keep away from me, helping me with the buttering and worrying about the toast. Delia says Icarus's what's known in the classics as a tit man, which I always thought meant some sort of idiot.

With the extra money from Loudolle's Easter time, Mrs Fry has decided to start opening the Toastie at luncheons as a jacket potato bar, and she's invested in some new ovens. She also wants to branch into Bistro for the evenings. This has given me the perfect opportunity to become a full time girl, and help carry the can at Green Place.

All the full time girls are called 'Potato Maids' and she has had it professionally sewn on our pinnys. I like to think that looking back years from now my grandchildren will say that Nana Sue had to support herself before she was published, and had many jobs including canteen apprentice and potato maid.

I am finding Joe somewhat irksome because he's always following me around at work or writing soppy poems at Group, which make Aunt

Coral and Delia behave badly. The more he tries to make love to me, the more I feel attracted to Icarus. It's the strange occasional quirk of love that the more someone loves you, the more you go off them. I wonder whether I should try to pretend I don't love Icarus and see if that would help.

At least I have managed to bond with Michael. She reminds me so much of Aileen. Like Aileen, Michael's mother is her father's second wife, and like Aileen, Michael's got scattered siblings.

Aileen and I were like sisters to each other when we were growing up in Titford. But of course we weren't sisters and it was hard to say goodbye at the end of a top notch day's play. So we made our own telephones out of old tin cans, with a hole drilled in the end for string to be poked through like phone wire, and we hung out of our respective windows, two houses apart and pretended to be on the phone. It did make my mum laugh.

There have been so many times when I have wished for those days again. Whoever said 'be careful what you wish for cos you'll get it' was a liar.

Coral's Commonplace: Volume 2
Green Place, Nov 6 1935
(Age 13)

Home news

It was bitterly cold today, especially inside. I woke very early to sunrays spread on the horizon like a fan; these are known as corpuscular rays, such as the ones that shine through the trees at sunset.

Cameo had cut the arms off my ball gown while I was asleep, so we went out to Crimson and Hopper this afternoon to buy me another. Cameo said she did it because she was feeling unhinged, and was eaten up with worry over a rare infection believed to be spread by paperclips. Mother was not calm. It took twenty-five minutes for us to talk Cameo past the paperclip pot in the hall on the way out. Mrs Morris was doing the polishing, and found it so entertaining that she polished the same figurine for the whole time. We shouldn't indulge Cameo's attempts to be arty, it takes us so long to go out.

I know I have no need of a ball gown quite yet, but confess I did enjoy wearing it round the house.

Emotional news

I want to have six children, in three sets of boy-and-girl twins, Robin and Robina being my first name choices. Cameo wants to be a pilot, like Amelia Earhart, or a racing driver, like Helene Delangle, who has a hundred boyfriends and is a nude dancer part time. 'There are two things I want to be when I grow up,' she said to me. 'One is a great adventurer, the other is taller than Dad.'

We have started ballroom dancing together in the woods on days when the weather permits. I am much smaller as Cameo's such a colt, so she has to be the man, which is very nice for me. It is wonderfully private doing it outside where Mother and Father can't see us. We foxtrot and waltz and tango, and Cameo likes a smooch. I have to be the man for this one so she can practise her 'things' on me.

Last night she crawled into my bed, as she often does and said, 'What shall we talk about? Boys?'

'Let's talk about going to sleep.'

'Why can't we talk about boys?'

'Because you're 8,' I said.

School news

We have a new class entitled 'Good Grooming'. The first lecture was taken up mainly with telling us not to pick at our spots. I resent the insinuation that I have any, and Cameo is the number one pin-up, in spite of her glass eye. They also talked about the importance of the frequency of washing the weevils from your hairbrush and the necessity of sleep as a beauty aid. What would they turn us into? Mrs Pankhurst would turn in her grave. If we followed their advice we might never know the ecstasy of intense moments spent on a blackhead, of a sleepless night following a pillow fight, or a rarely washed hairbrush kept in a secret drawer, and anyway, a Green Place girl's hair is self-brushing.

This is a two-minute puzzler by Cameo that she wanted me to add:

Can you spot the odd one out?

SUN
MOON
STARS
SOCKS

Sue

Wednesday May 27th

ADVERT FROM THE post office window:

Delia Shoot

HANDMADE GOWNS FOR PARTIES

Telephone Egham 69950

The income from the West Wing lodgers has solved our immediate cash flow problems, but when the winter comes round again it is likely the three of us in the Arctic Wing might perish. I am hoping that the auction of Aunt Coral's shoes will generate enough money to restore and let out some other rooms, but there is a lot that we need to achieve fiscally before that could happen. The squirrels have chewed their way through a lot of the wiring and we'll need to pay for electricians, plumbers, plasterers, painters, to mention a few.

The bank won't go near Aunt Coral and she won't go near the bank, having previously exhausted every possibility of each other. So I made enquiries into every lodger's skills and it transpires that Delia has a secret she had not revealed because of laziness. The secret is that she can sew. I have encouraged her to take orders from the wealthy Egham ladies by advertising in the post office and she has been able to get a couple of commissions. The choosing and sourcing of fabrics, the shapes, textures and colours etc., have really made her thrive. She also employs the labour of Georgette, Print and Taffeta, who are fashion freaks too. They sit out by the pool because Nanas love to be out in the open, and they gossip, eat sandwiches and sew. It is a cracking cottage industry and our best shot at serious money. The first gown they made was sold to a Mrs Fury of Virginia Water and netted a whopping £198. It was an aqua silk-satin dinner gown designed and cut by Delia, with sequin specks by Georgette, appliqué godets by Print, and matching beading by Taffeta. Job done. Mrs Fury was a head turner.

Delia has also sold her engagement ring, which she said she'd been dying to do, but the silly girls went to Harrods and blew most of the money, leaving only peanuts for Green Place. I was beside myself when I saw them coming home from Knightsbridge loaded with green and gold bags. Aunt Coral bought herself a new handbag costing £295 because she said it was her birthday in a few months' time. (Controversially, she has just *had* a birthday!) Her spending seems to go up as a direct result of her feeling down, and she is feeling down about her debts. It is a vicious circle. Spending has been her friend when she was lonely, but I'm determined that she won't be any more.

It's struck me that in an age where romance is declining, a product we might sell is chivalry, and I have been wondering whether the Admirals might host chivalry workshops, inviting all the Egham romantics. They are real gents and certainly know how to treat the ladies. I have never once had to close a car door, or put my own napkin on my knee if one of the Admirals is around to do it for me. During dinner, they help us in and out of our chairs, stand up if one of us leaves the table to go to the toilet and are experts in the art of complementing.

With only a small outlay, (such as the £295 from the refund of Aunt Coral's handbag), we could host catered weekend events employing the resources of Mrs Bunion, the grounds, and the Admirals. There are a hundred ways to make money if you have the space and good ideas.

Brackencliffe

By Sue Bowl

But Brackencliffe life tweren't no picnic, with twenty-five below stairs to be fed. If Cara was late to the fireside a-nights it meant she would have to sleep cold. Lest we forget, it was the seventeenth century and the only central heating was roaring log fires.

At the third night on the trot of sleeping too far from the hearth, Cara became sick and had to go up to the San, (the hospital wing for staff). There she recovered under care of Spinster Nurse Chopin, with Keeper in watch at her side. But while Cara lay sleeping a-bedde, Pretafer stole in to peep, and in a sudden girlish frenzy seized a locket from about Cara's swan neck. But Keeper darted from under the bed to his mistress's aid, shaking his prey till she dropped the locket, and plucking it in his jaws took flight.

'Find him,' whispered Cara to Fiona, who rushed to her bedside table.

'Silence!' said Pretafer as she turned away, ignoring the shredded garments adorning her tiny calfs.

Egham Hirsute Group
On Cliff-hangers

At Group this evening our efforts tied in nicely with our fiscal endeavours because there is the chance of prize money for the short story competition. I had just read out my latest instalment (above) and now Aunt Coral asked the Admiral to read out a taster of his. But he was gazing out at the empty swimming pool sewn with magnolia petals. He offered his little extract slowly, with a tired little voice.

The Socialites

By Admiral Avery Little

She awoke, the blue bikini peeping from its box. Yawning, she put it on, before checking herself in the mirror. The arms of a gazelle, two legs, a cascade of fragrant curls, and a sheen on her skin that would rival the freshest cherry. If this pretty socialite wasn't next year's model, there was no justice under heaven.

Society photographer, Danny De Zooter was set to shoot her at dusk, but till then she needed to swim, gliding through the water in dreams.

'Excellent Avery, really excellent, well done,' said Aunt Coral, forcing herself not to show any information about how his extract made her feel, underplaying the way she said 'Avery', as if it were just the name of some idiot student and not the man she loved.

'Joe?'

'I haven't done much yet,' said Joe, but he stood up.

Roger Mead

By Josef Fry

She awoke, and Hawley knew she was not thinking of him. Perhaps it was because he had seen the way she looked at Roger Mead. But there was still time. If he waited, it would happen. She didn't know the truth about Roger yet, and when it came out, as sure as the sun rose, Hawley would catch her.

'Excellent Joe, really excellent, well done, I'm dying to know what happens next,' said Aunt Coral.

Joe looked everywhere but at me, and I wasn't going to show any information on my face about the fact that I'd noticed him not looking at me. I pretended to make pencil notes as he was reading, so I'd have a reason to look elsewhere. The atmosphere was loaded. Aunt Coral was trying not to look at the Admiral, the Admiral was trying not to look at Aunt Coral, Joe was trying not to look at me, and I was trying not to look at Joe. The only person with someone not to look at was Delia and I'm sure she felt the lack.

'Delia?' said Aunt Coral.

Delia arose and held her handbag for support.

Don't Wait

By Delia Shoot

She awoke and wished she hadn't, wished she'd never been born. Never been born to such pain and regret. Another day to repeat the efforts of the day before, and the day before that, falling behind her, lost to possibility. But today might be different.

 She bathed and dressed, the fat woman in the mirror. Today she would do something about it. But by lunchtime the cold Pouilly-Fuissé had proven such a comfort from the lonely long day that she thought, 'Well there's always tomorrow.'

'Excellent Delia, really excellent, well done,' said Aunt Coral.

Delia took a hanky from her handbag and blew her nose, sitting down again with careful control of herself.

'Writing's a very emotional business, very emotional indeed,' Aunt Coral went on. 'But that emotional business is vital to engage the reader. Now, thank you for sharing your extracts, let's move on to a four-point plan: 1, the use of cliff-hangers, 2, the art of foreshadowing, 3, the creation of atmosphere and D, the transportation of the reader; that is, the art of sweeping the reader away on a journey, all for the price of two teas.'

She flashed a twinkle at the Admiral, who missed it, for his mind was still in the swimming pool. I felt sorry for him that he'd missed it, it was a beautiful gaze and never to be repeated. My antennae are hot for that sort of thing at the moment because Icarus misses all mine. Joe doesn't though. Even though they are not for him, he doesn't miss one. It is like working beside a microscope.

I typed 'Sweeping the reader away' on my notes, while trying to stop analysing group members' gazes. For how I long to cliff-hang and sweep and transport. And how I would love to foreshadow.

'The cliff-hanger,' said Aunt Coral. 'The cliff-hanger is a device or a tease for the reader, to bait them into continuing with the story. Can anyone spot any cliff-hangers in our extracts?' she asked.

We all put our hands up.

'Sue?' said Aunt Coral.

'What is the truth about Roger Mead, in Joe's story,' I said.

'Excellent Sue, yes, we all want to know the truth about Roger Mead and we sense the author will tell us if we keep on reading. Anything else?'

We all put our hands up.

'Sue?' said Aunt Coral.

'There's always tomorrow in Delia's story,' I said.

'Yes indeed, excellent Sue, "there's always tomorrow" draws the reader onwards, literally, to tomorrow. You've got the idea.'

I couldn't see much in the way of cliffhanging in the Admiral's story. It was clearly just a fantasy about Loudolle.

'Now, what is the question most people want to know about a story?' said Aunt Coral.

We all put our hands up.

'Sue?' said Aunt Coral.

'How does it end?' I said.

'Excellent Sue, yes, how does it end. Always remember, the reader wants to know the end – it's what keeps them turning the pages. Now . . .' She shuffled her papers and took a long swig of Sapphire which had become her group staple. 'Now, moving on to the art of foreshadowing, can anyone think what this might mean?'

We all put our hands up.

'Sue?' said Aunt Coral.

'Is it giving an impression of what might be going to happen later in the story?'

'Excellent Sue, well done. Can you think of an example?'

'The possibility that the pretty socialite in the Admiral's story is going to end up as next year's model?' I said.

'Good,' said Aunt Coral. 'And Joe?'

'Well, in "Roger Mead" I'm giving the impression that if Hawley waits, the girl might fall for him,' he said.

'Excellent Joe, well done, you're therefore somewhere between cliffhanging and foreshadowing, which is excellent. Now let's go to point three on the plan, the creation of atmosphere, or the world of the story. Here is an example of what I mean.'

Aunt Coral stood up in the conservatory window, her dear face swamped in apple blossom, and for the first time offered some of her own work as an example to the EHG. Her voice was clear and small, with only a slight vibrato to give away her hidden inner emotions.

'Looking out of the window, at the road down to the gates,' she said, 'could for example be built into: "She gazed out of the window, stuck closed with paint from that job that turned out to be a false economy, and watched the rain roll down the tarmac to the wet gates." And if we say something about how the rain fell it will further beef up the atmosphere. For example, "the rain fell like carpets", or "the rain fell like stairlets". Try to think of new ways to give the impression of what kind of rain it is, i.e. whether you want it to be teeming or spitting or cascading. But also and most importantly, you must remember to say how the woman is feeling when she looks out the window, to draw us into her emotional state, for example: "She gazed out of the window, stuck closed with paint from that job that was a false economy, and watched the rain roll down the tarmac like stairlets to the wet gates, behind which no one could hear her cries."'

We all sat in awe. Aunt Coral had filled her tiny passage with buckets of atmosphere, transporting us in a nanasecond to a badly painted window with a sad woman behind it. I was inspired beyond belief and could hardly wait to get on with 'Brackencliffe'. It was a very emotional moment for the Egham Hirsute Group.

'That's it for now,' she said, spent from her efforts. 'Next week we'll look at red herrings.'

We applauded her as she left the room, a tiny figure in a spring cardigan tottering unsteadily as she walked away. Was she thinking, as I was, of the cliff-hanger in our own story?

'I've got a big football match coming up, on Sunday 5th July,' said Joe, bringing me back to earth. 'I was wondering if you'd like to come.'

Though I was not plus about it I thought that I'd probably go. 'Thank you, that'd be nice,' I said.

Icarus plays football too and the thought of seeing him outside Toastie hours was quite overwhelming. I am now upstairs alone with his eye, my heart full of excitement and despair. But it is nice to have a date in the diary, albeit with the wrong man.

Coral's Commonplace: Volume 2

Cutting from the *Egham Echo*, May 30 1936

Poor Gollywhopper (daddy long leg)
By Coral Garden, age 14

Oh I am not long for this world, so I must savour every moment,

each leaf on the hedge thrills me, and how I wish for more.

It is light in the garden and green and we are many.

I am drawn to the light, when the sun goes down.

Is that some small sun?

I dance towards it for lo, there is the night sun!

I find a chink and I fly in, but how did I get here? How do I go back?

I fly at the light, I fly at the door, but I cannot find my way out,

With the last of my strength, I cling to life,

My legs fail one by one.

I land forever in a silver cup, it burns my wings, my last thoughts
are of the hedge.

And there you will throw me in the morning.

Sue

I AWOKE THIS morning from one of my nightmares, calling for my Mum, and Aunt Coral came running. She made me some breakfast on the terrace, and then gave me her one piece of published verse to critique in order to distract me. She had it pressed inside her Commonplace. Unfortunately her poem only made me feel more upset, and it was as though I were a fountain, raining tears on the frills of her collar, which luckily seemed quite waterproof, so they ran off to be baked in the sun.

'It's very depressing,' I told her. 'Perhaps you should have dwelt more on his life before he got trapped in the house?'

'You're right,' she said. 'Poor gollywhopper.' And we rewrote the poem from all the positive points of view about being a daddy long legs, such as being high on sweet air, and not knowing you're going to die, and nose-diving martinis and sleeping in herb tubs. Aunt Coral really has a talent for getting inside the minds of the small things.

The sun had risen like a fireball beyond the pool, with the plumes of buddleia like reeds in front of it. The Nanas were already at their sewing, discussing the Queen's holiday pattern. Delia was cutting trenches of calico and the Admirals were in the depths of the garden, so Aunt C and I found ourselves with a rare moment to talk un-interrupted.

'I feel as though I have lost fifty per cent of myself,' I said to Aunt C, 'and that I have to reassemble myself and find a new fifty per cent. If I'd still been in Titford it would have been a different fifty per cent wouldn't it? I'd have ended up in a shop selling car shoes, and grown up to wear frosted lipstick, and had so-called friends who didn't understand me and to whom I couldn't tell secrets.'

'Perish the thought,' said Aunt Coral. She stirred her regular powders into a glass and offered me a pastry. 'What happened in your dream?'

'It was like a Film Noir starring Mr Jewell, the librarian at Titford. He was the one working on the day Mum took her life and he was the one who found her. In my dream he was called away from the front desk and detained for a long time by papers in an office. Meanwhile Mum walked into the library and lay down on the floor by the Poets. If he hadn't been away so long, he would have found her sooner, but instead he put his feet up on his office desk and had a quick smoke. What bothers me is the thought that perhaps she didn't leave a note because she meant him to find her in time. Why else do it in a public place? But he didn't find her and she didn't leave a suicide note, so we either A, haven't found it, or B, she was expecting to be resuscitated, and this thought distresses me *so* much, to think that it might have been her cry for help and we missed it.'

'I know it's very hard, but you must try not to look backwards. It's awful, but it may be the case that she just didn't leave a note,' said Aunt C. 'You have no way of communicating with her now. There are some things that you just cannot know.'

'But I *have* got a way of communicating with her,' I said, 'I have messages from the other world.'

'Indeed?' she said, momentarily distracted by the Admiral jiggling grass off his trousers.

'Yes,' I said. 'When I open *The Dorcas Tree* to study in the evenings, it always opens at the same place, and my eye is always drawn to the same line which says: "I was sorry I left without saying goodbye." And even more strange is that it is given as an example of dialogue for a character who has vanished.'

'A coincidence,' said Aunt Coral, 'which is in collision with your quest.'

'But maybe she really is talking to me from beyond the grave and if so, maybe she will tell me where her suicide note is. I have to hold back so much you know, when I'm out in the world in public. I hope she has gone to Heaven, and if she has, I hope that she still thinks of me. But I worry that she doesn't, because in Heaven they say there will be no more suffering, so to think of me would make her suffer, so maybe she might not. Maybe I need to go back to Titford and have another look for a note,' I said.

'Maybe,' said Aunt Coral. 'If you think it will help.'

Thursday 18 June

I finally found out who Dean Martin is. He's Aunt C's stockbroker and looks after her portfolio of shares. Marks and Spencer is her spiritual home and unfortunately she believes she is helping to keep her own shares in it afloat by doing her weekly shop there. I've had the difficult job of persuading her that her shopping alone makes no difference to the share price and that the weekly groceries are better bought else-where whilst we are still in a state of economics. She's still rejecting my suggestion of reducing Mrs Bunion's hours and revealed a whole other side to herself when I raised the matter again yesterday, threatening to move into what she calls a 'death house'. She is strongly in denial, and her shopping list is full of dreams. She keeps it on the butterfly table in the hall beside the telephone and updates it daily. Here's an example of her latest version:

Shopping List

Brooch

Rouge

Handbag

Weedol

Truffles

Song book

Half the time she buys the items, then practises the art of unshopping them, which she says is almost as much fun as buying them in the first place, except with a tinge of regret.

She has also started to keep her latest To Do list alongside the shopping list, not only to remind her where she is up to in life, but I'm sure as a hint to the Admiral-handymen. She has no shame.

To Do List

Make will

Pump tyres

Clear bat box

Sort briefs

Telephone Badger

I check it every day, just to see if anything has been ticked off. 'Make Will' has been on there since I moved into Green Place, so thankfully there is no hurry.

I desperately want to buy back the handbag she had to take back to Harrods, so I have calculated that if I save a pound a week for 295 weeks, I'll be able to get it for her in six years, so she'll have it on her seventy-second birthday. But that is based on her having told the truth about her age which isn't in her nature.

I asked her how old she was again the other day, to see if I could catch her out, and she said: 'I'm sixty-one – no, sixty-two – but I don't have a good head for figures.' Sometimes she will admit to up to sixty-four in the mornings; for she's only to see a pillow for scars to play pirates on her cheeks. But anyway I have now put her handbag on *my* shopping list.

Saturday 20 June

It is spider season at Green Place and the ivy and hedgerows are alive with them. You can barely throw a blanket over your bed without one jumping out at you, and they *love* ceilings and piles of clothes, they just can't get enough of them. Aunt Coral is on constant patrol to the sounds of Delia and Mrs Bunion screaming, plastic cup and postcard in hand, ready to catch and return them to the wild. Every time I see one I am reminded of Mum. Spiders were about the only thing she was afraid of, so Green Place was pretty traumatic for her and the cellar in particular.

The weather is showing great improvements and we must host the shoe auction soon, so 'telephone Badger' has appeared on Aunt Coral's To Do. Badger the gardener has worked at Green Place on and off for ever, although Delia told me there is some awkwardness due to him having had a dalliance with Aunt Coral some years ago. This prompted me to ask Aunt Coral more about her love life. Luckily it wasn't difficult to get her talking!

Her first proper boyfriend, Gerald, was a letcherer from her Uni, but she never really liked him that much and was unfaithful with a double-first from Oxford. Then she fell for Stringer, a poet she met in an air raid, before meeting Edgar, the egotistical botanist. She was with Edgar for quite a long time – 'enough time for him to have had four changes of glasses' – but they never married. She says they each made her feel alive, though she feels that the beautiful affairs they had became the baggage of later years, adding that they were all still great friends, albeit friends who don't see each other. After all those dandies, I can see why she'd want to live quietly at Green Place, but she maintains she is the marrying type and lives to be in love.

Contrary to Delia's insinuations, Aunt C insists that she's only had two gentlemen callers since the sixties: Roy from the post office, and Badger the gardener, both of whom were beneath her.

According to Delia, the 'affair' between Aunt C and Badger was in the early days when Aunt C lived alone but for her Father, Mrs Bunion and her shoes. Badger was mad about Aunt Coral, but though he was dark and attractive, he was also married. They had some sort of liaison, which she says Aunt Coral never speaks of, for guilt about his wife, and when Aunt Coral ended it, Badger gave up doing the garden. He was eventually persuaded back by Mrs Bunion, but he is still very lazy – 'bone idle' Aunt Coral says. With this kind of work ethic, it's no wonder the garden is untamed.

Anyway, I imagine Badger has no chance now, as with Loudolle back in Alpen, the Ad is back to flirting with Aunt Coral. How shallow of him to flirt with Loudolle one minute, Aunt Coral the next. Who does he think he is? Gladys Cooper?

Aunt C has been reading a book on the art of horology so that she can chat with him about the recoil and anchor escapement on the pendulum clock. Sometimes her love of him seems to involve a lot of hard work.

Saturday 4 July

The Great Shoe Auction was held yesterday afternoon. Our ads about it were in the parish magazine and the post office for the previous fortnight so we were expecting a good turnout.

It wasn't the first time there's been an auction at Green Place – after the war there were many which they held in basic white tents put out on the lawn to make money. Many of the family airlooms were lost in this way, in order to raise enough funds to plough back into the house, or 'the money pit' as they called it. In order to pay his taxes Great Grampa Evelyn sold off all the family fireplaces, and he even had offers to buy the drawing room ceiling and the flagstones from the footpath in the garden. The Garrick of London was interested in acquiring the morning room – it was very common to sell whole rooms at that time. Fortunately he didn't go that far, or I wouldn't be sitting here now!

Everyone wanted to help at the shoe sale and the Nanas made glorious shop girls. Print was in a dress of tulips with flounces at the de collage, and she had an accessorised tissue bag for she suffers from the cold. Georgette was in cornflower wafts, with contrast olive booties, and Taffeta was in a caramel shift and had arranged her hair in four big curls to sit round her face like a hat. She had three strands of pearls to flatter her.

'One for each chin,' said Delia.

When laid out in the garden, Aunt Coral's shoes numbered two hundred, and as she'd kept all the boxes, the shoes were displayed on top of them in the fancy shoe position, with one shoe resting on the other at a jaunty angle. According to Mr Tsunawa, whose wife knows all about shoes, this is the optimum position in which to display shoes and encourages shoppers to imagine themselves at functions being jazzy. Where we could, we put the matching handbags beside them. There were slingbacks and mules in silver and gold, a batch of pink, blue, and nudey stilettos – she'd had a phase for those – sandals and boots, including short boots, long boots, zip boots, fur boots, knee boots, ankle boots and riding boots, though Aunt Coral can't ride. There was also a collection of pumps, which are between a shoe and a slipper. On the ground they lay, material evidence of a lonely heart.

The weather forecast had been good, so the event was held outside. Aunt Coral was happier that way; she didn't want a lot of strangers traipsing in to sit on the toilet. Delia painted a sign which was hung by the Admirals on the corner of Clockhouse Lane. It read 'Egham size 4 ladies' and it had a dainty arrow pointing up to Green Place and featured paintings of snazzy high heels.

By mid morning the garden was swarming with a hundred tiny ladies who fell like flies on the shoes, intent on taking them off to the world again, to be worn at a hundred parties. The Admirals made them all feel like a million dollars, so I foreshadowed hints about future events at Green Place such as chivalry workshops to send their menfolk to, like any entrepreneur would do.

Admiral Ted finally began the proceedings and a hush fell on the ladies. 'Thank you, thank you,' he began to a polite round of applause. 'Now, to kick off, I have lot 1, which is . . .' he read out the label which Aunt Coral had tied to them, 'gold and tan peep-toe stilettos . . . un-worn.'

There was a gasp from the ladies as he showed the dainty article and a hoard of little hands shot up.

'Do I hear twenty, twenty to the lady at the back, do I hear twenty-five, twenty-five to the lady at the corner, let's go to thirty, and do I have thirty pounds for lot 1?'

Admiral Ted continued until he was hoarse and all the shoes had been under the hammer, which took most of the afternoon. He was a terrier, and always held out for the best. Aunt Coral watched from the drawing room window with an obvious tear in her eye. Each unworn pair represented a lonely afternoon to her, a party she had never been to, or a luncheon she didn't attend. I comforted her by reminding her that there's no point in having lots of shoes in the cupboard – shoes should be out in the world.

'Lot 192,' said Admiral Ted. 'Strappy geranium slingback with matching silken clutch,' and once more he added in a sombre tone: 'un-used. Do I hear thirty-five pounds for the set?'

More gasps were to follow again and again in wonder at the items. Aunt Coral has impeccable taste. In her imagination she'd been expecting a million invitations, but in life she'd been a lonely lady in a mansion with her cleaner, laying out the doilies, spending her money on dreaming. But now I hope that her lonely days are 'Going going gone'. (I intend to put the money into a high security account, requiring two signatures and two passports for withdrawals.)

Sunday 5 July

Excerpt from Delia's calendar (by kind permission)

JULY 1987

Sun 12	Recital at the Wood house. Tasmanian Lunch. (*Kaftan*)
Weds 15	Dinner at Maison Bleu with Pedro. (*Floaty with grown up denier*)
Sat 18	Cocktails at the Ritz. Then Rodriguez on the South Bank. (*Matinee blouse, sew pearl buttons*)
Sun 19	Tea dance Waldorf (*print-front fastening*). Drinks with the Jeffreysons (*informal*) (*large ottoman bag*)

It was Joe's football match this morning and it was pouring with rain. So I rang him hoping it would be called off, but he said that they play in all weathers. Aunt Coral preferred to remain in bed mourning her shoes, so I had to go on my own. Though the sale made a whopping £2,000 they had cost her more like £20,000 to buy, and so the £2,000 back was a drop in the ocean, and she'd rather have had the shoes. I reassured her that investing it in more rooms meant she'd make the money back in rental within a year, and that she'd have the £2,000 back to buy herself more shoes, but she declined into her bed jacket and I didn't see her again till lunchtime.

At the match, Joe was gangly and kept on slipping over. Icarus was the winger and best-looking player on the field. It was freezing cold and I was glad when the whistle blew because my anorak was soaked through to the lining and I needed to go in and get thawed. They lost 4-nil and Joe gashed his knee and had to be seen by a matron. But over orange segments afterwards it was he who enquired after my health, which Aunt Coral has trained him to do.

'You look tired Sue,' he said. 'Have you not been sleeping? You're shivering, take my jacket.'

He is becoming Aunt Coral's protégé; I think she is grooming him to be a good boyfriend. (I wish she'd go to work on Icarus.) Joe always makes me feel like a lady, although sometimes he takes it too far and becomes winsome and unmanly. I don't actually like too many poems, I prefer a bit of tension, a bit of a challenge in a man. It's not that exciting if you think someone will marry you tomorrow and follow you about crying.

I told Joe over orange segments, all about my nightmares and he was riveted and offered to drive me over to Titford on his bike to help me to hunt for a note. He really, really likes me, there is no doubt about that. I wish I felt the same. But I decided to take him up on his offer of a lift to Titford (when the next good opportunity arises), so I suggested lunch at Green Place, and when we got back we were welcomed and sat down to Mrs Bunion's Sunday cuisine.

'Rainy isn't it?' said Joe.

'No, it's Sunday,' said Admiral Ted, who is a little hard of hearing because he has tittinus.

'Delia, I thought you were going to luncheon today at the Jeffreysons?' Aunt C said casually.

'No I wasn't,' said Delia.

'But it says on your calendar that you have luncheon today at the Jeffreysons,' said Aunt Coral.

'I must have forgotten to cross it off then,' said Delia, taking back the paper. Delia has her own private calendar hanging on the wall in the kitchen and there are often things written on there that bear no resemblance to what she actually did that day. Like Aunt Coral, I think she would enjoy a great many more appointments to go to and so I think she makes some up.

There was an awkward moment filled only with the sound of Joe and I at our dumplings. Joe was scraping his cutlery over Aunt C's special plate.

Aunt C realised she had inadvertently exposed Delia's calendar, and so attempted a rescue. 'Careful of the porcelain Joe, it's rather valuable. Porcelain is the most delicate and expensive form of pottery you see. It comes from the word *porcellana* which is Italian for seashell. If the pottery's not translucent, and doesn't let light shine through, then it's not porcelain. You are eating off the finest Queen's china in the south.'

'Wow,' said Joe, obviously very impressed. He placed his knife and fork solemnly on his plate without further scratching.

'I was thinking of getting a cat,' said Delia, unimpressed with Aunt C. 'Mr Waiting has just had kittens.'

'Oh Delia, don't get a cat,' said Aunt Coral, 'that means that you'll never get married.' She wasn't normally so tactless.

Delia arose complaining of heartburn and was shortly followed out of the room by Admiral Gordon, his stomach protruding through the gaps in his Sunday waistcoat.

Ever since Loudolle was here I've noticed that Aunt Coral and Delia have had some friction. Loudolle has driven a wedgie between them because, in Delia's eyes Loudolle could do no wrong, and in Aunt Coral's eyes I couldn't, and so they have had to take sides. As Aunt Coral has not had her own children – she always says it would have taken a team of PHDs to get her pregnant – the bond between us is very close. I am like the daughter she never had, so of course she would take my side.

'Is your young man spending the rest of the afternoon with us?' she asked me after a short pause.

'No,' I said.

'Yes,' said Joe at the same time, and we both laughed, a bit too much.

'Why don't you show Joe around,' she said, 'show him the cobweb kingdom?'

So I took Joe around and had a good look myself at some of the rooms I'd not yet been into, in the house that goes on for ever, room after empty room.

'You could have boat people living in here and never know they were there,' said Joe.

He was right; it would be easy to hide in Green Place. I spooked myself with the notion. I showed him the locked-room door, which always has an atmosphere, and then I took him up to my room. As we entered something happened to him – his colour changed and he grew quiet.

'This is my room,' I said. And when I turned round he was suddenly in front of me. He leaned in towards me and tried to steal a kiss, but he missed my lips and caught my nose by mistake, and then he trod on my toe.

'I didn't bring you up here for that,' I said.

'I'm sorry, I couldn't help it.'

'Thank you Joe, that's kind of you.'

'I love you Sue.' He looked into my eyes for several moments, waiting for me to say it too, which I couldn't, because I didn't, and I couldn't look away or say something else because he'd just tried to kiss me and so to ignore it or change the subject would be rude, so I didn't say anything at all, which was awful, and as time went on Joe went more and more red.

'Why do you like my brother so much?' he said. 'He doesn't respect women.'

'I'm sorry,' I said, but he was already leaving, putting his foot through a tread on the stairs on his way out.

Aunt Coral saw him out and I spent the rest of the afternoon and evening in bed with Icarus's eye, feeling bad about Joe but unable to help but love the man I loved.

It was the perfect night for bad dreams and I had the same dream about Mr Jewell, but with a different ending this time. In this version Mr Jewell did not stay for a cigarette, and got to my mother in time to save her. As he was walking away from the ambulance, he found her note in his pocket. Thinking nobody would read it now, he screwed it up into a ball. I was yelling at him that he should read it but he couldn't hear me because I wasn't there.

When I awoke at 3am the rain was falling like a million tears from Heaven. Perhaps she does think of me after all.

Monday July 6

Brackencliffe

By Sue Bowl

Keeper had run far away and lay asleep in a great black cave, spent from his flight o'er the moors.

'Good boy, Keeper, good dog,' said Fiona, as she found him and lay down beside him. She placed Cara's locket round her own bonnie neck, feeding Keeper the remains of her lunch. Then they rested together, but knew not to tarry, for great was their fear of discovery.

Bemeantimes back at Brackencliffe, Van Day reached out to Cara. 'Comely wench, aren't you?' he said 'whyfore haven't I seen you before?'

So he can speak if he has a mind to, thought Cara, defending her maiden's weeds.

'Come hither starlight,' said the Knight and he pressed her close to his westcott. 'My

name is Knight Van Day,' he said, 'and I come
from wither and yonder.'

   Pretafer returned from the water cabinet
and ordered Cara fetch her a plate of noodles,
for though she had tons of suitors, she was
jealous of the maid, and little knew what
would have hap if Knight Van Day had tarried.

I read my latest work to Aunt Coral this evening in greatest secrecy in
her bedroom. It has to be the last time I read her an extract, as we can't
afford to break the rules. (We are not meant to discuss our entries, so
our efforts are entirely individual.)

   'Excellent Sue, really excellent, well done,' said Aunt C. 'Did they eat
noodles in the seventeenth century?'

   'I'll change it to barley,' I said.

   It was a good observation, but in truth it dampened my firework, as
I only agreed to read it to her because she is still upset about her shoes.

Coral's Commonplace: Volume 3
Green Place, March 12 1938
(Age 16 but pass for 18)

Until today, it has done nothing but pour for a fortnight. It's like machines in the sky have been moving the rain sideways instead of letting it drop. This is what's known as drifts, or swathes. A swathe is a committee of raindrops that have been caught on the wind and blown sideways. Sometimes they form interesting shapes such as gentlemen's beards or coconuts. I've spent days looking out of closed windows, pondering the prospects of adulthood, but there is nothing in the paddock but a slick of water and Cameo's dear old horse. If the rain continues the sharp fragrance will be rinsed from the tulips and the wisteria will remain a shrill green, sodden and gasping for light.

You can imagine our intense joy at the break in the weather this afternoon, when we were able to sit out on the terrace with Brown Bettys, restored by the sun's faint heat, with distant rain fresh on the air and water gushing through all the ditches. Such a sensuous moment punctuated an otherwise dully repetitive day.

BROWN BETTYS

Water
Brown Sugar
Lemon
Cinnamon and cloves

1 Boil in a pot
2 Add contents into warming pan with:
> Four bottles of strong ale
> Six tots of brandy (per family of 4, or to taste)
> Half a dozen pieces of toast spiced with ginger nutmeg 'n' cloves
3 Float 'en crouton'

And Mother had an inspired serving suggestion. Surely the best thing in the world is a cocktail that's poured from a teapot?

Emotional News

Cameo and I, like Lady Chatterley, have both fallen for Sayler. He started gardening for us a week ago, since when we have been keen to assist with the weeding. I work myself into a state of classic gitters at the full panorama of his biceps. I have never known so divine a man and don't think I shall soon forget him. (I give him 15 out of 10, but he's potentially out of my league.)

Other men of my acquaintance:

Doctor John – reassuring, brains, nice pocket watch, but confirmed bachelor (7)

Father's solicitor Howard – Heathcliffian, miscast as a lawyer (a whopping 8.5)

Other charismatic corkers (not to be openly admitted!):

Daniel-the-useless, Mrs Morris's nephew – good-looking but very resentful. He's supposed to 'help as required', but he won't iron because it gives him a nose bleed. Mrs Morris loves him like a son. (7)

Mr D'Olivera, our grocer: painfully good-looking, knows the fine line between a ripe fruit and a rotten one and chooses out the best for his girls. (Cameo displays his fruits by her bed and calls this 'Still Lifeing'. Mrs Morris throws them away when they grow fur. Father rails that it takes three weeks to ship one banana here from the West Indies in a vessel with good refrigeration, and so it is very wasteful of us to let anything rot.) (9)

Johnny Look-at-the-Moon, our coal boy, so-called because of his prophetic dreams. In fact he is renowned in Egham for his important dreams, and can tell you the Derby winner, or a good day to go to the bingo. Mythical, lyrical in attitude with dreamy eyes, even if he is always filthy with coal. And how I love the way he pronounces 'Thursday' without an 'H'. If he were older I would definitely fall, but as he is only 14, this would be wholly unsuitable. (However, I still give him 10 out of 10.)

Cameo and I actually had a row over Johnny, because I told her I had a painful crush, so she said she had a painful crush too, but only because I had said that I had one. It is troubling however, because she happens to be the right age for him. To be three years younger than your husband is perfect. In the end we agreed to leave Johnny alone and divide Sayler and Mr D'Olivera between us instead. We came to an understanding that sisters will always come first.

'I cannot let there be hatred in my heart Coral, I love you far too much,' Cameo said.

'If there is no hatred in your heart, Cameo,' I said, 'then why is it coming out of your eyes?' It was one of our most literate quarrels.

Last night after we made it up Cameo came into my bed again, when I really wanted to be alone. I think she just wanted to check we were still a happy family.

'Don't tell me I can't talk about sex because I'm eleven,' she began. 'Sex is wonderful,' she continued, swirling an arm as if she were dangling it off a rowing boat.

'How do you know?'

'Everyone says so,' she said.

'Actually, I was rather hoping to crack on with my medical series – I've got prostates and sternums tonight,' I said.

This had the desired effect and she slithered off. They grow up so fast.

House News

The downstairs Mary, Miss Lunn, has been dismissed because she was delusional and convinced that Father wanted her to sleep with him in the afternoons, and that the reason for his withdrawn attitude was that she didn't, and nothing to do with his sternum. She has been crying in corners and, ultimately, it impacted too much on the household. Mrs Morris has kept a lid on it. Mother doesn't even know. I hope Miss Lunn catches a glimpse of comfort in the near future.

Father, in a bad mood because of his sternum, has accused us of laziness, saying we never lift a finger round the house. But we do our bit in our own way; I just don't think he sees it. Cameo trails her languid fingers through the dust, leaving symbolic drawings. She claims she has lost the ability to dust, as if it is evolution.

Sue

Wednesday 8 July

I've been trying to find out more about the mysterious Nana Cameo recently. As a child she fell down a mountain and a ski pole went through her eye. As a consequence she wore a glass one which Aunt Coral says did little to steal from her beauty.

'She had the face of an angel and hair as pale as Victoria sponge. She never once had to pay a bus fare if there was a male conductor,' she said.

Outside in the garden there's a plaque where Cameo buried some of her dollies.

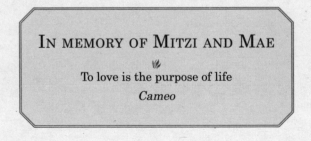

IN MEMORY OF MITZI AND MAE

To love is the purpose of life
Cameo

It was a great tragedy she died so young, although perhaps even more of a tragedy for Aunt Coral, who was left alone to look after their father, once Nana Pearl had also gone. During this period nobody in Egham saw her. She had all their food delivered and for some reason kept their calendar always to the same year. I wonder if she wanted time to stand still, or felt that she could save up the lost years for betterment? Great Grampa Evelyn became reclusive and took her for granted. She says that some days he did not come out of his room. They had no Mrs Morris any more, and the maids never stayed very long. Mrs Bunion didn't come on the scene until later. It must have been hard for Aunt Coral, I don't like to think of her fading like that, it wasn't right for her. She is a definite people person and so delights in a group.

My mother was around of course when Great Grampa Evelyn was getting old, but she had turned her back entirely on privilege when she left boarding school, found her job and married my father. But she often talked of her guilt at having not visited more often and having left Coral alone to manage. But in her defence, I think my mother felt banished by her boarding school days, because had Nana Pearl lived longer, it is very unlikely she would have been sent away.

But, as for Aunt Coral and Cameo, as in so many cases, it was the most dutiful daughter who was treated like an old slipper, whereas Cameo, prior to her death, had always been treated like a jewelled sandal.

Aunt Coral eventually confided one evening last week, after one too many Sapphires, that it is in the locked room in the East Wing that Cameo died, and that behind the locked door are all her things just as she had left them. I think this often happens when somebody dies suddenly; it helps them to last a bit longer in the minds of the people they've left behind.

'But it's not only her things, it's a feeling I get when I go in there,' said Aunt Coral. 'It's like there's something inside.'

'Imagination?' I said. (I was her true follower, choosing the pragmatist's view.)

'Must be,' she said, and then her defence gates burst under a rush of memories.

'The thing about losing Cameo is that it was such a shock. I was called back from Oxford and by the time I got home my sister was gone. It was all so sudden.'

'But how did she die?' I said, for I thought this might be a good moment to ask her. But Aunt Coral filled up at the thought of it all and asked if she could explain when she was feeling sober. It is odd she is so cloak and dagger about it; Cameo's death certainly seems shrouded in mystery. I did ask my mum about it once a long time ago, and she said she wasn't sure, but thought it might have been a stroke.

'I know you know how it feels,' said Aunt Coral. 'I loved her; I wanted to take care of her.'

I tried to comfort her with a nugget from my own life experience.

'I've always wanted a brother or a sister but now I think that not having one has been a kind of a blessing,' I said.

'How do you mean?' said Aunt C.

'Because I could never lose them,' I said.

Monday 20 July

The thing that I keep coming back to is that Icarus asked me out once, and if he's asked me out once, he'll do it again, surely, especially with Loudolle out of the way? Taking the extra care that is necessary over my appearance in the mornings is proving a time-consuming business. It means early starts and long trips to the bathroom to keep fresh and in tip top shape.

Aunt Coral describes me as girlish, Delia says I am cute, Joe said he thought I was gorgeous, (this was before I spurned him). Hopefully, I may be all those things, to all those people, but Loudolle is really beautiful, with coltish knees and glamour locks, and I don't know if Icarus sees me that way.

If I could just get close enough to him to ask him why he asked me out, then at least I'd know that he actually had, and that I hadn't just imagined or dreamt it. I try without ceasing to find a moment to talk to him, but every time there is one, my courage fails me. Asking him why he asked me out isn't an easy question. There are always so many people around to listen.

A new Maid has started at the Toastie called Charlie Harker. She comes from New Zealand and drinks Whisky Macs. She is the kind of girl who'd give Loudolle a run for her money, though she is not what you'd call a beauty. She has the smell of airports, or rather, the stuck-down bits in magazines which have fragrance you wipe on your wrists. I admire her a lot for having travelled from the other side of the world.

Mrs Fry has appointed her Head Maid. She's all about getting maximum performance from everyone and she gets it by operating rewards. Being Head Maid means that Charlie has extra breaks and doesn't have to wash any pots. My hands are peeling because they are always in water, and I'd have loved to have been Head Maid, but I don't think Mrs Fry has ever liked me that much.

At the moment I am working from seven in the morning till five in the afternoon, five days a week, sometimes doing extra hours in the evenings making picnic orders for deliveries. My earnings have shot up from £30 per week to £100, and I give most of it to Aunt Coral for upkeep, bar the pound a week I am putting aside to buy back her hand-bag, and three pounds a week for my personal savings. With occasional babysitting for Mary-Margaret Fry I am able to swell my salary further and afford occasional treats.

I babysat for Mary-Margaret the other day and got a sneak inside Icarus's bedroom. It was very much a child's bedroom with pictures of pop groups, and pants on the floor. There were teddy bears on his bed, which is crazy when you think how machismo he is. Though I did spot a big black machine in the corner which looked like a terribly loud gateaux blaster.

Joe's room by contrast had flowers in a vase and clean towels on his basin. His room resembled that of an elderly gay man and it was interesting to note that in trying to kiss me, he may have been fighting against his nature. I was fascinated to see both their rooms and how much they revealed about the men inside.

Things with Joe are awful at the moment, and most of the time he ignores me, and to make matters worse, he's even begun to skip Group. I asked him if he'd make good on his promise to take me to Titford, but he said that he was too busy.

Brackencliffe

In the morning Cara arose before dawn and went to the ridge to spy for the runaways. She had tarried there only a moment before Van Day rode up on Peril. The great stallion circled, its clipperty hoofs arucking the earth. The ridge was not like the bedchamber, there was none to save her here.

'Now where was I,' said Van Day dismantling, with his great mouth open in yearning.

But like bullets Fiona and Keeper came running, out of the darkness, out of nowhere. Keeper tore into the Master's trouser and brought him to his knees.

'Run!' he barked, and Cara and Fiona fled, leaving Keeper to fight Knight Van Day, who seized the dog by the scruff and took out his revolver.

'You think that I would be thwarted by a spaniel?' he said, and threw back his head in laughing.

'Fuck me' said Fiona, 'what are we going to do now?'

'You're very unusual you know.' That's what Aunt Coral said when I read my last excerpt out to her.

I haven't told you yet about the strange new noises I've been hearing at night at Green Place. As I mentioned some time ago, Delia says 'Fuck' in her sleep, so I put most of the noises down as part of her night-time regime. And Aunt Coral's bed squeaks up against her desk whenever she turns over. But about two weeks ago I registered a sound as being nothing to do with Delia or Aunt C. It was on a black and starless night, the sort of night that is suffocating. I heard a distinct thud coming from somewhere below me, then all was quiet again, but there was an atmosphere, a presence, like someone was there. My own ability to listen was soon drowned out by my heartbeat, which was so loud that I had to cover my chest with a pillow in order to hear the sounds of the house.

The thud has happened on every consecutive night since, so the night now has a tune that goes: 'Fuck, squeak, thud, Fuck squeak, thud.' I can account for the fuck and the squeak, but I can't account for the thud. It is troubling.

I am not an easily frightened girl; in fact I used to be quite the opposite. Back in Titford I used to spook Aileen when she came to stay by telling her I could see floating heads. Of course I couldn't, but I loved to scare her, it made me feel I had power. Poor Aileen; I feel bad about it now. No wonder she got in my bed for safety.

It's not the same at Green Place, however, and I am beginning to feel afraid. Coupled with what is going on in my nightmares, it makes me feel quite dreadful. At about ten I get into bed, exhausted from the Toastie, so I drop off quickly. But then I find myself at the suicide bank reading the notes of every language. Then I awake to the sound of the 'Fuck, squeak, thud,' then lie there and hold on to my pillow. Then I fall off to sleep again to see Mr Jewell with his feet up smoking and my mother lying dead on the floor. Then I repeat the process over and over again for the rest of the moonlight hours. It's always a huge relief when it is time for morning, when I wake up calling and Aunt Coral rushes up to me, avoiding the gaps in the stairs.

Not surprisingly I have been late for work on some occasions and Mrs Fry has said I am on a promise.

Aunt Coral is not alarmed by the thud, and has declared that in her opinion, it must be caused by something which is naturally occurring, such as a badger going for a walk. She says that in all her years at Green Place she has never known any intruders, supernatural or other. Mr Tsunawa is of course delighted by it, believing it to be the work of grey ladies or phantoms. Admiral Ted and Delia don't even hear it, Delia because she makes so much noise herself, and Admiral Ted because of his tittinus. Admiral Little and Admiral Gordon have said that they can hear it, only faintly, but they agree with Aunt Coral that it must have its origins in nature. Nevertheless, in order to settle my mind, everyone did a full sweep of the house to look for the cause, but we found nothing.

The mere fact that we were searching the house made me step up my search for a suicide note from mum, which up till then had only been happening in my dreams. I can't stop thinking about looking for it, though I know it's unlikely I'll find it. But the more tired I get, the more I want to find it so that I can get some sleep.

I have begun to hunt in Green Place, because I think it is *possible* that my Mum may have travelled to the house and may have hidden the note somewhere, not wanting my father to see it, and she might have guessed that I would visit Aunt C at some point, or even that Aunt C would find the note and give it to me. But looking for a note in Green Place could take years.

I have even had a look in the Toastie, in spite of the fact that mum could never have known that I would work there. But she might have given the note to someone, who might have followed me when I left Titford, and they might have planted it somewhere for me to find. Plus I really don't trust Mrs Fry – maybe she'd found it, maybe she'd moved it. It doesn't take much for me to develop theories.

Perhaps the thud is another message from the other world? Perhaps Mum wants to alert me to something? My poor mind never stops trying to make some sense out of the senseless.

With the work I am doing, added to the nightmares I'm still getting, I am often very tired, which, when you are grieving, makes you feel very raw. I cry at the slightest thing, and am getting a reputation for doing it. I cry when Admiral Gordon talks of the sea, I cry at the sight of small rabbits, I cry when the moon is full, and I cry when it isn't, I cry at the Toastie and I cry at Group, and I cry when the robins land on the buddleia.

Meanwhile Aunt Coral is defeating the point of having paying guests by hiring more staff. She has got Mrs Bunion back each weekday and has hired Badger full time, and his son, and Glenn Miller the builder. She is unstoppable in her self-destruction! If she even thinks of buying a new handbag, I think I will smack her.

Wednesday 29 July

My life is a dreary toil of pots and potatoes, dreaming of notes and sleeplessness, and into this situation has come another strange noise, as well as the return of my nemecyst.

At the front of Green Place there is a patch of gravel where Aunt Coral grows bamboo. If you tread on it, it makes a loud noise, so when I heard this last night, after hearing the thud, my alarm bells started ringing. I dashed on to the balcony, holding on to the French door in case I fell through, but I could not see anything, not even a badger.

'Perhaps the badger is varying his route round the front, and he's too daft to avoid the gravel?' said Aunt Coral when I asked her about it this morning.

She is very gung hoe about the thought of potential intruders, supernatural or other. But Aunt Coral comes from Aunt Coral land where children run beside bicycles and go to bed at seven, and badgers and ferrets eat shepherd's pie and all old ladies have chauffeurs.

Luckily there's always so much to do at the Toastie that there isn't much time to dwell on things. I have moved on from canteen apprenticing to creating some of my own fillings for the potatoes and also to some casual waiting. My speciality dish is coleslaw, for which I use apples spiked with tomato ketchup to give it that extra zip. Waiting tables is certainly nicer than the lonely hours of buttering in the bare back kitchen. The workmen from the tyre place swallow such volumes of breakfast that I wonder where they put it all, and they make me feel a million dollars with their bawdy and flattering remarks. I love being front of house, I feel like I belong there.

The best time of day at the Toastie is after hours, when Mrs Fry takes Mary-Margaret home for her dinner. We do prep for the next day, and then we take cappuchinos. Charlie has taught Michael and me to play poker, which she says normally you'd need alcohol for. She had a big win at a party where she drank 75cm of wine. Michael talked a bit about Icarus and how he had dumped her, but confided that she still loves him, so I kept quiet that I do too.

And Joe is thankfully being a bit less frosty, which I think is because he is worried about me, and because he's fundamentally a nice guy. I wonder if I could ask him again about running me to Titford, as a friend, that is. In many ways it is the last place on earth I want to go to, but I need to check for a note. But I can't go when Dad and Ivana are there. So I have to wait for an opportunity.

Thursday 6 August

A pro-po my secret love for Icarus, the worst possible thing that could have happened has happened. This morning, after a particularly bad night of dreams and noises, I was looking for the note at the Toastie when Icarus came into the kitchen. Michael and Charlie were front of house, Joe was on the frother, Mrs Fry was on the till and Mary-Margaret was still at school, so we were quite alone. This was the moment I'd been waiting for.

'What are you doing?' he said, because I had opened up all the flour jars.

'I was just looking for . . . nothing,' I said. And then, as if from out of one of those jars, I heard my own voice waft serenely, saying, 'Why did you ask me to Sandy's party?'

Yet it wasn't really my voice, but the voice of exhaustion that takes over when your editor's sleeping.

'Actually Sue, I didn't,' he said. 'It was Joe that asked me to ask you.'

Coral's Commonplace: Volume 3
Green Place, September 12 1938
(Age 16 but pass for 18)

The fiddleback or violin spider: native to the United States, a fiddleback lives for one or two years and their offspring take a full year to grow to adulthood. They do not usually jump, and only attack when provoked. You will find them in occasionally used bed sheets, such as those on a spare bed, (watch out visitors), and they will hide in shoes, gloves and items of clothing which have lain still for a long time, e.g. stockings strewn on the floor, (watch out messpots). Any disruption to its nervous system can cause unpleasant aggressive behaviour. The way I remember this spider is to imagine it playing the violin. This distinguishes it from its close neighbour the trumpet spider.

This brief study was done as a means of peace-making after a painful dispute with Father. I told him I wanted to study literature at University and he returned that a girl blessed with a scientific brain should not waste it on confectionary, as if Tolstoy, Dostoyevsky, and Chekhov can be described as so. For I know beyond any doubt, that all comfort is to be found in literature, all that I need is there in the recordings contained in books. But no, Cameo is art and beauty, and I am brains and duty. One is typecast at birth. It seems I must die to my poetic side if I am to please Father.

My problem is that I do so wish to make him proud. I can't bear it when he shuts me out. I also drew him a picture of the goliath bird eater which features in my jungle guide, which met with some approval. I didn't show him the one I did of him later, without his toupee; Mother thought it was a great likeness. He misplaced it after our talk and became in an even fouler temper. We searched the house high and low, before launching a sweep of the gardens. Finally, Sayler discovered a fox's den in the woods, and inside there was a newspaper, a couple of potatoes and Father's toupee.

'I wonder what the foxes wanted with that?' said Mother, as Father stormed back for his dinner.

But my suspicion that this was NOT the work of the foxes was confirmed by Cameo's coded winks. If ever I could be accused of being jealous of Cameo, for being allowed to be all the things that I'm not, it wouldn't last more than a minute before she'd disarm me like this.

And anyway, the bigger picture in the world is giving us all a sense of perspective, with every day rumblings of an outbreak of war with Germany. Just thinking of it takes me far from the mood for Mirabel's party tonight. But nevertheless I shall record here our outfits, which every other day than today I would have relished, and which walked straight to us out of a dream:

CAMEO will be in charming peasant flounces, in one of the most lovely straw colours which are all over the place this season. Her shawl is a contrasting delicate morning-mist blue. She has based her look on Shirley Grey who has been seen out in it at the 400 Club.

MY DRESS is of tender green crêpe, and I have a headdress of silver rain urchins. It is not unlike a dress you would spot in the carriage drawn by the Windsor Greys.

Our shoes have come from America, on diversion from the Cape. Ecru sparkle T-bars for me, of a shade not seen in this country. Cameo's are sky-blue and mimosa sandals with stiletto heels which she says are stinko to walk on. But she has been specially allowed to wear a heel, so she is grimly determined to bear it.

They took snapshot photographs of us in our gowns before we left, which are heading for the album labelled 'Fit for the King'. Being a girl is not without its delights.

Sue

'THE BRONTËS WOULDN'T give two brass fittings for structure,' said Aunt Coral this morning, as we walked and talked writing on our way to sit outside. She was rehearsing some research about the Brontës on me, for a group that she had in her pipework.

We settled on the terrace and she opened up a deck chair dressed in a modest little bathing suit, and a late summer beetle ran out. The buddleia was host to a great many birds; it was a sad delight to see them. Loudolle was swimming in her bikini and all the Admirals were sunbathing.

I decided to distract Aunt Coral and myself by moving the subject on to some more of the practical issues we faced.

'Have you bought another handbag Aunt Coral?' I said, noticing a small tote in hiding under her chair.

'I told you I was lonely.' It is becoming her stock answer.

'Then there's money to be made out of loneliness, isn't there? How about the chivalry workshop in the conservatory? Shall we fashion a budget?'

To be honest it is beginning to seem like a silly idea, but at the same time I will try anything, for our prospects of staying at Green Place are growing dark in the shadow of debt. Paying the staff Aunt C insists on employing means that all the extra money from the Admirals' rent is going straight out again rather than into refurbishing new rooms. On my urging she tried the bank one last time, but she called the bank manager by her Christian name, Linda, which was over-familiar and didn't afford Linda her status. As a consequence Aunt Coral found herself with a deficit in her over draught.

She owes £4000 at Harrods, her backlog of other unpaid bills is another £3000 on top of that, and those are just the things that I know of; it is obvious that someone like Aunt Coral is going to have more up her sleeve that she hasn't declared, such as a share in a racehorse called Treasure, on which she flutters each Saturday.

'Could one of the Admirals apply for a mortgage on the house?' I said, for it dawned on me as I watched them sitting on their deck chairs that instead of paying rent, maybe one of them would like to buy a stake for their retirement. Aunt Coral sat for a long time watching the Admirals watching Loudolle.

'I don't know about that,' she said. 'But you could, couldn't you, with your steady earnings? You could get ten times your salary or whatever they offer . . .' She left it there like a cliff-hanger, and of course I took the bait. Aunt C has never been very moral when it comes to money.

It could be worth a punt, so I put 'telephone bank' on my To Do list, rising above the knowledge that at present I have only £16 in my savings. What we need more than anything is a lump sum to clear things, so at least we can start from zero, rather than a minus.

Aunt Coral looked excited for the first time in ages as we planned the chivalry budget, and she rushed off to find Mrs Bunion to discuss menus, taking Delia with her. Nothing gets them going more than planning an event, nothing, not even Group. I made her promise to come in at under £125 for a whole weekend based on there being fifteen modest students for the workshop. They don't have to eat caviar. But when Aunt C goes to bed with a figure in her head, she will have added more zeros to it by the morning.

We have set the date for three weeks' time to allow business to build. It will be a total experiment, but Aunt Coral is thriving, and if it is a success, then maybe we can hold more workshops here and find our way out of the shadows.

Monday 17 August

TOASTIE ROTA
Via E. Fry

Loudolle – Front of House

Icarus – Chief of Staff

Charlie – Tables

Michael – Tables

Joe – Beverages

Sue – Back kitchen

I was at the Toastie this morning buttering up a picnic when Mrs Fry came in and told me I was to be taken off front of house, and put into the back kitchen for the rest of the summer holidays. She said it was because I had been late on more than three occasions and that the customers need to know whom to expect when they come into the café.

I know the real reason of course. It's because Loudolle is back and Mrs Fry wants her front of house. It really isn't fair as she's often late for work too, but she blames it on jet lag, so Mrs Fry never disciplines her. At least I won't have to suffer the sight of her and Icarus canoodling whenever his mother isn't looking.

In fact I am beginning to think she can keep him, that it is time for me to let go. I've spent the whole of the spring and summer being disappointed by Icarus, and I need to try and move on. Indeed the only significant time I have spent alone with him is when I have been in bed with his eye. It isn't exactly the love affair of the century, it's more of a crumb from his plate.

This evening Aunt Coral hosted a special dinner and Mrs Bunion came in to cook: gamey pâté to start and venison sausages to follow, with the Admirals taking charge of a pudding called 'Officer's Mess' so that Mrs B could knock off early. One of the dinner guests was Daphne Podger, a very old friend of Aunt Coral's and the sister of a former beau, who is extremely rich, so Aunt Coral was going to ask for a loan. It is not something I approve of, but we do have great need.

I offered to waitress, as it was a swanky affair. Loudolle of course stuck her oar in and offered to waitress as well, but I think that was only because Icarus was away so she didn't have a date. I was not looking forward to working with her, and I made it plain from the start I would not be engaging with her as a woman.

By four o'clock the kitchen was a hive of activity, Mrs Bunion whizzing the pâté and the Admirals dipping their fingers into the pudding cream to check up on the flavours. Loudolle was assisting the Admirals by glorifying in herself, which they seemed to enjoy. The Nanas, Delia and I were out by the pool helping Aunt Coral lay the grand table. She had brought out the silver and some of her most valuable china, to try and impress her guests.

In 1774 the Empress of all the Russians, Catherine the Second, commissioned England's greatest potter, the late Josiah Wedgwood, to make her some crockery. This beautiful china was known as 'The Imperial Russian Dinner Service'. The collection was painted with views of various castles, ruins and streets, presumably so the late Catherine could get an idea of England. But there were three or four pieces made by the great potter that he did not consider good enough for shipping to Russia, one, because there was an imperfection in one of the trees,

CAMPARI FOR BREAKFAST   143

and two, because of a chip, and these pieces he bequeathed to his friend Lady De Mallet Simpson who is a distant relative of Great Grand Nana Pearl. This is how the extraordinary items came to reside here at Green Place, surviving every auction and car boot sale because they're so very precious.

'The pieces are important,' explained Aunt C, laying out a soup plate showing a view of Hampstead Heath, 'because they depict an England that is gone for ever and London as it was two hundred years ago. The shape and proportions are exquisite and the mulberry colour unrivalled . . .' She had just drawn a breath to continue when suddenly we were interrupted by a shout from inside the kitchen.

'The sausages!' screamed Mrs Bunion.

We all ran into the kitchen where there was a rumpus.

'I put them on the table here under the net to sweat,' said Mrs Bunion. 'Which one of you took them? I need to get them started, or they won't be ready.'

She became increasingly agitated as we all denied any knowledge as to the whereabouts of the sausages.

'Let's calm down and think about this rationally for a second,' said Admiral Ted, taking a notebook from his pocket to write down salient points. 'When you arrived at Green Place earlier, Mrs Bunion, what did you do with the sausages?'

'I put them in the fridge with the butter, and then at half past three I took them out and put them on the table, under the net to sweat. I know I did, because I always do. I sweat them at room temperature for an hour before I cook them. It's the correct way with a sausage.'

'Are you sure?' said Admiral Gordon.

'Of course I'm sure! Why would I lie over such a thing?' She was by now in a terrible state and had been placed on a chair and given tea.

Then Loudolle, who'd been giving me bad eyes all day, stepped up and said: 'Look, I really don't like to say this, but I'm going to have to, because Mrs Bunion's so upset . . .' Everyone was silent, riveted, waiting, held in the palm of her hand. 'I saw Sue drop the sausages in the swimming pool. Sorry Sue, but I can't stand by and see an old lady in distress. You want me to go get some more Mom? I could take the car and be back in twenty minutes.'

You can imagine how shocked I was. It was a total made-up story.

'That's not true,' I said. 'I never touched the sausages, let alone dropped them in the pool.'

'Why are you lying?' said Loudolle.

I took a step up towards her to give her a piece of my mind, but Delia held me away.

'Come now,' she said. 'There's no harm done here. Loudolle will go and get some more sausages. We all have mishaps; it's not your fault Sue. At least we know what happened.'

'But, I—' I looked around me, and words faltered. 'Check the swimming pool if you don't believe me, there's no sausages in there.'

But judging by everyone's faces the only person who believed me was Aunt Coral. Loudolle swalked off to get the car keys, with a terrible conceited face on.

It is a bitter pill to swallow, being blamed for something I didn't do. The only way to clear my name is to find the real culprit. Someone obviously sabotaged the sausages, but who? It can't be the Admirals, for why would they bother, and it can't be Aunt Coral, for why would she sabotage Daphne's enjoyment of the meal, and it can't be Delia for the same reason, and it can't be Mr Tsunawa, for he is away. Which leaves Loudolle herself. But why, why, why would she want to? She already is the favourite of almost everyone we know, so of course everyone will believe her. As long as Aunt Coral believes I am telling the truth, I didn't mind too much about the others. But from now on I will be keeping my eye on Loudolle Shoot.

We went back to laying the grand table outside, but all the stuffing had gone out of the day and I asked if I could be excused from waitressing, as I couldn't promise I'd be able to work with Loudolle without stepping up to her.

Brackencliffe

By Sue Bowl

'Ha hah!' said Pretafer viciously, tossing her flaming curls to one side. For there she spied in front of her, cowering in the thicket, the maids to whom she gave chase.

'There you are, I knew I would find you! Seize them!' she cried to her man guards, and Cara and humble Fiona were captured and taken unto the Brackencliffe dungeon by the bodies of six fullsome men.

Pretafer laughed and she laughed till her mouth frothed and her eyes shrivelled and the Spinster Nurse had to be called to come and take the Missie home.

Egham Hirsute Group
On reinventing the cliché

'The Brontës wouldn't give two brass fittings for structure,' Aunt Coral began at the next group of the season last night. Joe had returned to the group after his attempted kiss and was concentrating hard on his jotter.

'What we need to do to enthral the reader is reinvent the cliché. Consider, does being a spinster make you any less of a person? *No.* For example Sue's character, Spinster Nurse Chopin, is an example of the reinvention of a cliché. We've all come across spinsters and nurses, but not quite in the context we see here. Similarly,' she said, fixing her eyes on the Admiral, 'in a descriptive sense, we are used to hearing about heavy and pendulous breasts. But to say someone's got a heavy and pendulous face would be reinventing a cliché.'

'And also very insulting,' said Delia.

'Perhaps the desired effect is to be insulting?' said Aunt C, trying to throw it open. But no one put their hands up for fear she might bring up breasts again.

'Likewise in Charlotte Brontë's *Jane Eyre*, we see Mr Rochester and Jane's love flourishing, and we make assumptions. But no, he has an insane wife he is hiding. Charlotte Brontë, like Sue, is reinventing a cliché,' said Aunt Coral.

'Can any of you think of any other examples?' she said, moving forward with the session.

We all put our hands up.

'Sue,' said Aunt Coral.

'In *Wuthering Heights*, Emily Brontë puts the ghost outside the window instead of inside the house like most ghosts,' I said.

'Excellent Sue, really excellent, you've got the idea. Now I want you to quickly each call out a "type" of character for me . . . anyone?'

We all put our hands up.

'Sue,' said Aunt Coral.

'A bachelor.'

'A bachelor, good,' said Aunt Coral. 'Delia?'

'A gardener,' said Delia.

'Good,' said Aunt Coral. 'Avery?'

'A princess,' said Avery.

'Good, Avery,' said Aunt Coral 'And Joe?'

'A boyfriend.'

'Good,' said Aunt Coral. 'So, to recap, we have a bachelor, a gardener, a princess, and a boyfriend. Now, I want you to each select one character from the list and create a reason for them to be in some way unexpected, thereby liberating yourselves from convention. Then we will share and discuss them.'

The conservatory was hot and the evening was light and easy. I remembered so many groups where I'd sat in my hat and coat, with my fingers freezing round my pen. As nice as the summer is, I do hope we can raise enough money to see another winter at Green Place.

'Ready? Who's going to go first?' said Aunt Coral, with her eyes magnified behind her gin glass. We all put our hands up, for we were inspired.

'Sue?' said Aunt Coral.

'I've chosen a boyfriend,' I said, and I read aloud, not looking at Joe. '"Her boyfriend was the sort of person who ignored her and treated her like a rag and looked at other women all the time,"' I said.

'Good,' said Aunt Coral. 'Not the sort of boyfriend I'd want. And Avery?'

'A princess,' he said. '"Princess Melanie was so beautiful that no gentleman in the kingdom was safe from losing his heart. But Princess Melanie could neither sing nor sew, neither read nor write – Princess Melanie was a halfwit."'

'Excellent Avery, really excellent, well done,' said Aunt Coral. 'It's totally unexpected to think of royalty in terms of being, ahem, half-witted. And Delia?'

'I've chosen a bachelor,' she said. '"He had never married and this was not because he had not had offers, but rather because he was more in love with himself than with any woman he'd ever known."'

'Excellent Delia, yes, a bachelor who is vain,' said Aunt Coral, her eyes flickering towards the Admiral. 'And Joe?'

'A gardener,' he said. '"She would not be a gardener for ever; it was only to pay the rent, and the garden provided a good place to bury the bodies."'

'Oh Joe!' said Aunt Coral, 'a psychotic lady gardener! Excellent. And well done everybody, you've really got the idea. Of course the same theory applies to the story or "plot" as we call it, so always be aware of twists and turns and possibilities, and – just as in life – anything can happen!

'Now, I'd like to set you some homework, which is a confidence-building exercise, designed to enhance your creativity. I want you to write a letter to yourself from someone who you long to hear from, for example, Mr O'Carroll, Sue, or Marlon Brando, Delia. Perhaps you'd like to hear from Kate Bush, Joe, or Bette Davis, Avery. I'm not suggesting you choose the above, but the idea is that it should be someone positive, exciting, beneficial; not Ralph, Delia, or the council, Avery. Everyone understand?'

We all nodded and the session ended, Aunt Coral tottering out of the conservatory followed by the Admiral on his way to join the other Admirals in the drawing room. Delia had a dinner appointment in Egham, although I think she actually just went up to her room and wrote letters to herself. (Which she has adopted as a healing habit ever since Group began.)

I walked a little way down the drive with Joe freewheeling along on his bike. I wanted to try and reconnect with him, but he was curiously distracted by my feet.

'The sound of summer,' he said, involuntarily flirting with my flip flops.

I passed him his helmet and put the visor down for him, which he seemed to enjoy very much. As I said goodbye I had a curious feeling, a strange sort of longing for him to ask me out again, which of course he didn't. But I felt something a kin to disappointment after he had left. It had been nice, flattering, I suppose, when he had wanted to spend all his time with me, I have missed it. That is to say, I have missed that he made me feel a bit special. But I am still angry with him for making Icarus ask me out and sending me on a wild goose chase with my feelings. And I am guessing that he is still angry about that unwanted attempt of a kiss.

But as usual after one of Aunt Coral's groups, I was inspired and raced back upstairs to Brackencliffe, where I fell asleep over my notebook.

Tuesday 25 August

At 3am, I woke once again to the 'Fuck, squeak, thud,' and a few seconds later there was a step on the gravel, and then another, so I froze.

I'm not sure how long I sat there, possibly four, maybe five minutes, but eventually I plucked up the courage to go on to the balcony and look outside. All the night was quiet, lit by a purple moon. There was nothing there, no badger, no ghoul. I reassured myself that old houses make noises and young animals scurry and I went back to sleep singing from the logical explanation school of thought.

I have noticed that sometimes life can throw you a pleasant event to balance a scary one, and later on this morning Delia found a tortoise that was staying in an East Wing bathroom! She has christened it Bertie, though she is not sure if it might be a Betty. It is amazing to see how something so small can be the cause of so much delight to someone. Life never ceases to amaze me in that respect; there really is a lot of pleasure to be got out of small things, and no one better than an old girl to make you see it.

Anyway, after going to the bathroom to have a look at Bertie, I got back to my room and found Loudolle there. It was quite a shock. She was standing by my bed in her airline pyjamas with a nasty look on her face, the sort of look that will eventually swallow up her beauty and leave its print instead. So I hope.

'What are you doing in here?' I asked her.

'Just looking for something,' she said.

'What? What can you possibly be looking for in my room?' I said, itching to give her a bitch slap.

'Oh, nothing,' said Loudolle, '. . . or *this*,' she said. She was holding Icarus's eye. The world seemed to float for a moment as I thought of all the things she could do with it. She could show it to Icarus. She could tell Mrs Fry about it. She could steal it.

'How much would you give me to keep this a secret?'

'Five pounds,' I said. 'It's all I've got.'

'That'll do,' she said, 'for now . . . I'll hang on to this for you, shall I? We wouldn't want anyone to find it.' Then she left my room, taking the eye with her, and I was left alone, like a small sheep on a hill who has been separated from its mother.

Why, why did I play into her hands? What does it matter if she tells Icarus I kept a piece of his eye? (Apart from the obvious humiliation and embarrassment, which might indeed cause my disintegration.) There should be no shame in having liked someone enough to have kept their eye under my pillow; the classics are full of such passion. But if I'm honest I think the reason is that exposure of the eye would be certain to make me look an idiot. And part of me still wants Icarus to love me, as hard as I am trying to forget him.

But these emotional things take *time*, and I calm myself with the notion. After all, the Cistern Chapel wasn't painted in a week.

Brackencliffe

Pretafer was recovering under the Spinster Nurse Chopin.

'Get off me, woman!' cried she. 'I want to make mischief with the maidens. Lah hah! Hah, hah, hah, hah hah, hah.'

'Missie, come back, you're not well,' cried the spinster, preparing her syringe.

'Funny smell,' said a footman, as Pretafer passed him by, for she had soiled herself in all her excitement, cruelty and cunning.

Coral's Commonplace: Volume 3
Lady Margaret Hall, Oxford, July 3 1940
(Aged 18 but pass for 21)

The whole of the south coast has been evacuated and occupied by our troops. There's barbed wire on the beaches and oil in the sea, and they are going to set the sea on fire if anyone tries to come.

Green Place has been requisitioned, so Mother, Father and Cameo had to leave. They have gone to stay with Aunt Fern in Somerset, and I will have to stay here and go and join them in the holidays. Giving up one's home bears with it a strange feeling of detachment. The day-to-day inconvenience is accompanied by a deep knowledge that to do right we must. I miss silly things, such as the tin cupboard. I asked Cameo to pack my pyjama case, but she couldn't find it in all the hurry. If I were to go into my bedroom now I would find twenty soldiers billeted.

We had a long phone call during which Cameo told me that they've had to shoot Alto, her adopted horse. He had sweet itch, which was getting harder and harder to treat. They can go on and on with sweet itch, so it was a terrible decision. Cameo had been bathing his blisters with geranium oil which she crushed herself. And only a couple of weeks ago she had asked Sayler to drain the pond, so the midges that lived there would head off and leave Alto alone. The vet told her an injection would be too slow on a horse of his size, and that he wouldn't know a thing of the bullet. I'll miss the thud of his hooves in the morning when he suddenly decided to canter, and the way he took sugar from our hands and then flashed his teeth in something between a smile and a bite.

They wouldn't have killed him yet if the soldiers hadn't come according to Cameo. They are coming to Green Place for the greater good but, oh God, what of the smaller?

I also heard that Daniel-the-Useless applied for a job with the railways in order to escape being called up, but he was turned down, so now he's got to go. I don't think it makes him any less brave because he shows he's afraid. He's one of those transparent people who can't hide his emotions.

They reckon on the requisitioning of our house and land for a term of up to twelve months, initially, for the purpose of billeting fresh forces and for food production, as we expect three million Americans to feed on our shores. They are also recruiting for some 'classified training' which Father says means that they get candidates drunk and practise interrogating them to see if they give over secrets. He says that most of them succumb to the loosening effects of alcohol, but the ones that don't become the crème de la crème of special operations.

Cameo wrote from Somerset and told me that our young nephew Oliver is a hero because he discovered not one but three Germans in the trees near their village, who, in spite of their injuries, found the strength to surround him.

'Which one of you three's the strongest?' Oliver asked.

'*Er ist* (He is)' they replied, pointing to the big one.

'OK,' said Oliver to the tough guy. 'You and me against them two.'

At least that's what Oliver says!

It's so frustrating for me, being away from all the action. My contribution to the war effort is tiny; only some light volunteering at present, digging veggies at Brownscombe Farm. I have hours to spend in pursuit of my studies, but I wish I was doing something more helpful. Maybe I could specialise in military entomology? Eradicate the threat from insects of the trenches? Develop a vaccine to combat lice or stop the spread of typhus?

Study news

Contrary to popular belief, the Daddy long legs is not a spider but a fly. Interesting. But what I want to know, is why are so many spiders called widows? Professor Podger of Evolutionary Biology says we will go into the matter very fully. He has set us a short essay on the subject of 'highly organised bacteria' (bacteria with specs, briefcase, and a pie on the go in the fridge?). He states that these organised bacteria are more successful than others that are lazier in multiplication, and claims to be a fan of *lactobacillus* and *streptococci*.

Going to Dicken John's study for cocoa tonight. I know he has eyes for Consuella, but . . . 'Don't let one cloud obliterate the whole sky' (Anaïs Nin).

Sue

Friday August 28

FINALLY, ON WEDNESDAY, my chance came. A letter arrived from Dad telling me that he and the Dane were in Venice on a mini break, therefore I knew the coast would be clear and I'd be able to search the house in peace. I was very hopeful of finding a note from mum.

I rang in sick, saying that I had a terribly infectious skin complaint, because I knew that would worry Loudolle. Mrs Fry would have to find another dogsbody.

Titford is a relatively dull place, jazzed up by groups and societies: the walking group, the ladies pottery set, the gentlemen's club for crown bowels. The history group preserve the bones of the town and offer up information about the blue plaque, and maintain for the streets their oldey back drop, by fighting a valiant fight to keep the bus stops thatched. Mum never liked those Titford types much, she thought they were small-minded and pokey hole, but she did have one or two friends dotted about to keep loneliness in check.

The High Street is cut into segments by four sets of traffic lights, with the library right at the bottom. It's a high street like many other, the only difference being that in Titford they love to demonstrate about things. It's because the town is so boring that they need to liven it up. I passed the car shoe shop on the left, and by car shoes I mean the sort of backless loafers that mothers keep in the car to ferry children. Ivana had several pairs, though not the reason to wear them.

Nothing had really changed. There was nothing extraordinary, no notes on the ground behind lampposts, no banners saying 'welcome back Sue'. I passed the bookshop, where Aileen had a Saturday job and the brick used to be tied outside, and Flowers 'n' Cards and the Titford Gallery and Je T'aime boutique and, finally, the library. I tried to ignore it just then, and turned off the main road and into Addison Drive, where I looked down towards my old house. It was like looking back in time, like I could just walk up to the door and my Mum would be there to meet me. I must have walked down that road a thousand times, maybe even a million. It was such a familiar stranger, or maybe I was the stranger, reborn in the eight short months since I'd left.

I went in and stood in the hall. Standing at the bottom of the stairs, I realised that actually I'd remembered wrongly, I *did* get scared in Titford. Mum made the mistake of telling me that I mustn't be afraid because the fear attracts things to you, and that made me even more afraid, so I often used to debunk into her bed and Dad would be pushed out and go and sleep in my room and we'd all wake up in different beds in the morning. It was quite chaotic.

Such memories were accompanied by the smell of rain on a Titford morning and of burnt toast coming from the kitchen, and the sound of mum scraping the char off the toast before calling me to get a move on: 'Quick Sue!'

Her voice filled the quiet of the hall until I tripped on some car shoes and the past was broken away. I picked them up and noticed that they were tied together with a cobblers label which said: 'This pair should not be together because they are a mismatch. One is a 40 and one is a 42.'

It was clear as day: a message from the other world. I took the label as evidence and put it in my pocket. I knew they shouldn't be together. Dad was forty and Ivana was forty-two.

Somewhere in the kitchen lurked a cheese that was jumping. I buried it in the garden, so they would not have to return to smells. Further along the counter there was a card on the kitchen pin board, which had two names in gold leaf: Nicholas James and Ivana *Beverley*. I'd forgotten her Nana was English.

I trawlered through some correspondence, and beneath a stack of letters I found a birthday card to Mr Edgeley from my mother. How odd that Mr and Mrs Edgeley had given it back to my Father, but perhaps they thought it was the correct thing to do for posterity. And on closer inspection of the post mark on the envelope, it appeared it was posted *the day she died*. It read:

> *Dear Mick,*
>
> *Happy Birthday. Hope you have a lovely day. I'll be thinking of you and wishing you well.*
>
> *Much love,*
>
> > *Blue xxxx*
>
> *PS don't forget the embroidered cloths.*

It was galling to know that her state of mind had been good enough to remember a birthday, and only added weight to my theory that she had meant to be revived. I don't understand why my Dad hasn't told me about it, how he could *think* that it wasn't important.

The sight of Ivana's things round me made me sick; it looked like we had a squatter. I went up to the bedroom, to check it hadn't all been a mistake, to check I wouldn't find Mum sitting in bed and so surprised to see me. But of course she wasn't there, and there was no trace of her on the surface, only Ivana's face creams and collection of small furry animals gathering dust. Although behind the scenes there were still tracks to suggest mum's existence; the circle where she put her tea mug and the worn patch on the rug where she stood at her basin that retained the shape of her feet. So many traces of her, beneath that squatter's top note.

In my experience I have noticed that the backs of drawers seem to be a good place to find things, so I started my note hunt there. A lot of Ivana's rubbish had to be gone through, nasty bedside potions, a letter from the doctors, and one of those Red Indian dream catchers for the prevention of nightmares. But at the back of the chest, in accordance with my theory, I did find a clump of paper. It was one of those fortune tellers you make at Christmas, with my hopes for the future written under the blue flaps and Mum's written under the green. Mine said things that I wanted to happen like, passing my driving test and falling in love and getting a puppy. And Mum's said, 'Grow old gracefully and keep jogging'. If those were her hopes for the future, no wonder she did what she did.

I finished upstairs, having ploughed every furrow, including behind books, under the mattress, and in Dad's papers, where I found a box labelled 'Blue', which when I opened it, proved to be empty. Where had he put the contents? Had he thrown away her old letters, the ribbons from her bouquets, the birthday cards she treasured? The thought was so overwhelming that I had to sit down for some moments.

Downstairs I continued and my eye fell on two photographs on the mantelpiece, one of Dad and the Dane at a dinner, and the other of him, Mum and me when I was a baby. In between the photo and frame, there was a yellow piece of paper. I had to sit down with it in my shaking hands. Could this be it? Could this be what I came for? There aren't many situations in life where you can feel such dread and excitement. The familiar threads of the sofa tickled the back of my calfs and I held my breath as a voice inside said, *open it, open it, open it*. I unfolded the paper and gasped to see her handwriting, but then immediately was disappointed as I realised it was only a label for the picture.

'This is Sue!' it said. I must have been only a few months old at the time when the photo was taken, and she was very pleased with me. *This is Sue!* And the 'S' was super flamboyant and the 'e' was close up against the 'u' and it had a flourish through the bottom and to the right that was utterly unique and enviable.

I had thought about spending the whole day in Titford, but when it came to it I didn't even stay the afternoon, and I spent no time at all in my bedroom. It was so small and suffocating and like a coffin compared to Green Place, and in the backyard a weed had grown up round a broom where it had been left standing still for too long.

The front door gave its familiar plastic click as I left like a thief with my treasure: the fortune teller, the birthday card, the label, all of them messages from the other world.

I passed by the library on my way back to the station and planned to go in and check in all the sleeves of the Poets, but it was no easy place for me to go to, so I stalled for a while in Je T'aime. Aileen used to treat herself from Je T'aime all the time with the money she made from begging.

I thought about what Aunt Coral would do in such a distressing situation and so I bought a dress. It was pink and lacy and frilly, and made good company for me as I finally plucked up the courage to go into the library, holding the raspberry coloured Je T'aime carrier bag for security. The first thing I saw was Mr Jewell with his feet up on the desk, smoking. But as I walked up, he stubbed out his cigarette and flapped at the smoke, embarrassed at being caught with his trousers down.

'I do apologise Miss,' he said, briefly glancing towards the smoke alarm which was covered with an Elastoplast. 'I know I shouldn't, but I'm not allowed to leave my desk, not if I'm here on my own. I do apologise, I'm trying to give it up!'

He cleared his throat and flapped at the smoke again then resumed his librarian's air.

'What were you looking for?' Then he looked at me closer. 'Do I know you . . . ?'

The sight of him just as in my dream was so unnerving that I had to excuse myself and go, which left him bewildered. How do you find the words to say, *Yes you do know me, I am the daughter of the woman that you found – the woman in the incident – and I would like to check in the sleeves of the poets to see if she left me a suicide note.* It was like a gloved hand held hostage my vocal chords.

I practically ran back to the station, where there were leaves on the tracks and pigeons were grumbling in the concourse rafters, and in the distance the top of the Titford church tower was the only thing left in the sun.

Back on the train I watched out of the window as the sheep went past from county to county, and the buildings changed and grew less provincial, for Titford is nothing like Egham. And when I got off back here at Egham I couldn't wait to get back to Green Place, where Aunt Coral ran out to meet me.

'Sue, I've been so worried about you,' she said, 'Loudolle said you had a skin disease.'

After a dinner of mince when everyone else had gone to bed, I showed Aunt Coral my cobblers label – my message from the other world. 'This pair should not be together, because they are a mismatch, one is a 40 and one is a 42.'

'I'm not sure that it *is* a message from the other world,' said Aunt Coral.

'It *is*,' I said. 'Because Dad is forty and Ivana is forty-two, they are a mismatch, don't you see?'

'You're being a fool to yourself Sue; you're looking for a message where there is none.'

'In order to be a fool, Aunt Coral, you have to *not* know that you are one. So to be a fool to yourself is impossible, if you already know that you *aren't* one.'

'I'm not sure I follow,' she said. 'I think you're over-tired. Being a fool to yourself means you are being a fool to *yourself* as opposed to being a fool to *somebody else*. It isn't to do with *knowing* or *not knowing* that you are a fool.'

Sometimes she can be obtuse.

'I'm not sure I agree, but I do see your point,' she said after a pause. 'And I know you are searching for why she did this, but it may be that unfortunately, *we just don't know.* Even if you live with a person for years, it's still possible to not really know them; we only ever know of a person what they choose to let us see. And what is inside can be opposite to what is on show.'

But of course I knew my mother a lot better than she did. I showed her Mr Edgeley's card.

'She sent this to Mr Edgeley,' I said, 'from number 42. He was her ballroom partner.'

'Let me see,' said Aunt Coral.

'This could have been what she meant by the numbers forty and forty-two. Maybe she is trying to tell me something that I cannot interpret.'

'Possibly, or it might just be his address,' said Aunt Coral.

'You think my messages from the other world are rubbish.'

'Not if they help,' she said.

It was going to be impossible to make her see, and I had to forgive her, for I knew she was unable to see things another way. She is just too pragmatic and sciencey.

'Do you have any idea what she might have meant by the PS?' I said.

'It sounds like she'd lent him some cloths,' said Aunt C.

'But why would she bother about cloths if she was going to end her life in the afternoon?' I said.

She gazed into the middle distance. 'I don't know,' she said after a while. Mum leaving me as she did was the *ultimate* in not caring. Sometimes I feel so angry with her, which is then accompanied by guilt. Being angry with a person you love is such a vicious opposite and a never-ending conflict in your never-ending life.

I went off to bed feeling deathly but not so deathly that I didn't put a note under Loudolle's door:

Loudolle

Hope you don't catch my skin disease, which is very itchy. I just wanted to warn you that my face has been up against that eye.

     S

The moon is full, the wind tussling the tired leaves of summer, and soon Mr Jewell will appear and light up.

Coral's Commonplace: Volume 3
Aunt Fern's, Whistlers Corner, Sleep, Somerset, August 12, 1944
(Aged 22)

Mother suns herself on the beach, seizing the wonderful moment, remembering when the Junkers 88 kept flying over on their way to take part in the blitz. The hamlet here was too small for the Germans to bother with, but they did once take a pop at a fishing boat. Mr Donaldson dived into the sea to slow down the bullets. He was lucky.

Aunt Fern's boys Alleric and Oliver play nearby, running races through the barbed wire tunnels on the beach in spite of the possibility of mines. They were well drilled in earlier days when the skies were still full of bombers, as to what to do if they discovered a German pilot on the run. Aunt Fern says the drill went like this:

Aunt F: 'What should you say?'

Alleric and Oliver: 'You are my prisoner.'

Aunt F: 'And if he becomes aggressive?'

A and O: 'I am your prisoner.'

Enemy paratroopers had been known to disguise themselves as nuns and vicars. As a consequence the locals have become highly suspicious of the Church.

The others are well. Mother drives a food truck in the village, and yesterday she misjudged its height and took a short cut under the bridge to make her delivery. The recipients of the food have been complaining of nuts and bolts in their rations.

Cameo had a job for a short time, driving the pilots to the airfield. That was until they discovered that she had lied about her age to get it! (Her driving was self-taught in the Bentley up and down the drive at Green Place. Mother and Father didn't know!) Her cunning plan was to meet all the pilots and get invited to all the dances and it worked. Now she has an American boyfriend who has taught her 'the jitterbug'. He thinks the Somerset accent and the American accent are similar! His name is Lieutenant Chadwick Clements. She waits for him in the woods behind his barracks . . . oh my! She explained that nearly every time his squadron flies out on a mission, somebody doesn't come back, and the ones that do have lost a friend who didn't. They drink gallons because of the pressure. It's not surprising.

Before the war we knew very few men, and now there are all these soldiers. It's hard not to fall, with the constant reminder of the shortness of life intensifying every moment. If I thought it was my last day on earth, I would want to spend it in love. The most popular woman in the village is the seamstress, Mrs Allsuch, who can remodel your dress and make even a frump feel pretty. A new collar here, a contrast belt there – it all saves on the ration book. Yet it seems so shallow to be even thinking about romance, when every day, people are giving their lives.

I wish it were my turn to wait in the woods for a pilot. Almost everyone I know is having some sort of dalliance; even Mother has a General with a twinkle in his eye who makes sure he passes when she's gardening. I must have an invisible sign on my head which reads, 'Desperate, Proceed with Caution'. I worry that it's because I'm too old, the plain one, the swot, the geek, one of the privileged few who are lucky enough to study, who are expected to deliver honours unto their family. I must try and rewrite the sign on my head so it reads something less unsettling. I must not look like I'm searching, in spite of the fact that I am.

Johnny Look-at-the-Moon is stationed in Dorset. Father saw him on a trip to Bournemouth. He told Father he had dreamt the date of the Normandy landings, but he couldn't tell anyone sooner because it was an official secret. Father passed on a message from him that he hoped the tide would bear him back to sail again in our waters.

He's a true Celt, Johnny, a dreamer and a poet, and now because of this war, he's a warrior too. He is with the sixth battalion of the Dorset Regiment, which is soon being sent to the front. The local girls plan to line the street and sing to them as they march. I wish I were in Dorset.

CAMPARI FOR BREAKFAST

Perhaps I might write to him? Perhaps it would boost his morale? No one would ever know except Johnny, and it doesn't have to be a love letter, but then again, I might die tomorrow, so perhaps it should be? I've admired him since I was a girl, what's the harm in confessing? But expressing emotion is not something that comes easily to me. I prefer other people to do it for me.

Cameo is much better at these things, and she says she thinks that I should. 'What's the worst that could happen? It would make Johnny smile?' she said, before she skipped off to meet her Lieutenant.

When Father writes to Doctor John they use a code that they agreed on last time they met, in which the first words of certain sentences, a certain number of sentences apart, spell out another sentence. Father won't tell me what it is! They came up with it to outwit the censors. Maybe I could do something like that, or, I don't know, maybe not. I wish I didn't torture myself over men so much.

Cameo and I both thought for ages that a censor bar was where the censors met for drinks, but censor bars are actually black or grey boxes which obscure sensitive words in documents. Of course in the current climate they cover everything, because, 'Loose lips sink ships'. The wireless frequently goes quiet with broadcast delays, especially before the news. We are now used to sudden birdsong or music over the airwaves, usually right in the middle of a good bit. There's no way to ensure privacy. The world is a web of scramble.

Alleric and Oliver are now sitting on a towel eating Bournville sandwiches. They break the chocolate up into loaves of bread to make it go further. Sweet coupons are like gold dust, so chocolate's a big theme in their day. It's the same for the other side, where I read that the Hitler youth are encouraged with extra rations of sweets.

Things are quite different in Oxford. I flash my torch on the ground in the dim yellow light they allow on the street at night and hurry home for the curfew. And Somerset may be awash with exotic soldiers, but at college there's a sorry lack of male undergraduates. Most of the girls have now been conscripted, but only to work in reserved occupations so that the men who were previously exempt can now go to war. I volunteer at St Hugh's, which is a women's college that they've turned into a military hospital specialising in head injuries. They produce the metal plates for skull repair at the Morris car factory locally in Cowley; all car manufacture has been halted. The rear gunners fare the worst, because of their position in the aircraft. They get shot to bits. The children visit with flowers; they think the men without faces are ghosts.

Dr John's based nearby. He's part of a Medical Corps Royal Air Force Regiment, who make up mobile units that perform operations on the injured as close to the front as possible, which greatly increases their chances. The wounded are then sent back to Oxford by air. This is at great risk to the doctors, though Dr John says they are lucky to be 'three steps back from the front'.

'Never in the field of human conflict has so much been owed by so many to so few.' (Winston Churchill after the battle of Britain.)

Copy of letter sent to Johnny:

Aug 12 1944
Whistlers Corner, Somerset

Dear Johnny
I hope that this letter brings you cheer as you go to war. I'm sitting in the kitchen at Aunt Fern's. The sheep outside have made a den in the hollowed-out tree trunk of a giant oak brought down by the weather.

Love of the warmth and cover must drive them to run inside it. But how funny they look when they're running. After all, if you were a sheep, what on earth would be your hurry?

You will be glad to know we are all well, and very much hope that you are. I hope that your dreams keep you safe. I hope they protect you from harm.

Come hell or high water we must have hope, mustn't we? It's

the little things that keep me going. Like a group of birds I am watching, who've just taken off from the road and flown up into the hedge, like a tiny fleet of torpedoes.

Back in Oxford they stay well away from civilisation. Even the birds and the bees are afraid at the moment. I miss Green Place.

Home is where the heart is, though it looks very different now. The garden is a boggy veg patch; the drive is lined with trappings of warfare.

To say that I miss my home would be such an understatement, for I would miss it anyway, even if I were a person living in an ordinary time. I was stopped the other night a minute after curfew; the guard asked me where I was going.

'Me? I'm on my way back to the hall,' I said. 'Please let me go on my way.'

May God bless you dear Johnny as you go on yours.

With my love and my hopes for your good luck and protection.

Coral Garden

Sue

Tuesday 1 September

> ## CAN YOU HELP?
> ### MISSING TORTOISE
> ### BERTIE LEFT HOME ON WEDNESDAY SHORTLY AFTER SUPPER
> ### ANY INFORMATION PLEASE RING
> ### EGHAM 69950
> ### REWARD OFFERED

'DON'T YOU THINK you are over-reacting?' said Aunt Coral.

But Delia was already on her way to the post office in a state of devastation. Bertie had stolen her heart. Until I met Delia I thought Aileen was the saddest person I knew, but Aileen was a child when she had the pet brick, whereas Delia is a full grown woman.

She has started spending two hours in the attic every Tuesday evening; when Aunt Coral asked her what she was doing, she said she was teaching Admiral Gordon Italian. Maybe he feels sorry for her, with her self-letter bonfires and her endless search for funds to keep Loudolle up to date. Aunt Coral raised her brows, but I do believe they aren't up to anything other than what they say. Admiral Gordon wouldn't

168 CAMPARI FOR BREAKFAST

presume, he's not a Don Wan type, and Delia has been badly hurt, so I think if lie-down loving is on the cards, they will have time to learn Italian first.

Talking of lie-down loving, Badger and son are gardening *every* morning at the moment, and Tornegus (the son) is quite something. He is a tanned boy with a pony tail, hoop earring and tattoos. Amongst his other attributes, he can talk and he can wink. Aunt Coral told me that prior to the 1960s she'd never seen a young man with an earring, and as a result she can't see in him what I do.

Before I left Titford my only boy experience was Pete. He used to walk me home sometimes and we attended a couple of parties. Aileen called him 'Dead Pete' because he was so quiet, but I knew he was only quiet because he wasn't confident enough to speak. But Aileen was super confident and so *open* when her bosoms came in, whereas the moment mine did, that was it, duffle coat on.

Anyway it still didn't make her an authority on men. She went to Australia with a boy called Jonathan who, before he left, had business cards printed which said: 'Jonathan Chardeley, Actor'. But in her last letter, she said they were in the Northern Territory working with sheep.

It didn't last with Pete. For some reason I couldn't quite bring myself to kiss him. I think you have to like someone a lot to do that.

Thursday 3 Sept

There was a 'Late Summer Tasting' given by Mrs Fry at the Toastie last night, as she wants to expand into Bistro. She held it in what she now calls 'The Function Room' and invited the whole of Egham, including Aunt Coral, thinking that she might be an investor!

The night was particularly humid. Everything was drooping with moisture – my hair and make-up, the food, and the flowers outside, which hung limp on their branches, smouldering with fragrance. I was feeling much better after a good night's sleep, and Michael wore a pinafore and foot-loss tights in homage to me, which was such a great compliment as I'm hardly ever copied.

Mrs Fry had spent all day creating a Bistro-inspired theme, the tables were all dressed in gingham and the walls hung with straw dolls crowned with garlic pigtails. On every available surface flickered a hundred tiny candles, just like in the picture she'd cut out of a magazine which had been hanging in the Toastie all the previous week.

Her hairdresser Stacey was there when I arrived to aid with last-minute décor. 'I'd like it more sweeping and bouncing and the heaviness cut off the front,' said Mrs Fry.

'I thought we were growing it,' said Stacey.

'We are, but I just want more bounce,' she said.

'OK. So more bounce and sweep and the heaviness off the front.'

They must have spent an hour going over the details.

Guests were to be given a Hollandaise crumpet on arrival and chocolate roses when they left and I must say that Mrs Fry showed tremendous Bistro flair. There were special menu cards featuring a photo of Loudolle posing with a fake smile, pretending to serve a customer.

Joe looked quite different when he walked in. Gone were the turn-ups and specialist shirts and in their place were jeans and a T-shirt that showed off a lot of his muscles. Michael nudged me as he wandered by and I had to acknowledge it was quite a transformation.

Aunt Coral came with the Admiral and was having problems with her sandals. He had to keep putting his hand out to steady her, which of course she was enjoying.

'I am not giving in to the gravitational pull of the slipper,' she had told me in private earlier, mournfully demonstrating her swollen joint which I was not allowed to call a bunion. She is in total denial about being a Nana; it is marvellous and sad at the same time.

But I can't deny her efforts have made a new man of Joe. He was by far the man of the evening, and when he gave Charlie a lift home on the back of his bike, I have to admit I was disappointed to have missed out on the excitement of travelling pillion. Excitement, for the sake of my writing, is something I am extremely keen to get into.

Icarus and Loudolle swalked off early to a party, which was a mercy because every time Loudolle caught *my eye*, she pointed to *her eye* with a nasty circling finger, and I had to operate quite hard to keep my cool.

All the adults said they thought that Michael and I looked sweet, referring to our pinafores, which made me feel quite a wally. At seventeen you're not quite a woman; neither something at once not the other. It's one of those difficult ages where you fall between two stools. I long to be twenty, which is the reverse of Aunt Coral who longs to be thirty. Neither of us can speed up or reverse the process, and neither of us really likes it. She always quotes Oscar Wilde on the subject: 'The tragedy of old age is not that one is old, but that one is young.' Sounds to me like he was in denial.

Later on, when I was back in the privacy of Pearl's room, I got my own back on Loudolle by drawing a full moustache and bogies on her face in the photo on the menu card. Revenge is sweet – I slept like a light.

Monday 7 September

Last Friday Mr Tsunawa went back to Japan, so Aunt Coral decided that on his last few nights, we should give him a haunting to remember. We began by moving objects around the Grey Room so that he couldn't find things where he'd left them when he returned home from work. Then we took it in turns to go and knock on his door every night at midnight and then, before he answered, we'd run away. As a consequence, he became more and more excited, and proudly began to refer to himself as the clairvoyant of Hong Kong.

On his very last night I dressed up in a maid's costume and stood in his wardrobe with my face partly obscured, so that when he opened it to pack he saw a ghostly maid in there hiding. He ran off to fetch Aunt Coral, at which point I escaped. It all worked like clockwork.

But then something strange happened. On my way back, I noticed that the shower was running in the Admirals' bathroom, which was strange, because Mrs Bunion had left for the day, the Admirals G and T were abroad and the Admiral was at his club. Delia was out at a real dinner with Loudolle and Aunt Coral was in the drawing room with Mr Tsunawa, which accounted for everyone. So who was in the shower?

If I'd had the nerve I would have gone straight in to have a look, but I didn't. Instead I went back to Pearl's room, changed out of my costume, then went to fetch Aunt Coral and Mr Tsunawa. We all went to the Admirals' bathroom together to see if anyone was there, but there was nobody, and the shower was off. But the floor was wet and steaming. It only further agitated Mr Tsunawa who suggested that it might have been the maid who had gone in to clean.

Aunt Coral was nonchalon as always and said that there have been leaks in that bathroom for years. I suppose that when you have lived somewhere like Green Place on your own for a long, long time, you have to develop a way of explaining strange things otherwise you'd be too frightened to stay there.

'Maybe it was the badger,' I said.

'Maybe it was,' said Aunt Coral.

'I was joking,' I said.

Aunt C has withstood far more mysterious things at Green Place than freak running water. She used to find Cameo sleepwalking into East Wing cupboards, and would have to go and wake her, and she'd have no idea where she was. And Great Nana Pearl often complained about an old lady looking back at her when she looked in the bathroom mirror. But Aunt Coral, as usual, was adamant it was just Nana Pearl's own reflection, joking that if there wasn't an old lady looking back at her, there'd be a dead one and this cheered Nana P up no end.

Whatever the spiritual activity here, be it supernatural, natural, or other, there are certainly mysteries mounting on mysteries, what with the thud and the sausages and the shower. Maybe they are *all* messages from the other world and maybe I just can't translate them?

This advert appeared in *Reuters* after Mr Tsunawa left:

Accommodation 50 mins from London, highly recommended by Tommy Tsunawa.

Are you looking for accommodation? Business or pleasure? Look no further than this country house separated from rest of world by three quarters of a mile-long drive. Unique décor, glorious gardens, faultless cuisine and ambience, distinguished society-beauty hosts with unparalleled grace and charm.

Individual requests catered for.

Enquiries Ms C Garden, Green Place, Clock-house Lane, Egham. 69950.

(I suspect Aunt Coral dictated it!)

Egham Hirsute Group
Early Autumn Special

'Continuing from our last session, I'd like us to share our letters,' said Aunt C, at the hottest group of the year. 'And just to remind everyone, our letters are from someone we've been longing to hear from. So who'd like to begin? Avery?'

The Admiral stood and read aloud.

Dear Rear Admiral Little,
It is with great pleasure that I am writing to you to confirm that
there will be traffic calming measures in place in Clockhouse
Lane by spring 1988. We agree that most motorists have no idea
of the quiet residential nature of the Clockhouse and need clearer
signage.

Any further comments will be respectfully taken on board.

Bill Rigger
Egham District Council

Aunt Coral was a little taken aback at first and didn't know what to say.
She was clearly expecting our letters to be of an emotional or romantic
nature. At least it wasn't a letter to himself from Loudolle, which would
have been embarrassing.

'Excellent Avery, well done,' said Aunt Coral after a while. 'Yes, you
have had a long battle haven't you?'

She paused for a moment, still thwarted by the ordinariness of his
material. Where was the cousin of Lord Byron that he'd shown himself
to be? Had he been replaced by the most boring man on the planet? But
because she is such a brilliant guru, she quickly recovered her face.

'Delia?' she said, after a sip of her nourishing Sapphire.

Dear Delia,
I'm so sorry about Ralph. I had no idea what a twat he was and can
now only sympathise with what you must have gone through.

I hope that it is some consolation to you to know that after
the accident on the mountain he suffered a lot before he ran out of
oxygen, and that his girlfriend, Hilary Shitface, left him for dead,
making her own way down from the hillside, where she went off
with a Brazilian.

He hadn't updated his will, and so everything, including the house and all his assets, naturally pass to you.

I hope that this letter finds you well and looking forward to your future.

Kind Regards,

Mrs June Colbourne
Solicitor

'Excellent Delia, well done,' said Aunt Coral. 'Managing to get Ralph in somewhere . . . and not so much someone who you long to hear from, but some*thing* you long to hear. Right, yes . . . and Joe?'

And Joe stood up and read his letter.

Dear Joe,
I don't want to be your 'better than nothing person'; I want to be the one. I don't want to be your 'she'll do for now' person; I want to be the one.

To me, love is phone calls followed by letters because you cannot bear to say goodbye. Beating down my door, not knocking on it.

Whoever it is that is filling your head is a very lucky lady. I can wait.

Love and feelings,

Kate
xxx

'Excellent Joe, really excellent. Goodness! From Kate Bush, I presume? And if she is your better-than-nothing person, then who is your number one? Excellent Joe. Full of longing, and, may I say, mystery.

I was wondering who his number one was too, with Kate Bush in the queue. Joe has stopped looking my way, and it's hard to tell what his feelings are now that he's become so good at hiding them.

'Sue?' said Aunt Coral, 'have you written a letter to yourself?'

Of course I had, but I had gone down the emotional route, and I was worried about reading it. I wrote it one night after a nightmare, and it seemed to calm me down. I was going to write one from Mr O'Carroll but I thought I might be too harsh on myself. Sure enough, as soon as I stood up my knees gave way and I had to sit back down again.

'I can't read it,' I said. 'Could someone else?'

Joe was on his feet in a nanasecond.

'Sue's letter,' he said.

Dear Sue,

I am sorry I left without saying goodbye. I had expected to be resuscitated. I never meant for this to happen, or I would have left you a note.

I want you to know that I am all right, that I live in Heaven with all my dead relatives, and dream in vales of buddleia, which are blue. I have sent you messages from the other world and hope that you understand them.

Although I cannot visit the earth, because that is a rule of Heaven, I can still hear you, I listen with the ears of a spirit. It's like when the clouds are very still and high, but low vapour is blown fast across them – I am the Eagle that's coasting on the current between the two. I watch over you.

I just wanted to let you know, as I know that you have been longing to, that although I do not suffer, I THINK OF YOU ALL THE TIME.

Mum xxxxxx

When he'd finished everyone was emotional, except the Admiral who must have still been thinking about the council.

'Excell . . . rea . . . exce, w . . . done . . .' said Aunt Coral. 'Goodness . . . wel . . . do . . . S . . .'

We disbanded early, as the group were too moved to continue. Aunt

Coral had prepared a whole section on interpretation which would have to be postponed.

I am lying in bed now, caressed by the heavy summer air which is laced with the scent of the buddleia from the trees down Clockhouse Lane, my thoughts drifting from Group to death and then to the loss of the eye.

I can't tell you how much I'd love to lie with it, to hold it in my hand. Until it was gone I never knew how much I'd miss it, or what a comfort it has been. Maybe I am as sad as Delia, building my future on something so small. But it's surprising how little a thing you need to do it: a tortoise, an eye, a handbag. I dread to think what Icarus would say if he ever finds out that I kept his eye. He would think I was mad, but worse, he would think I was *sad*. Most girls my age have got real boyfriends' eyes to look into, but I have been reduced to a relationship with a small piece of photo. Just what sort of woman am I to get excited over so little? But then I have never even been kissed. Aunt Coral says it's because I am innocent, and I'm still young enough to be getting away with it. She makes me sound quite saintly.

But there is no way on earth that I will *ever* let Icarus find out about his eye, so, short of stealing his eye back, I will have to pander to Loudolle. It has just occurred to me that the eye, which has given me so much joy and pleasure, has now become a source of evil. Hold on, there's somebody at my door.

How ironic. It was Loudolle, with another demand.

Coral's Commonplace: Volume 3
Green Place, Aug 5 1946
(Age 24)

Green Place has been returned to us in a shocking state of repair. It seems the troops found it hard to keep warm, so they put a random mix of wood up the chimney, including some of the back stairs, wall panels, banisters, floorboards, some furniture, and a thirty-foot beech from the garden, which was the only giant beech in Egham. But we try not to resent it; our home is as nothing compared to the millions who have died in the war.

Despite that, F and M are naturally heartbroken and struggling to come to terms with it, and have been further crippled by the new taxes brought in by Mr Attlee. They have to pay ninety-five per cent on their savings and sixty-six per cent on their income, and if they die the government get sixty-five per cent. Britain is bankrupt. Father's aristo friends the Oziases have had their assets stripped by two sets of death duties – poor Julius himself and now their eldest Julius Caesar. I don't think Mr Attlee approves of the rich at all.

Mother has not had a banana for seven years, and is now in the grip of a demoniac craving for one. A sure way to create a luxury item is not to be able to get it.

'This war wasn't fought so that you could enjoy a banana,' said Father.

It is one of his favourite ways of coining the greater perspective. And we do feel guilty, and lucky to be standing here, free and full and alive.

Mother replied with poignancy, though it was after he'd left the room.

'Yes it was.'

Joy, pleasure and abundance are all part of freedom's gift. But the lights in the world are still on, and there is a naked lady in red pen on my bedroom ceiling. There are also the following inscriptions on the walls:

Arthur Marks, 8th United States Army Air Force. 400 days.
Flight Lieutenant Dorian Campbell loves the WAF in the secret bunker. Sweet voice in the night.
Squadron Leader Benedict Dunford. Balloon Squadron supreme.
Pilot Officer, Colin Anderson, no 615 Squadron RAF.
James Anderson, Royal Auxiliaries. RIP my brother.

I have added two of my own:

RIP Sayler
RIP Daniel Morris

It really feels in both a great and a small way that the old world has gone for ever.

Earlier today Dr John looked in to pass on his condolences about Daniel and Sayler. It is believed that Daniel 'had become separated from his unit'. Mrs Morris will not hear of anyone putting it another way. In the last Great War, desertion carried a maximum sentence of death, as did cowardice. Leniency is thankfully shown nowadays, except for treason and mutiny. Whatever has happened to him, Daniel is still lost, and so therefore is Mrs Morris.

It turns out that Dr John's unit was part of the team sent in to recover bodies on D-Day, and he spent thirty-six hours operating nonstop, one man after another after another. Not surprisingly he is even now a little done in.

Mr D'Olivera has not come back. He is MPD, and my heart goes out to his family.

But as the grim news trickled in about all our missing friends, thank God there has been some good news about Johnny. Although he has been held as a Prisoner of War, he was apparently liberated from a

German Stalag. I didn't even know he had been taken as a prisoner of war. But our only link with Johnny is his Father, Jackie Isles, and it was not until Mr Isles called in to the house that we knew a thing about it. Mr Isles was brimming over with pride and joy to have his son back. He said that when Johnny was sent to the front, he wasn't expected to make old bones. So understandably Mr Isles is now unable to contain his relief. It is like a miracle. He has visited everyone he could think of. He wanted to tell the whole world.

He told us Johnny is still weak and suffering greatly from shell shock. He'd been living on a bowl of gruel and a pound of bread a day – that is, if he completed his work. If he didn't, his rations were diminished, and the hungrier he got, the less he was able to finish his work. Such tortures. And his feet are in a terrible state from jungle rot which took hold because he got too tired to take his boots off. If you don't take your boots off, your feet are constricted and damp, and when sores develop they can turn to gangrene. The condition can occur with as little as one day's exposure, so he is lucky to have any feet left at all. I hope they will be warm and dry for the rest of his life.

Mr Isles said Johnny wakes in the night with a desire to end it all, because he feels he cannot recover from the horrors he has seen. It seems that even though he is home and safe, that still the danger threatens. I wonder if he ever got the letter I wrote to him while I was at Whistlers Corner? I hope that it gave him some cheer.

Hundreds of children rescued from the camps have been brought to London. It was announced on the radio and makes a very harrowing story. Most of them were very weak, and some were close to death. The stronger ones carried the bags of the weak, tiny heroes supporting each other. They assembled at Victoria station and were taken to a nearby church hall, where they were lined up and instructed by gymnasts to do star jumps. This seemingly cruel exercise was a short cut, designed to determine which of the children needed emergency treatment, and the ones that collapsed were taken straight to hospital. But the remaining children began to cry, believing after their long journey that their friends were being taken away to be killed. Most had grown up in the camps, and did not know of any other reason for a person to be 'taken away'.

Rumours abound that the man responsible for all this terror, Adolf Hitler, is working as a waiter in Switzerland, though this probably came from the Department of Liars in an attempt to catch other criminals.

With the economy on its knees odd things are happening. Photographic film and the metal it comes in has been reused and sold again, so you can get photographs of strangers coming up on your family shots. Dr John showed us some of his pictures of the war, and there are also some pictures of a pale stranger photographed holding a baby. They are under the trees in a forest; Dr John thinks it could be in Poland. She looks afraid. Was she in hiding? Could it have been from the Nazis? Could the picture have been taken by her husband, who feared they were close to capture? Is she still alive? And what of the baby? I dream of her being reunited with all her loved ones who may've been stolen away. How lucky I am to be here. But for an accident of birth, it could have been me.

And I have nothing but respect for Winston Churchill, whatever his cost to the economy. His booting-out has shocked the whole of Europe, especially Mother. It was a sad day for the man who's achieved so much. And I will never forget his talent for comedy either – 'Hitler's tattered lackey Mussolini'!

But enough of war. I have got a degree! Although my class two did not meet with much approval. But I can say hand on heart that I tried. There are other things in life besides reductionism. You are reading the words of the woman who has read *Anna Karenina* three times.

Some private news:

In these days of shortage and austerity, Cameo's cup floweth over. She got a job in a cigarette factory because she was heartsick about her American and needed a diversion. And at the factory she met and fell in love with a Major Jack Laine. He came on a private matter to meet with the owner. (Some sort of trade-off for cigarettes is my guess.) He is devilishly handsome, but unfortunately, already married.

Nobody knows except me, and one close friend of his, who, I have it on good authority, has only told four hundred of hers. In spite of my inward misgivings, I expect I am possibly jealous, having no one to write home about but a salty academic who can't keep his lunch off his shirt. Still, it's reassuring to know I'm decent enough for a proposal. Gerald asked me to marry him, but I couldn't countenance being a Podger.

'I know it's a secret for it's whispered everywhere' (Congreve)

Sue

AT ABOUT SEVEN o'clock this morning, when we were all still in bed, there was a terrible crash. I thought a tree must've fallen into the house. It was ferocious, like a demolition gong, or a plane falling out of the sky, or a thunder clap that was strong enough to bring down an entire forest. I heard Aunt Coral run downstairs and the Admiral following after her. When I caught up with them, they were in the kitchen, as were the rest of the tenants – all that is except Admiral Ted, who slept straight through all the noise.

'Maybe they left an unexploded bomb here,' said the Admiral.

'The house is falling down,' said Aunt Coral. No one accused either of them of melodrama, just in case.

Then there was a second crash, even louder than the first. We were so frightened that we all got down on the floor. A few seconds later came the sound of what I imagined to be a volcano. It so jangled our nerves, that it was ages after peace came before anyone dared to break the silence.

'I'm going upstairs,' said Admiral Little bravely.

'I'm coming with you. Ted's up there,' said Admiral Gordon as he followed suit.

And not wishing to be left alone, we women went up too, convinced we were going to find Admiral Ted splattered all over the floor. We edged in through each door as though we'd had special training, checking each room methodically; it took us quite a long time. Eventually we discovered the problem. The ceilings had come down in two of the East Wing bedrooms. But the knock-on effect looked perilous for *the whole Wing.*

'I shouldn't like to say, Miss Garden, I couldn't put a figure on that,' said Glenn Miller, arriving within ten minutes of Aunt Coral's urgent call. 'You've probably got some rot, or woodworm in those timbers. But I can't understand for the life of me why it should fall,' he said.

He pulled at a bit of plaster that was hanging by a thread and a whole lot more fell down behind it and disappeared into powders. What I thought had been a volcano was in fact raining masonry.

'Oh dear,' he said.

Aunt Coral was in pieces and was having to be given the Admiral's gooney.

'So what ball park figure would you say,' said the Admiral, 'to put it all back up again?'

'Well, cor, I think . . .' said Glenn Miller, 'I think it's going to be dear.'

'Is it too early for a sherry?' said Aunt C.

The most chaotic morning followed. In between the ceilings coming down and our hasty retreat out of the East Wing, there were frequent visitors to the front door all bearing tortoises. Aunt Coral wasn't coping, and Delia couldn't identify Bertie. Emergency scaffold was arriving, and Glenn Miller called in his men, who came rushing like a boiler-suited cavalry. I was making tea for everybody, and trying to move my things out of the East Wing, and trying to get ready for work, knowing I was going to be late. Loudolle had already swalked off after her usual swim, having milked me the previous evening of a further £3.50.

'You gonna be late for work, Sue? You want me to tell Mrs Fry?' she said.

'Tell her what you like. I hope you fall in a cowpat.'

'Oh you're gonna regret that,' she said. 'Don't forget I know things . . .'

'And I know you come from Ealing and not Alpen, Colorado,' I said.

But it made no impact. She has no humility about having reinvented herself, and was not to be out-embarrassed.

I tried to comfort Aunt Coral, who was being assisted by the Admiral. Her main concern, as was mine, was the thought of having to leave Green Place.

'This will wipe out the shoe fund completely,' she said. 'We won't be able to do anything up.'

'Let's break the problem into small chunks, which they say you should do in a crisis,' I said.

But she was beside herself and had lost all sense of proportion, railing that we were all going to have to go into homes because the building was unstable.

'Mrs Bunion won't have to go into a home,' I said. 'I've never heard of a home for cleaners. She has a family she can go to. Besides, Mrs Bunion doesn't even *live* here! *Nobody's* going into a home Aunt Coral, except hopefully Loudolle. We might go to a hotel or somewhere. We could go somewhere nice.'

This perked her up, and when the Admiral returned I went to phone in sick, which I knew would inflame Mrs Fry, but as Aunt Coral was in no fit state, I knew I had to prioritise her. When I returned she had been given an aspirin and the Admiral was kneeling by her chair.

'There's no need to upset yourself, Aunt Coral, there now, there we go,' he said.

'But I don't want to live in a Tupperware, I love feeling the draughts all around me,' she said, trying to be amusing.

Slowly and gently under the Admiral's care Aunt C was beginning to rally, but then the moment was gone, to be replaced by a mystery development. Above the suites where the collapse happened there is an attic space, which has been the store for a surplus of boxes and old toys. It is accessed by a pull-down ladder through a hatch in one of the bedrooms, (one of the nooks and hidey holes for which Green Place is famous). Anyway, in amongst the debris Glenn Miller and his team had found an unusual gentleman's hold all. It was packed with a few items of clothing, which Glenn felt looked 'too ragamuffin' to belong to a resident of Green Place. His team had made enquiries among the male residents of the building, and even telephoned Badger to check that the hold all wasn't his, (at which point Aunt Coral became momentarily mortified), before they came to the conclusion that the hold all didn't belong to any *official* inhabitant of Green Place. And so, putting two and two together, 'and making ten' according to Aunt Coral, Glenn and the team came up with a theory. They were convinced it was the mystery owner of the hold all, a stranger, who had put his foot through the ceiling when he was rummaging in the attic. So by lunchtime, Green Place was crawling with policemen.

'What I think you've got here, Ms Garden, is either a trespasser, or a tramp,' PC Pacey told us. 'There's no sign of breaking and entering, you see, so it's unlikely to be a burglar. You've got a tramp I 'speck. We do see a lot of them out here in some of the larger houses. But the finding of a hold all of clothing on the bed doesn't necessarily mean that the trespasser damaged the ceiling. From the looks of those timbers those ceilings could've come down on their own. If you *were* to manage to catch him, we could charge him with civil trespass. But, unless you catch him red handed, there's not a lot we can do.'

'I see,' said Aunt Coral. 'Do you mean by civil trespass that the trespasser's more polite?' A poor attempt at a joke, but it showed her indomitable spirit.

'No, it doesn't mean that the trespasser is more polite, it just means that they haven't broken and entered.' PC Colin Pacey was without a sense of wit.

'Are you telling us that the law considers it acceptable for someone to walk into a house and *sleep* here, as long as he keeps the place tidy?' said the Admiral, shaking his head in appaulment at this loophole in the law.

'No Sir, the law doesn't consider it acceptable for someone to walk into this house and sleep here, but it happens all the time on the borders and people don't even know it. He might have been here a while.'

By this evening, we were all quite stressed and tired from the events of today. The sultry day led to a sticky night without a breeze to release it. We sat together on deck chairs beside the pool, the Daddy long legs were in the hedgerows and the martinis were on ice. If we hadn't been in a crisis, it would have been blissful.

'How are we going to catch him?' said the Admiral pacing around the terrace.

'With a trap?' suggested Delia.

'With a trap!' The Admiral was getting excited.

'What sort of trap?' said Aunt Coral. 'You can't just put a trap out, the fellow might get hurt. And what if it isn't a tramp, what if the bag of clothing belonged to someone who stayed here once and left it behind when he went? Those clothes might have been there for years. Just because there are bumps in the night, doesn't mean there's someone living here. I'm certain no one's been in that room for years and years and years.'

But the Admiral was inspired with all his hormones raging. 'If he's coming in and going out the same way as the rest of us, it should be relatively easy,' he said. 'It's a question of surveillance, of sealing off the exits.'

'But there are a hundred ways into Green Place,' I said.

'What about digging some traps in the woods like you see in the films?' said the Admiral.

'*Where* in the woods?' said Aunt Coral. 'And what if you catch a jogger?'

'You would have to be careful that no one gets hurt,' I said. 'You have to act within the law.'

'Baloney! The law's an ass,' said the Admiral. 'Just look at what's happened here.'

After a great deal of argument we agreed that in the first instance, Badger and Tornegus will dig some deep holes to act as traps, at vulnerable areas of fencing. To accommodate my safety concerns they will pad the holes with soft landings and leave out food and water in the unlikely event that a jogger or rambler should be caught in one by mistake. Plan B is surveillance. We will take it in turns to watch the exits, particularly at 2 to 3am, when the thud tends to happen.

And the greater plan is to re-erect the ceilings as quickly as is possible, and try harder than ever to raise some cash for all the work.

Meanwhile we have moved ourselves back into the West Wing, like refugees from disaster. This time I have the attic where Delia was doing her Italian. It has a skylight, and if I stand on my suitcase I can see out all across Egham. High above everything, from the elite vantage of my eerie I can see, to the left lies Titford and to the right lies Egham and to the front lie the armies of buddleia. The affluent borders sprawl beyond with their twinkling evening lights, where a hundred cars are sealed into a hundred sliding garages, and a hundred sets of car keys are cast on a hundred tables, and a hundred dinners are taken before a hundred fires, and a hundred hungry husbands rush and kiss their hundred wives.

Brackencliffe

Down in the dungeon, Cara's guard was a good man and could see nae reason not to be nice.

'What ails ye?' he asked the maids, when he took in their dungeon meal tray.

'I n'ery know where my beloved Keeper is,' said Cara. 'Last I saw he was held captive by the scruff of the neck.'

'Whyfore!' said the guard. 'You mean Keeper the spaniel? Why, he is yonder in the dog house — the Master has kept him for sport.'

'We must free him, please help us!' said Cara.

'The Missie will kill us all!' said Fiona. 'This dungeon ceiling, it pounds!' For the weight of the Missie dancing with Knight Van Day above them was a fair threat to the building.

And so the guard took pity on them, and freed them under cover of darkness, reuniting them with their spaniel Keeper, whilst above them, Pretafer's waltzing shook the earth.

Once they were free, they ran and they ran, Mistress Cara, loyal Fiona, and fleet Keeper, ran far, far away from Brackencliffe.

And as they approached safe haven, Fiona whispered gently, 'Here lest I forget,' and handed Cara her locket.

Coral's Commonplace: Volume 3
Oxford, May 15 1947
(Age 24)

Telegram from Mother and Father:

> MAY 15 1947 GIRL. BUDDLEIA ROSE. AT GREEN PLACE

> 8AM GMT. 6LBS. ALL PERFECT.

More than shocked, as Mother didn't know she was pregnant until she went into labour. She's had what is termed a 'surprise pregnancy', which, though baffling, is apparently not totally unheard of. She continued her cycles all the way through, if a little irregularly, but that was the norm for her anyway these days, and she had no symptoms. Dr John says the baby was most likely carried very far back in her womb, and as she has always suffered with her digestion, it would have been hard to tell the difference.

What a total miracle, and the greatest possible shock! But she's always wanted another.

I said I would come straight away, but they have put me off till the weekend because Mother needs absolute bed rest and Mrs Morris is caring for the baby.

Green Place, May 21 1947

Buddleia waved her arms in the air for a few moments this morning like she was conducting an orchestra on the ceiling. The rest of the time she has only woken up to feed, before falling back to sleep again while she is still on the job. She is tiny, not even as long as Father's forearm. She looks like a little tadpole.

Apart from the obvious physical stresses, Mother is overjoyed. Father is somewhat distracted and Cameo is very quiet. She has been in bed most of the time since I've been here – she says she is feeling coldy. But I think it's more than that, I think she is nursing a broken heart. She's not been herself since Major Laine ended their relationship shortly before Christmas last year. He moved away with his wife, saying he could never leave her. I never thought he was going to anyway, but it was easy to pull the wool over Cameo's eyes. She's only nineteen so she believed in all his rubbish. Cameo could have any man she wanted. I wish she hadn't fallen for him.

I've tried to comfort her but it has been terribly awkward because nobody knows here except me. To his friends who know, he will be that poor chap who some young girl got smitten with, and didn't his wife give him stick, and poor fellow he's trying to do the right thing. But to me he is less than a bastard.

Other news:

Johnny Look-at-the-Moon's Father, Jackie Isles, called in again to tell us they plan to go back to Ireland. My heart did a back flip when I heard his voice, because I thought Johnny might have come too. Sadly, though his health has improved, he wasn't able to come today. I am disappointed not to see him. That is a fact.

Mr Isles says he is getting out of the coal business, as there's too much competition from gas. He plans to try his luck with a smallholding in Donegal where he hopes that his family will have a higher standard of living. Father asked him in and they enjoyed a smoke together with Dr John. The war's been a great leveller!

Jackie wouldn't take the third light, so Father had to light another match. I asked Dr John about this later and he told me it is considered bad luck for three to share a light from the same match, because when in trench warfare, at the first light the enemy can see you, at the second they can take aim, and at the third light they fire. But Dr John said it's rubbish; you can't be seen in the trenches, that's the whole point of them. It's because some fellow wants to sell more matches – he must work for Lucky Strike.

Mrs Morris will be retiring to the seaside at Eastbourne at the beginning of August. Losing Daniel has knocked all the stuffing out of her. She truly loved that poor boy, had her life mapped out around his. Without him she seems somehow unhinged, unrooted. Mother and Father are providing a handsome pension. I know they would have given even more if it hadn't been for the new baby.

Despite her sadness, she (Mrs Morris) somehow found time to update her log book. There have been no such additions to the family names in the log for the last 19 years! Normally she only puts in a new entry when we move rooms or have guests to stay (in case Mother can't remember where they are).

FAMILY ROOMS, May 1947

Trout Suite (West Wing) – Mr Garden

Pearl's Room (East) – Mrs Garden

Bluebell Left (East) – Ms Coral

Bluebell Right (East) – Ms Cameo

Grey Room (West) – Ms Buddleia

She has also given Buddleia a gift – Granny Morris's copy of *The Poetical Works of Mrs Felicia Hemans*. Felicia Hemans was a late-romantic poet, but Buddleia's a bit young for it yet!

Sue

I SHOULD HAVE known that there wouldn't be much of a market for chivalry. Today, with only four days to go till the workshop and half the building under scaffolding, there were only two places booked, and those to Tornegus and Badger on freebies from the Admiral, promising great results with women after attendance on the course. And I still haven't had time to approve Aunt Coral's budget, which is sure to be inflammatory. I do wish she'd hand it in.

Thursday Sept 17

We are now up to five students, which is an improvement but still a bit embarrassing. Aunt Coral has invited Joe of course, for he is her own young protégé. Then there will be Badger and his son Tornegus, and also two pest control men, Derek and Pigpen, who I propositioned in the toilets at the Toastie earlier on.

Friday Sept 18

There are still only the same five students booked on the chivalry workshop. Unless a bus-load of boy scouts gets lost up the drive, it looks like that will be it. I'm sure if we were better business people we would cancel and not continue, but it isn't the Green Place way, plus Delia has got carried away and has invited Nigel from the *Herald*, which will at least mean good publicity.

We've decided that the press launch, (which is what Delia's calling it!), will be a two-pronged event, with a special women's EHG to run in conjunction with the workshop, and then the men and the women will meet over luncheon so that the men can practise their skills. Chocs away!

Saturday 19 September

Chivalry Weekend Special Ladies' Egham Hirsute Group

This morning found we women in the conservatory commencing our special group. The day was sticky and close, every glass panel intensifying the heat and making you wish to run outside and throw yourself in the pool. For the gentlemen the day had already begun with some basics such as jousting, for the purpose of which the Admirals had hired a pony. It was lucky to be outside in the paddock under refreshing spits and spots of rain.

'Welcome, Ladies, to the special chivalry EHG,' began Aunt Coral. 'Who can tell me, what is the most famous example of chivalry?'

We all put our hands up.

'Sue?' said Aunt Coral.

'Walter Raleigh's cape,' I said.

'Excellent Sue, Walter Raleigh is correct. Any others?'

We all put our hands up again.

'Sue,' said Aunt Coral.

'The rescuing of Rapunzel,' I said.

'Excellent Sue, Rapunzel, yes. And Delia?'

'Prince Albert taking the bullet for Queen Victoria,' she said.

'Excellent Delia, yes. Prince Albert. And Loudolle?' Unfortunately Delia had asked her along for the special.

'I'll take Prince Albert,' she said, misunderstanding the concept.

'Thank you Loudolle, not quite, you'll need to listen more carefully.'

Tensions between we ladies were at slightly unchivalrous levels!

The men outside had moved on to a lecture, and we caught their voices through the open conservatory doors.

'Ladies do not need to be pulled out of cars, but they may require some easing,' said Admiral Little.

'Good. Now . . .' said Aunt Coral, pulling our attention back, 'I want you to write a short piece on the most romantic offer you have ever had.'

'The purpose of the exercise,' said Aunt Coral, 'is to let your imagination run free, so be as far-fetched as you'd like, as you would be in your dreams.'

We jotted down our thoughts and then stood up to share them.

'"I did not know my destination, but was to collect my ticket at the airport. 'Venice', it said on the envelope, and when I opened it there was a note: 'Marry me tomorrow,' it said. The note was signed 'Count Jason'."'

'Excellent Sue, really excellent, well done,' said Aunt Coral, 'my goodness me, Count Jason . . . And Delia?' she continued.

'"Ciou Caramia Deliaissima,
Amore Signomi Vittorio, amore, amore, amore. Amore grande, mi dispiace amore amore amore.
Vittorio"'

'Excellent Delia, goodness, how romantic.'

'In the event of an argument remember, NEVER SHAKE A LADY,' said Admiral Ted from outside.

'And Loudolle?' said Aunt Coral.

'I'll take Count Jason,' she said, misunderstanding again.

'Thank you Loudolle, but you've missed the point, never mind, we can't all be Einstein.'

You can imagine that this remark put the cat among the pigeons, and several daggers flew across the conservatory while we took part in silent clashes. I think Aunt C was trying to be funny, but it didn't go down that way!

Loudolle did not show any reaction but was certain to be hiding a vengeance which would be sure to come out later in the day and explode all over the workshop. It appeared that the real jousting that day was taking place at Group.

'Now, chivalry is a tradition, a defence, and an honour. A truly chivalrous man would give up his life for the lady he loves,' said Aunt C.

'Stand when she leaves the table, and finish her food if she can't,' said the voice of Admiral Gordon.

'Which leads me on to favours,' said Aunt Coral looking rather disappointed that the chivalry of English men was more ordinary than she had hoped.

'Favours were traditionally a hanky or a garter, which would be given to a man to wear before he jousted for good luck. It was also a sign to all the world that the man had a special feminine friend. You might have a little think about who you would choose to give yours to!'

This caused somewhat of a rustle amongst the group!

'Always attend to the taking off and putting on of a lady's coat,' came the Admiral's voice from outside. 'Some ladies like to have their bonnets taken off too.'

Aunt C looked dangerously wistful. No surprise who she would choose for a favour, for she gazed with such longing out the window at the Ad, standing on the lawn in his full naval uniform, (bar his sandals). I sensed her wanting to abandon Group to go and fetch a bonnet and she almost ran out of the room a short while later when Mrs Bunion rang the lunch gong.

On the way into the dining room I overheard Aunt Coral discussing menus with Mrs Bunion, and was staggered to learn that they weren't discussing lunch for the workshop, but what food should be served in the trespasser traps. However Mrs Bunion had excelled herself with the cuisine for lunch and came in bang-on budget with a banquet of chicken and oatcakes and a four o'clock mug o'soup.

Nigel, the Head of Events at the *Herald*, arrived in time to eat, and was given lashings of wine to encourage a good review.

Afterwards we gathered together in the garden, so that the gentlemen could walk the ladies, blessed by a rare appearance of the sun. I pinned my proverbial favour to Tornegus, which caused a hundred million opinions.

'This is the correct way to lead a lady when walking along, and should prevent any tantrums. And remember to speak softly to ladies, they like deep resonant voices,' said Admiral Ted, demonstrating with Mrs Bunion by placing one hand in the small of her back and the other under her elbow, and gently encouraging her with a barotone, 'There now, that's the way.'

Tornegus put his hand in the small of my back as we walked, and encouraged me along as per the Admiral's advice, as if I were a dog. None of the ladies I know need to be encouraged to walk along, not even the Nanas who admittedly tend to drift.

'If your stride is a good deal faster than a lady's, never walk off and leave her,' said the Admiral. 'And never take a lady for a walk when it's windy, she may fall over.'

Tornegus and I walked into the orchard, and as soon as we couldn't be seen, he stopped being chivalrous and seized both my hands spontaneously. One minute he was standing opposite me and a nanasecond later, he had pinned me up against a tree. The moment was rather steamy.

'That's not very chivalrous,' I said, with a twinkle, for I found myself getting arouselled.

'I wondered if . . .' he trailed off, and then he totally lost his patter.

I didn't understand why he had dried up until I heard footsteps from behind my tree. I think Tornegus had been just about to try and kiss me, but he had spotted his Father come looking for him! And so we sprang apart and he abandoned his advance, for we were now in full view of the approaching Badger.

'This one will need pollarding before Spring,' said Badger as he joined us, referring to the very tree I had been up against.

'I'll say,' I thought quietly to myself. I almost got a kiss.

We all walked back to the house together to find romance flooding the place at every single corner. Nigel was running around the garden, pretending to be Victorian; Derek and Pigpen were in the conservatory writing poetry to their wives; Admiral Ted was in the kitchen attending to Mrs Bunion; and Delia and Admiral Gordon were upstairs talking Italian. The sun teased the dust into kaleidoscope tendrils of love.

Aunt Coral was busy fiddling with her bonnet, temptingly near to the Ad. He was as amorous as he was able to be whilst filling out forms he'd requested for loans on listed buildings.

'We might just qualify,' he said.

'We might,' said Aunt C throatily, incorrigibly playing with her bonnet.

It hardly mattered when, as expected, Loudolle retaliated over the earlier slights with another ransom demand. I found that the prospect of giving her money didn't bother me as much as before. Maybe because I felt rich, not in money but in moments, and my moment amongst the apples was mine for ever; it could never be stolen away.

Of course Tornegus is no match for Icarus but he has given me a new perspective, which is a blessed relief. And he took my hands in the orchard, in a flash of rare sunshine and apples; it was not the hand of the man I love, but that of a traveller along the way.

Very late this evening, when everyone was in bed, Aunt Coral came up to the attic.

'I didn't want to spoil your day,' she said. 'But is it what I think it is?' And she handed me a card addressed to me in my father's writing and bearing the Titford postmark. I didn't need to open it. The bad news inside burned through.

To

Sue and Aunt Coral

Nicholas and Ivana

request the pleasure of your company

at their wedding on December 22nd

at the Titford Town Hall

If only life could be like the films, where painful nights just melt away into rapid changes of season, to 'two years later' or 'in the end'. If only the pages of the calendar *could* be blown away by the wind and jump-cut to the happy ending. But not so life. You have to live through every heartbeat; there's no escaping the bad bits.

'I thought it might be, so I went to fetch this,' said Aunt Coral, settling on my bed in her cosy. She was holding the bottle of wine from the cellar that she had laid down for my 18th.

'But I'm not eighteen till January,' I said.

'I know, but I think it will help.'

She pulled a corkscrew out of her pocket like an alcoholic.

'It's a Bordeaux, so we need to let it breathe,' she said, studying the seventeen-year-old bottle. Although a great connoisseur, she is not above buying a wine because she likes the picture on the label. She gently blew off the dust.

'I had the telegram about your birth and the next day I chose this. It's a Château Lafite. The finest. For good luck, long life, and bless—'

She stopped to examine the vineyard closer, and something came off in her hand. It was a damp clump of paper, on top of which you could still see the handwritten letters 'S' and 'U'.

I recognised mum's writing immediately. I'm not certain if Aunt Coral did too, but I think she took her cue from my face. I remember so clearly the way the 'E' would have been had it not been washed away. It would have been up very close to the 'U', as if it did not want to be parted from it; it was mum's trademark way of writing my name.

There was no more script to follow, no point of familiar reference. My teeth chattered, though it wasn't cold, and Aunt Coral was white as snow. I hadn't looked in the cellar because Mum was afraid of spiders. She must have really wanted to be certain to hide it away from my Dad.

'I thought we'd never find it. I stopped believing,' I said.

'I don't feel ready,' she said. Her voice was fragile but it was as if her hands belonged to a strongman. She opened out the note steadily in preparation for reading. But how could anyone ever be ready for such a thing as this? If we'd been in a film, we would have had special clothes on; we would have been in a solicitor's, with professionals on hand in case one of us couldn't cope. But instead we were in an attic, in ordinary lamplight and dust, with no one but each other. It wasn't enough. We couldn't have been any closer, yet Aunt C was far away, and at the end of the awful hunt, we were each on our own.

The sound of footsteps down the passage released us into action.

'OK,' I said. It was as good a word as any.

My darling Sue,

There is not a word or a number that can ever express how much I love you. I'm so sorry for what I have done. And I hope that if you are reading this on your birthday it means that you are with Aunt Coral. She is the best of aunts and sisters, and I know she will take care of you.

I was so lucky to have had you, had the joy of you all your years. The fact that I can't bear my sadness is my weakness, not yours.

I've left you a bundle of things in a locker at Titford Station. The key is under the floorboard in my bedroom, and the locker is 402. This is just between you and me, please keep it private. I am sorry to be so secretive, but I do think it's for the best.

I wonder if you'd ask Coral to put a little plaque up for me in the garden? Maybe out next to my mother's? It's somewhere I always liked to be.

I'm so sorry I left without saying goodbye, but you know I couldn't have managed it.

Forgive me my darling, please forgive me.

I love you so very much,

Mum XXXXXX

Sometimes it feels as though every silver lining has a cloud. The answer I've been searching for ever since Mum died is finally there on paper, dotted with Aunt C's tears and made a mash of by the drips in the cellar, but it isn't the answer I want. It is the dawn of many more questions.

There are some things she said I feel I understand, and some that I really don't. I understand what she means by not being able to bear her own sadness, that must be about Dad and Ivana I'm sure. But why would she go to all the trouble of hiding things in a locker? And why did she feel the need to be secretive, and why did she think it was for the best? She didn't have anything to hide, or anything to be ashamed of that I know of. Perhaps feeling that Dad didn't care about her drove her to hide her precious things.

Although in a way it is a grisly relief, to be sure that she really *meant* to do this. That it wasn't an accidental cry for help, and there was nothing I could have done to prevent it. And maybe Aunt Coral is right. Maybe finding out she wasn't who she thought she was did hurt her. She was such a sensitive person, it must have been such a shock. And she didn't even have Dad's companionable shoulder to cry on when she found out, because of Ivana. These thoughts are unbearable and to survive I must stop.

Aunt C checked on me about ten times before I persuaded her to go to bed. She knows that sometimes all one can do is stand by on the same roadside. I know how she'll get through it; she's pretty classy at comforting herself. She'll go down and rummage in her papers, keep her radio on and get an extra quilt.

But I just want to be alone, I feel hollow, as though I have no blood, bones or veins inside me. I can only tell you that finding that note actually physically hurts.

I have put it in my sock drawer, where I can catch a glimpse of her lovely writing. To have put it in my treasure box would have felt like excluding her, shutting her away from the light, and under my pillow was too painful, and under my bed too dark. But the sock drawer is sometimes open, sometimes closed. It is very much part of my actions, and my actions are still alive. I cling to these little things like odd bits of ship wreck drifting about in an open sea.

We must carry on, we mustn't collapse; I've learnt this very strongly. And if we do stop carrying on for a while, life carries on without us. And so when the sun rises, if it does, I will face the second day of the Chivalry workshop, with the best courage I can.

Even at such grave moments as this, my mind tries to balance itself with the practical. How am I going to get the key from under the floorboard in Dad's room? He barely leaves the house when they're there; they prefer to stay home, loving. And what could there be in the locker that is so dire and dreadful? I think there will be little sleep for me tonight.

At about 9am, the tired sky let through a single shaft of light, which looked briefly like a followspot falling through my skylight. It woke me and I went to look out over Egham in the brand new day. But the beam was gone in a nanasecond and the clouds reformed their cover.

Loudolle has such a strong nose for unrest that she sniffed out my upset's region, like an emotional sommelier who wanted to add some depth to it.

'Have you got an admirer?' she asked at breakfast, eyeing my gift of Sunday chocolates. Tornegus had brought them for me, but even they had failed to lift my mood.

'Nice for you to have someone to take to a party – or a wedding?'

I don't know how she knew – maybe Aunt Coral had said something – but I am constantly staggered at the extremes of Loudolle's cruelty. My Mum is dead, it is no joke. I wonder how she would feel if, one night, after sitting up writing letters to herself, Delia committed suicide, and under a year later Ralph and some awful woman got married before Delia's shoes had gone cold. But, as much as I hate her, I hope that she never has to know that pain, which is something I would not wish even on the devil himself.

'It's an admirer more than you've got,' I said in reply. 'You can't even pull the Admiral. And it's downhill from here on as far as your looks go, Loudolle. Then what will you have left?'

'I think you should show me some more respect or I'm going to tell Icarus about you and his eye.'

I should've said 'Tell him, then, I don't care', but the thought of working beside Icarus, with him *knowing I bedded his eye*, was just over-whelming. Though what on earth does it matter in the light of finding Mum's note? I must have terrible pride for his dumb eye to affect me that much.

*

By eleven o'clock the gentlemen were forced indoors by the rain. The sky, which had been bulging with hot air, finally burst, and the roof, the gutters and the buddleia did not do well in the deluge. The rain was so heavy it sounded like waves crashing against a piano. I imagined when it finally stopped and the sun came out, it would be accompanied by a Caribbean steel band.

Prior to putting out buckets in which to catch all the water, Aunt Coral had arranged for Loudolle to do our hair in the drawing room before the finale banquet. It wasn't possible to say no, because Aunt Coral wanted to wave an olive branch at Delia for being rude to her daughter. And once it became a decision, she got carried away and set up the drawing room as a salon, with nail wear and lady materials. She placed the hot seat in front of the window, so that the reluctant customer could view the downpour whilst having their hair done. Before my turn, I tried to ease my countless tensions by replying to my father's invitation.

> Dear Mr Bowl,
>
> Your affair with Ivana Schwartz was the cause of the turmoil and distress which killed my mother and it will not surprise you to hear that I will not be attending your wedding.
>
> You drove her to despair, you dance on her grave, and you are an offence to her memory.
>
> S.

He no longer deserves anything from me: compassion, empathy, not even the three letters of my name. How can he marry so soon after losing her? Let alone marry the biggest moron in the whole of Scandinavia? It is an abomination. I hope that my absence at the wedding will speak much louder than words.

'Sue,' said Aunt Coral, leaving the hot seat. 'Your turn.'

Aunt Coral and Delia were now both pouffed to the nines, with

Aunt Coral's hair a vengeful purple. I went into Loudolle's chair like she was my executioner, and she went to work on me in a frenzy, while behind us the ladies applied creams.

'Mmm, your hair is gorgeous,' she said, but I could tell what she was thinking. *Mmm, nice hair. Let me glue it and maul it for you and make you look twice your age and five times as depressed.*

And my thoughts replied: *Thank you, whore of deceit, but I'd have been happier without a birds nest.*

She drew blood from my scalp with a deep scrape of her comb. 'Sorry,' she said, before whispering, 'I'll need to buy a new one . . .'

Then she backcombed my hair savagely, and wedged it out at the sides like giant wings. I did not dare to try and flatten it, I was too afraid of the consequences.

The total ransom from Loudolle's various demands now wratches up to a £50 tariff, and as I was sitting there I realised a new problem: I don't care so much if Icarus knows about the eye, I've had months to come to terms with it, but I *do* care if he knows I've been *paying* for him not to know. But at least Loudolle is going back in a week, so I will be able to catch up fiscally after she returns to Alpen to learn how to arrange cakes, or whatever she does when she is there. But oh, how dishonest is nature to package such a rotten fruit in such a pretty casing! It is one of the most deceitful habits of all creation.

Icarus was such a dream, and they can be difficult to let go of, every bit as difficult as trying to let go of my Mum. But that is what I need to do – let them go. Mum to her Heavenly home and Icarus to his Earthly one. But I know now that it doesn't happen in a nanasecond, but little by little over time, with no short cuts, and this is a natural consequence of being alive – unless you are a recluse and live your life without the consequences of knowing anybody.

I wonder if I fell so badly for Icarus because I was starving for love. If I hadn't been so starving, I probably wouldn't have even looked at him. It was the starvation that needed attention. I needed to find other food.

But in the meantime I still felt an urgency to prevent him from knowing how starving I'd been, so I found myself in the dreadful position of having to ask Aunt Coral for a loan. We sat woman-to-woman in the drawing room, she in lavender hell and me with my bleeding stumps, and it all came out. I had no choice but to confide in her, it was the only way to survive.

'She's a nasty piece of work,' said Aunt Coral, before salvaging. 'But never mind, I think it is an enviably romantic thing, to yearn over the young man's eye, and nothing to be ashamed of. It means that you are capable of deep love and passion, and that is a gift and a wonder. I'll ask the Admiral if he can lend me £50 and then you can pay me back once you've saved up. But I'd tell Icarus about it soon, and then she won't have anything over you. And there'll be plenty of other Icaruses. They just don't know you're on the loose yet.'

She made it sound like there were hundreds of others just waiting to be informed I was free, and that when they were, all hell would break loose and I would be inundated with appointments.

'That's impossible,' I said.

'Nothing's impossible,' said Aunt C. 'They gave medals to pigeons for bravery in the war you know.'

'You're joking.'

'No I'm not – the Dickin Medal goes to animals that have been brave, and during the last war it went to pigeons who had been spies. I always remember that when I think that something's impossible,' she said. Having come through the war, Aunt Coral's got different perspectives.

Then she added, before leaving in search of Mrs Bunion: 'If you think too much about Icarus you will miss the rest of life going on round you. Try and think about something else, and I promise it will get easier.'

She was like a gentle tide that stroked my eroded shore. That is one of the joys of talking with someone who has lived for a long time – you know that they will have done much more embarrassing things than you, and got over them, and lived long enough not to be embarrassed about them any more.

*

Loudolle's plan to execute my hair worked well, for at the Banquet Tornegus looked unsettled and kept staring at it, trying to see past my wings. He wasn't the dream like Icarus, but I knew I must try and be kind.

'Thank you for the chocolates,' I said, with a wink to keep him guessing.

Nigel from the *Herald* read us his review with our starters, which is to be four stars in this week's issue! The excitement levels were high. Delia said she was going to explore the concept of a fashion show, with Georgette, Print and Taffeta to model. And Aunt Coral was considering therapy EHGs, for there was money to be made in despair, and the Admirals were in talks over romance, which they hope to take into consultancy.

So, contrary to preconceptions, it looked as though quite a lot could be achieved by two old ladies, three Admirals, one cleaner, one waitress-cum-author and an Egham mansion with sixteen bedrooms and rotten timbers. The fact that we made a loss on the fiscal side was small beans compared to the possibilities.

Unfortunately the day did not end at that high point.

'Did you take the fifty pounds from my bag?' said Aunt Coral a while later, over the coffee and petty fours.

'No!' I said. 'Of course not! I wouldn't. I didn't. Of course not!'

'Well, it's gone,' she said. She left it hanging there and it was urgent to convince her, so we went into the conservatory to discuss the matter further.

'Please believe me, I would never go into your handbag, I know that your handbag's your cave.'

'Yes, of course – of course you wouldn't. I'm going to call a meeting.'

The Green Place residents were quickly gathered in the conservatory and Aunt Coral did not beat around the bush before stating her business.

'We have a magpie in our midst,' she said. 'I am missing fifty pounds from my wallet.'

An invisible camera rolled around the room, zooming in on the three Admirals, Delia, Mrs Bunion, myself, and Loudolle. Nobody spoke for several seconds, and then the menace began.

'I saw Sue go into your bag, Aunt Coral,' said Loudolle.

'It's not true!' I said. 'She's lying, she's always lying.'

'Please leave us,' said Aunt Coral, and the others left the room, exploding with opinions.

'I got you that money from the Admiral, Sue, I was going to give it to you, you had no need to take it. Tell me the truth, and I won't judge you.'

'But I didn't take it, Aunt Coral; you've got to believe me.'

'I'll be in my room. I need to think.'

She tottered out with her head at an angle, for she was in deep contemplation. I wanted to run after her and wrap myself round her legs to prevent her from going, to prevent her from thinking badly of me, to make her know for sure. Instead I sank into the chair by the window and watched the rain pour like a million angry needles from a black and tarry sky.

This is Loudolle's finest achievement to date, driving a wedgie between me and Aunt Coral.

But what no one has suggested is, what if it was the tramp?

Brackencliffe

After Van Day had departed, and idle dancing was done for the day, Pretafer learnt of the maidens' escape, and ceased to be in good humour. She was so full of vengeance and spite, that she fell ill with the fever, and she lay bedriddled with a pox on her skin, and the Spinster fell on her knees in the chapel to pray for the Missie's pitted face.

But just when they thought they had lost her, Pretafer Gibbon rallied. Yet when her cure was achieved, her face was so scarred by blisters that she needs must wear a box on her head to prevent her from a-fearing the children.

Bemeantimes, Cara was fast becoming the most beautiful girl in the land. She had tarried with loyal Fiona and Keeper in the Pasture of Sage and Parsley and they fashioned a humble dwelling in a rickety shepherd's hut under the sky. And here they passed their days at the hearth, in peace, if in a little hunger.

'Whyfore will you not let me look in the locket?' said Fiona. 'Whofore is inside it? 'Tis some handsome cousin, some Master at Arms?'

''Tis my Mother,' said Cara, 'lest I forget her image.'

Coral's Commonplace: Volume 3
Green Place, June 16 1947
(Age 25)

Excerpt from the paper, June 2 1947, *Egham Echo* 'Births Marriages and Deaths':

> The Garden family of Green Place announce the sudden loss of Cameo Garden. Memorial service at St Jude's. 'She that loveth, runneth, flyeth and rejoiceth; she is free and cannot be held in.'

I have not been able to do anything for the past two weeks. My pen is too heavy, and my legs give way if I try to get up. But there are no answers up there on the ceiling, nor any under the sky.

I'd only just got back to Oxford from my visit to see the new baby when I got the call.

'You must come back home again,' Father said. 'It's Cameo.'

'Is she all right?' I said.

And he just said, 'No.'

I left everything upside down and came running, but I was too late. That's what Father meant when he said 'no', but he couldn't say it. He couldn't say those three words. I only just arrived in time to see her dear face once more before she was taken away. She was pale and beautiful and still at the end, and so very cold.

Her death was sudden and without symptoms or warning, and Dr John believes it was caused by an aneurysm in her brain. He believes that it might have been there ever since her eye accident, that it was only a matter of time. I haven't even considered the effects of her accident since she was tiny. It happened when she was five, I thought she was totally healed. But he explained that a clot from a head injury, even if it happened at birth, can sit like a ticking time bomb, and there is no way to detect its presence until it's too late.

Surely this hasn't happened? Surely I'm going to wake up? It seems five seconds since we were kids in the Eastern Tree House. She was only here long enough for a quick kick in the leaves.

We have known Dr John all our lives; it would be an insult to question his diagnosis. Father doesn't want Mother more upset and anyway, nothing will bring Cameo back. But are they sure that someone didn't break in and murder her? That she wasn't poisoned by a lunatic? No one will listen to me, they say my ramblings are pure shock and grief.

How can I not have known that something like this would happen to her? If I'd have had any inkling, I'd have wrapped her up and never let her out of my sight. I feel so foolish for not being, somehow, prepared.

All my life I've interpreted myself around Cameo. Who am I without her? Who shall I be now that I have no reflection? I feel like an elastic catapult shot forever from its base.

Out in the woods I can hear a bell ringing, and my first thought was that it was Cameo trying to ward off the snakes, but then I remembered. Today, it must be a stranger on a bicycle passing somewhere nearby.

Sue

EMERGENCY ARRANGEMENTS HAVE been made in a hurry. The source of the problem according to Glenn Miller's report is dry rot and galloping woodworm. Floors must be lifted and the house injected ASAP to contain the outbreak of building-eating fungus. It's only because Green Place is so big that there are still some parts left unaffected. I have offered to stay and oversee everything while the others abandon ship tomorrow. Aunt Coral goes to her friend Daphne, in Knightsbridge, Delia will visit Loudolle, and the Ad goes to his club. The other admirals are getting lodgings in London.

I'm not afraid of being alone in Green Place. If I see a spirit or a ghost, I will be more than happy, because it will be evidence of life after death, and therefore a hope for Mum. It was a year ago on Wednesday that we lost her. It still doesn't seem real. Dad rang and spoke to Aunt Coral who passed on his message to me. He said he was there if I needed him. She suggested that Dad would be suffering too, and offered to relay a message to him, but I had none in my heart to give.

I didn't want to make a big fuss over it, after all it isn't something to celebrate, just a cross on the calendar that denotes the mad march of time. So I stayed up in my room reading and writing most of the day, and my housemates were very respectful.

I have heard that in the spiritual world, when you are thinking of someone you have lost and you see a white feather, it means that that person is trying to talk to you. There was a white feather on the floor on Wednesday, but perhaps it was because I remade my bed. But perhaps it *was* mum trying to talk to me.

I must go and fetch her key just as soon as Dad and Ivana are out of the way again. She did not want Dad to know about this, and I must honour her wishes.

But there is, of course, also the possibility of a living intruder staying secretly on the premises, but I have maintained that I am up to the challenge, which just shows you how much I do not want to go back to Titford.

Chivalrous as ever, Joe has offered to come and stay with me should the need arise, which is kind, as he has a warm bedroom to go to and Green Place is nothing but a home for spiders. I said no thank you, but it has made Aunt Coral much happier to know he is standing by.

Egham Hirsute Group
On Interpretation

Although Aunt C's primary focus is on how to get the money required for all the building works, she still found time to hold one last Group before leaving. There was a forlorn atmosphere, due to finding mum's note, and all the unpleasantnesses that have gone on, with the theft of the fifty pounds and the ceilings coming down, and the tenants' imminent departures. And the feeling was matched by the small acts of summer's slow death outside, one apple after another, and the last few handfuls of rose petals now turning brown on the damp ground.

'How do you interpret your surroundings? How do you interpret events?' said Aunt Coral, sipping the first of several Sapphires that went down her neck that evening. 'A tree falling across the road may be interpreted by one person as a bad omen and by another as a good excuse not to have to go to work that day. Being ditched at the altar may be interpreted as total heartbreak, or the best way of going on a diet. Can anyone else think of any examples?'

We all put our hands up.

'Sue?' she said.

'The dry rot, or rather, the travelling fungus in Green Place may be seen as a disaster, or an alarm call that saves the building.'

'Excellent Sue, and I hope so,' said Aunt Coral. 'And Avery?'

'The travelling fungus in Green Place may be seen as a disaster, or as an opportunity to go and stay at my club.'

'Excellent Avery, positive spin on the same point. Joe?'

'The travelling fungus at Green Place may be interpreted as a disaster or as a chance for Sue to be courageous.'

'Excellent Joe, well done, but not all the examples need be to do with the travelling fungus. Delia?'

'The travelling fungus at Green Place may be seen as a disaster or a reason to go to America.'

'Yes excellent Delia, same point differently interpreted. Goodness, aren't we all obsessed with the travelling fungus. Loudolle?'

'The travelling fungus at Green Place may be seen as a disaster or as a chance to learn about travelling funguses.'

'Thank you Loudolle,' said Aunt Coral, in a manner of friendly contempt.

I should point out that Loudolle has continued to attend enough Groups to be considered eligible to enter the short story competition. This came about when Delia told her that the prize money was £250. Admirals G and T have now joined up too, having become hooked in over this weekend.

'And now I have another exercise for you. Imagine, if you will, a scenario such as the one we had at the close of the chivalry weekend, when fifty pounds went missing from my handbag and we had a witness accusing Sue. Now, it reminded me of the time when we had a witness saying it was Sue who had stolen the sausages. And so, bringing the great Agatha Christie into our thoughts on interpretation this evening, let's ask how might we, taking this scenario as our crime, interpret things differently? All the evidence in both instances seems to point to Sue. There has even been a witness to the fact . . . I throw it open.'

We all put our hands up; you could have cut the evening in half.

'Sue,' said Aunt Coral.

'Just because someone says they saw something doesn't actually mean that they did. Maybe they said they did. Or maybe they *thought* they did.' (I added the last bit to save Delia's feelings.)

'Excellent Sue, well said, and Avery?'

'There may have been a perfectly innocent explanation whereby the witness saw what she thought she saw, but interpreted it wrongly,' said the Admiral defending the mermaid-witch.

'That's another viewpoint Avery, well done. And Joe?'

'It could be that the witness was a liar and didn't like the person she was accusing,' said Joe.

'Excellent Joe, really excellent, yes, it could well be. And Delia?'

'Or it could be that the witness was telling the truth, and was brave enough to say so, and was only acting in the best interests of everybody, even the thief.' She did have the wool over her eyes.

'Thank you Delia, and Loudolle?'

'Maybe the witness saw what she said she saw but nobody believed her.'

'Maybe,' said Aunt Coral. 'But we can see how many different possibilities there are within a single scenario. Now, all this is leading to something important. I, Coral Elizabeth Garden should like to bear my own witness, to tell you that Sue did *not* take the money from my handbag, and I'll tell you why. When the sausages went missing from the table, I thought it was most out of character for Sue to have dropped them in the pool and not to have apologised, or gone to fetch more sausages. I therefore suspected at once that there must have been foul play. I still didn't know who did take the sausages, but I knew it wasn't Sue.'

We were gripped.

'Ever since then, I have been on my guard against similar incidents.

So when Sue asked me if she could borrow a large sum of money, and I had put the cash in my handbag, I took the precaution of marking the notes by drawing a small red circle on each one, and then, when Loudolle accused Sue of going into my bag and taking the money, I followed my instinct which had been aroused by the sausages and I went straight into Loudolle's room and searched for the money. And there I found it, hidden in her sponge bag.'

She threw the wad of marked bank notes down on to the table, triumphant, and Loudolle opened her mouth in an unedited cry: 'So it was you who took my money!'

'Is that a confession?' said Aunt Coral, and fear made Loudolle shut her mouth.

'And furthermore, ladies and gentlemen, I know that the foul play went even deeper than that, because Sue had earlier told me that the reason she needed the loan in the first place was because Loudolle had been blackmailing her, and that the various ransom demands now amounted to the £50 sum. The ransom was to be paid in order to buy Loudolle's silence over a romantic secret, and Sue had no choice but to ask me to lend her the money, because she didn't want her secret exposed.'

Please don't tell them about the eye. Please don't tell them about the eye, I was thinking in every part of my being.

'And therefore . . . if Lucinda Shoot had succeeded in stealing the ransom money from my wallet before I could give it to Sue, thereby preventing Sue from paying it to her, and then making Sue pay the ransom again, then Lucinda Shoot would be going back to college with a hundred pounds and not fifty, leaving Sue bankrupt and taking all the blame.'

There was silence.

'But Lucinda Shoot made *another* major error,' went on Aunt Coral. 'She did not understand that nothing on earth would induce me to allow her to commit such an offence against a cherished member of my family.'

Well, all hell broke loose. Delia scraped her chair back, and the Admiral scraped back his, and Loudolle ran out crying. Joe was in shock and I was gobsmacked, and eventually Admiral Gordon and Admiral Ted managed to calm it all down.

I am overwhelmed with blessings to have an Aunt such as my Aunt Coral. For loyalty and ingenius she has no rival. I know I shall really miss her while she is at Daphne's. I am determined to save Green Place from falling down. I would hold it up myself if I could.

This is my bedtime reading, which I do not wish to show Aunt Coral, but which seems particularly apt:

serpula lacrymans (dry rot)
Although it is termed 'dry', it requires a level of moisture, and often outbreaks begin due to an escape of water. Traditional hot beds for outbreaks of *serpula lacrymans* were sea ships, and costs of repairs usually exceeded primary building fees.

The insidious, rapidly spreading decay produces a foul odour, closely akin to damp. Unlike wet rots, soft rots or honey funguses, it has the ability to 'jump' over materials other than wood, which is why when treating *serpula lacrymans,* plaster, coverings and floors must be stripped back two to three feet in all directions from the outbreak in order to ensure containment.

Metaphorically used to describe unseen corruption in society, or hidden individual difficulties, leading to catastrophe.

Coral's Commonplace: Volume 4
Green Place, July 4 1954
(32)

Eat, drink and be merry! Final restrictions lifted! At long last, after fourteen years of food rationing, Mother can burn her ration book. We shall celebrate with bacon, potatoes, bananas and the words 'as much as you like'.

My new job is at The Hospital of Tropical Diseases, researching bites and venoms. Which is sadly ironic because Mother is battling with malaria, or river fever as she calls it, that she contracted in the Bush. She may prefer the red desert to the green borders, the camp fire to the cooker, but such joys of the open air come at quite a high price, and they had to get the fastest ship home.

Little Buddleia has now been packed off to boarding school in the Pennines, Australian accent and all – I wonder what the nuns will make of her! Of course she didn't want to go but Father says it never did him any harm. And mother is quite unable to move, let alone look after a child.

Poor Buddleia has to endure ice baths and corporal punishment, and complains of a complete lack of toast, though she can smell it coming from the nuns' kitchens. I felt bad for leaving her in school on her last exeat, but a greater force swept me away in the form of the Botanist . . . more on which later. She sent me a mournful letter, saying she was sorry that no one wanted to share in her leisure time.

On our last visit to Green Place Father went out shooting rabbits and wanted to take Buddleia with him.

'I will shoot with a camera but never with a gun,' she said solemnly.

And each time she heard him fire she hung her head and prayed. She loves animals, just like Cameo.

'They have no voice,' she says.

It's awful being seven, particularly if you've an old head on your shoulders. She even claims to have joined the school Freedom Party. She and select classmates have requested my help in writing up a leaflet. 'A way to change the world' is the title. It'll be a better place for rabbits.

Green Place news:

The country's economy and buildings have both been devastated by the war, and some ministers are suggesting that caravans are the solution to our housing crisis. And there I was actually thinking of moving out of Green Place permanently to be with the Botanist. But I don't feel I can leave Father on his own, what with Mother in the hospital and the papers saying that one large mansion is demolished every five minutes. A demolished house can't be valued for probate you see, which is why so many have gone.

Father is applying to make us a listed building to preserve us and keep our land. It would be easy if we were Strawberry Hill Gothic or something very definitive, rather than just a lowly, latter-day Queen Anne. He states in his application that the gardens were planted by Gertrude Jekyll, with the supports to the balconies to the front of the building being of a pioneering construction (which is probably why they have rusted through and collapsed). I suggested he add that Green Place was once visited by the Double Duchess of Devonshire, Louisa Frederica Cavendish. The town and country planners go crazy for anyone famous, and might give us a grade 1. (Building of exceptional interest.)

The Botanist:

Edgar Van Campen. 5 feet 6 of perfection, and a genius in the lab. He was saying in the refectory how much he loves quirks on a woman, such as widows peaks, overlapping teeth and cowlicks. I don't quite have all of them, so I better watch him around Doris Trent.

$\mathcal{S}ue$

THE DAYS OF Green Place guardianship are long. I get up and make the first teas before 7am – Glenn Miller and his men need so much tea all the time and one of the plumbers requires a biscuit every eleven minutes. Then I put in a full day at the Toastie before returning to make final beverages and then go to my camp in the attic where I write by the light of my candles. Glenn has been considerate and tries to leave me with electricity at the weekends. He loves a chat and tells me lots of stories about the house. He seems to know a lot about my mother, but then he knew her as a young tradesman.

'I found her once in the potting shed,' he said. 'She was about eight or nine at the time. Mr Garden had banned her from reading *Black Beauty*, so she'd snuck in to read in secret.'

'Why did he ban *Black Beauty*? It's not rude is it?'

'No, it's not rude at all,' said Glenn. 'I think it was banned because it was sad.'

Glenn must have been a nice, reassuring presence around the place for my mum. Over the years Aunt C remembers him hanging out of windows, (paint brush in hand), never quite making an impact on the enormity of the building.

During the weeks the house is busy with the boiler-suited cavalry, and when I am alone on a Sunday, there are always the gardens to hike in and the trespasser traps to check for ramblers. It's difficult to dress for the weather though. I walk out with my jumper and coat on, and then I have to take my jumper off, and have just my coat, then I have to take that off too, then I end up with both of them round my waist, then I have to put my jumper back on again, then my coat back on too. And so on it goes in the Autumn–Winter crossing.

My favourite spot is up by the Croquet Hut on the sun lawn. It's a wooden lodge, almost swallowed up by the blackberries, with a staggering view over Egham. If ever, God forbid, Green Place does fall down, I'm going to ask Aunt Coral if I can live here.

She has written to me from Knightsbridge, from a flat with bars on the windows and only a courtyard garden. She has to share her bedroom with Daphne's cat and she is very agitated about her clothes. Not surprising when she packed near to two hundred dresses, in the hopes of being invited to all the functions of Belgravia Square.

In order that I should still have a part of her with me, as if being in Green Place isn't enough, Aunt C has left me her Commonplace Book for my bedtime reading. Five volumes of thoughts and cuttings about her life. I'm finding it riveting. But it's funny to think of Aunt Coral having a past. That's one of the problems of ageing, it can look to the people outside you that you were born the age you are now.

Dad left a phone message to say that he is always around if I want to talk, and asked me to reconsider not coming to the wedding. I'm glad I did not pick up the call, but I wish I knew if they have any plans to go away. I constantly dream of collecting the key and finding mum's secret treasure.

I have now been here on my own for just over two weeks and I have finally become used to all of the nocturnal noises, for which I have built up a placenta of explanations . . . pipes, creaks, drips, damp, bats, badgers, perhaps the slipping of a workman's tool.

Sometimes from my bed at night, I travel Green Place in my mind, passing around the building, stopping to snap some pictures. Delia's bathroom with the tortoise tank, the Admirals' towels as they left them, Aunt Coral's pink bed with one swaying tassel, the conservatory hung with doilies of frost and laced with tingling spiders.

When the power is on the lights flicker, especially when it is stormy, struggling to keep their connections. At these moments I feel certain that the ghosts of Victorian school children are running into wardrobes the minute I turn my back, and I have to reassure myself.

Coral's Commonplace: Volume 4

Cutting from the *Egham Echo,* November 18 1955, 'Births Marriages and Deaths':

> Evelyn William Garden of Green Place, Clockhouse Lane, regrets to announce the passing of his beloved wife Pearl Ellen Garden 1900–1955, after a long battle with malaria. She is survived by her remaining daughters Coral Elizabeth and Buddleia Rose.

It was not a shock, and in a way it was a relief. She rallied for a time after coming home, but the fevers kept on coming back. It's so rare here, perhaps she wasn't given quite effective enough treatment. But they tried, we know they really did try.

And as having to die goes, I could not have hoped for better for Mother. She did suffer a bit, and I wish that she hadn't, but there was time to say goodbye and to prepare ourselves. We had some nice trips to the coast and there were hours to reminisce and to fit in all she wanted. She was a chipper soul, and a great valuer of life's little things. In winter she liked to leave one of her feet out of the covers in bed, just for the sheer pleasure of tucking it back in again.

Towards the end, when she became very ill, she decided she wanted to return to Green Place to die. Not in her bed, as everyone had expected, but out under the stars, and she asked to be carried to the Croquet Hut with a view out over the world.

She was my echo, sometimes loud, sometimes soft, but always gently around me, calling me to the sun.

Sue

Wednesday 21 October

IT WAS ABOUT ten to nine when it happened. I had just finished dinner in the conservatory, which I had eaten with a blaze of small candles, when I heard the sound of footsteps upstairs. It didn't concern me at first because I had trained myself to think logically. Maybe Glenn had forgotten something – maybe it was a badger – but as I listed the options the footsteps came downstairs, and this time it was more worrying, as there was no way they weren't human. I ran outside, where I hid behind a mound of clippings, expecting to see the ghost of Cameo. But it wasn't a lady in a filmy gown or a ghost or a ghoul or a spirit, but a *man* I saw coming out. A man with a full beard, long hair, and a long coat. He walked briskly down the drive and towards Clockhouse Lane where he was swallowed up by the shadows.

I waited for some moments, and when I was certain he wasn't coming back, I went straight and rang the police, hovering all the while between calm and terror.

'It sounds like a tramp, Miss Bowl,' said PC Pacey, arriving within twenty-two minutes of my call. 'And he went out the front door you say?'

'The front,' I said.

'Brass neck! What I advise you to do is keep a close watch on security. If he went out the front door, he may come back in that way. He might even have got a key.'

Then he filled out some forms, before leaving me with a radio and heading out into the night.

Thinking about it as a logical adult, I told myself that this tramp, whoever he is, has been taking great care to be avoided, so he obviously isn't an axe murderer, as he'd have already pounced by now. He is probably a very nice person who just needs somewhere to live, and he probably wandered in one day, and saw that the place was empty. He is probably very spontaneous, as I imagine most tramps would be. In fact if he is hungry and poor I should share my wealth. Maybe I should leave him a picnic in the hall and show him I am a friend?

The power of this theory reassured me to the point where I felt calm enough to get into bed, where I tried very hard to distract myself with the correspondence of the day. It isn't until you are in a situation like that, that you realise that courage is a decision.

The first was a letter from my dad:

Dear Sue

I was devastated to get your letter. I'm so sorry that you feel that way. Whilst I do understand how angry you feel, and that the wedding may seem sudden, I want you to know that your mother and I had grown apart long before I met Ivana. And your mother, God rest her, did not know. I know you will find it hard, but I feel that it's time for the truth.

I hope that you will reconsider coming, it would mean the world to me. There is nothing but love for you in Titford, and the truth, if you want it.

Don't be a stranger.

Dad x

After I finished I tore it up, and went to leave a ploughman's in the hall for a tramp, with a notelet saying simply 'peace'. It was the action of my inner Caroline, and made me feel serene. (NB Aunt Coral has a strong temperament which if I had to name it would be a 'Caroline' – someone very cheerful, who advises the picking of flowers. Following this theory on, I think the Admirals would be Brians, who are calm and advise reading books, and Delia would be an Ogera, being prone to the melancholic.)

I have now returned to the attic to lose myself in 'Brackencliffe' and escape any thoughts of doom. But as I write, a dark patch of thunder is building up behind the trees down Clockhouse Lane. The leaves look like they are about to fall from the trees more from fright than because of the season.

All my life I've wanted to write about how it feels to be alive, and I hope it will be reflected within the walls of 'Brackencliffe'. I intend to fully subjugate myself to it while I am here in splendid and squalid isolation.

Friday 20 November

The weeks have flown past and Dad's nuptials are hanging over the horizon. But on a positive note, the opportunity I have been waiting for has finally arrived.

Aunt Coral rang this morning to tell me that she'd spoken to Dad, and found out that he and Ivana are going to be away for the weekend. Something to do with some hideous joint stag and hen night, which they are having in a hotel.

Loudolle has been at home for a college break. Mercifully she isn't staying at Green Place, not being one for the icy conditions. She is staying with the Frys, on a futon with mirrored wardrobes and pot pourri. Mrs Fry is always talking about her 'luminous elsewhere quality', but what use is that in the café or helping around the house? She tails me like an odour, following me at my chores, her eyes craven and watchful and full of her plans.

Early this morning I was in the Gents hanging up some hand washing signs for Mrs Fry. She is keen to take part in the government's hand washing scheme, encouraging people to wash their hands, especially the gentlemen, who, she said, were ten times more likely to have poo particles on their hands than the ladies!

I was thinking about how to get myself to Titford, what with my work and Green Place duties, so I had much bigger things to think about when Loudolle came into the loo. She put some air freshener into the cubicles, and then looked me over slowly, before her eyes finally alighted on the top of my head. This made me fall into a self-conscious coma about my hairband, which earlier I had thought so jazzy, but which was such a decision for work.

'How are you Sue?' she said, addressing my hairband sympathetic-ally. 'Getting ready for the gala? I really think you could win.'

For a brief moment I was flattered, but I knew she was just being creepy, because she risked the wrath of Aunt Coral if she tried any business again. She went for a piddle in a cubey, I could hear her fierce tinkling, and then she left the room without washing her hands, ignor-ing the expensive new signs.

'Clever you,' she said in farewell to my hairband.

I breathed a sigh of relief when she was gone. She doesn't have any power over me any more.

It was some time before I returned to the café, minus my hairband. It was crowded with heavy German teenagers; the air was thick with hormones. They had teamed with a Group from Oxford, who were wearing long jumpers and looking intelligent, debating about the menu and asking for things chargrilled.

But life is full of terrible things: spots, heartbreak, Loudolle. Aunt Coral always says that age and experience will catch up with me, and I'll laugh about it all one day, but I am currently having difficulties turning it all into the fond remembrance of tomorrow.

'OK Sue?' said Joe as I walked back in.

'Yes, I've just taken off my hairband,' I said, 'and it's left a bit of a shelf.'

'No, I mean you look worried,' he said, 'anything I can do?'

'My Dad and Ivana are away for the weekend and I need to go to Titford. There's something I want to collect,' I said, knowing that I was fishing.

'I can take you tomorrow evening if you like. We'll be very quick on the bike.'

It was with a grateful feeling of uneasy dread that I left Joe on the frother – yet back home all was quiet. There were nothing but the trees standing in the sky wondering what all the fuss was about. I stood for a moment on the terrace watching a spider climbing a strand of human hair. When it got to the top it threw itself off and began ascending again, just for the joy of being a spider. Inside the house was peaceful and the ploughman's remained untouched. And Glenn had left the hot water on, which meant I had no excuses.

After my bath I went to place flowers in the Grey Room, which I picked by torch light from the lean pickings outside. (It says in Aunt Coral's Commonplace that it used to be Mum's room when she was a little girl home on the holidays, which makes it even more special.) It was a long time since I'd been in there and it wasn't as I remembered. Rooms suffer from absences and are better with light and footsteps. I placed the flowers on the window ledge looking out at the dusky pool, remembering the waves rippling over the tiles when the water was warm in the summer.

The bed was slightly pulled away from the wall, and a long black coat lay across it. Glenn Miller's perhaps. Or a tradesman's?

'It belongs to Glenn, it belongs to Glenn,' I repeated to myself as I went back to my room.

Later on, when I was on bat patrol, I saw a light shining under the locked room door. I thought at first Glenn must have left it on by mistake, but I know that can't be possible, because there is only one key to the room, which is held by Aunt Coral in private.

Could it be the tramp who put the light on in the locked room? And if so, then how did *he* get the key? Or is it really a tramp at all? Could it be a spirit?

It is now 3am and I've just dreamt that it wasn't a man I saw leaving Green Place, but a woman. But dreams can be misleading and are often badly miscast.

Saturday 21 November

I had a surprise visit from the Nanas today, who arrived just as I was finishing my breakfast. I hadn't seen them for ages, because there'd been an outbreak of flu in the home. They walked up the drive having had their taxi drop them at the bottom. Print was wrapped in a rug and Taffeta was wearing home-made pop socks. Obviously there comes a point where being cosy replaces any desire to look nice. They'd been cooped up for ages, so I toasted some crumpets which I served by the pool under blankets.

'Where are your friends?' Taffeta asked me somewhat obleakly.

'They only come out in the evenings,' I said.

'Mine only come out in the afternoons,' she said, completely missing my joke.

'We came as soon as we could,' said Georgette. It seemed they had come on a mission.

'You see we were catching up with the papers,' said Print, 'and we would not have put two and two together had I not had a visit from an old friend. She was in the area for a bowels match and she spotted your advertisement.'

'I'm sorry, I don't follow,' I said, confused by the Nanas' ramblings.

'Her name is Emily Laine,' said Print, 'and Emily is Jack Laine's widow.'

It wasn't long before they were back on their favourite subject, (the

Duke of Edinburgh), but all I could think of was Emily Laine amidst the talk of the Duke's plus fours. They stayed for an hour or so before returning to the home, and their taxi had barely pulled away before I telephoned Aunt Coral.

'Are you going to contact Emily Laine?' I asked her, once I'd filled her in.

'I don't see how I can,' said Aunt Coral. 'What if she doesn't know about it?'

'Maybe you could get Print to try and find out if she knew?'

'No, Print knows nothing about Jack and Cameo and I'd have to tell her, and she'd feel awful for Emily. No, dear me, I'll have to think about it.'

I also told her about the man I'd seen, and the coat.

'Are you sure it was a man? Are you sure it wasn't a ghoul?' she asked.

I found this quite unsettling – that she would rather believe in a ghoul than a man! Seems to me she'll believe whatever is most reassuring. She's a Caroline through and through.

I am sitting up in the Grey Room again, trying to commune with mum and prepare myself for later, when Joe is taking me to Titford.

In the early evening Joe came for me on his bike, as promised. It was the first time I'd ridden pillion, and a moment I was not unaware of.

It took us only 45 minutes to get there – it takes an hour and a half on the train. But it feels a lifetime away from Green Place and the Egham borders.

Once inside, I slipped straight upstairs to retrieve the key as per the instructions on Mum's note.

'I wish my Dad had left me something like this,' said Joe, of his own distant grief.

'I'm so sorry, sometimes I forget that you've lost your Dad.'

'It's all right, I'm over it now, I've grown up,' he said, trying to be jolly and manly. 'So it's a key to a locker your mum has left you in secret? Goodness me.'

'It's under a floorboard that only she and I know about,' I said.

'Wow,' he said, closely following me upstairs.

Dad and Ivana's bedroom smelled like the foyer in a department store, and there was flat champagne in the tooth mug.

I lifted the board up gently, looking down into the hole underneath it as though I were looking down a precipice from which I was about to fall off.

'Joe,' I said.

'What is it?'

'There's no key.'

Coral's Commonplace: Volume 4
Green Place, Dec 2 1962
(Age 40)

I'm off the botanist again; much more off than on lately in fact. Daphne is convinced it's because he finally proposed, and that if he hadn't, I would be much keener. The minute I've got him, I don't want him and the minute I haven't, I do.

For all these years, when it comes to romance, I had thought that I was quite traditional. But it turns out that I just can't breathe when I feel tied. And Edgar is so very similar to me; like a cosmic reflection. But am I spoiled? Am I ill? Am I greedy, to wonder if the grass may yet be greener? Am I to stay a child, when all my friends have grown up?

As I look out of the window, I can see clouds of smoke from a bonfire. The window pane is misted up, apart from one central patch that's been blown clear by the new morning. And on the other side of the window, we are totally enmeshed in webbing. Maybe it's the spiders that have held this dear house up so long. Each frail fingerprint sparkles like fibreglass. It's as though they have cast their nets in the air and captured the entire house.

There's an island off the coast of Madeira they call Spider Island, which apparently is inhabited ONLY by spiders as big as the average boy's hand. I'd love to go and see them, but who would dare to come with me? Edgar would've enjoyed it, but there's no point in thinking about that . . . Still, at least we only had plans for bonfire night this time and not for the rest of our lives.

He wrote me a pompous letter about his various reasons for ending it, it was written with a third eye over it, in case his biographer ever gets hold of it. He's moving to Hampshire with a woman with a pronounced widow's peak. But if I am forlorn I remind myself that I could never see myself doing his dishes, or feeding his ravening guests, or walking from his bathroom to his bedroom dressed in his flannel pyjamas. I could never live in a flat, and I don't ever want to leave Father. It's not hard to imagine why Edgar decided to call it a day!

My friends it seems are happier with my being alone. Daphne prefers me to retain what she calls my 'mad Aunt' status, because it makes the toil of motherhood seem so stable and reassuring. 'Aunt'; the word conjures to me a tweedy, lonely figure or, God forbid, a type of Miss Havisham. No, if Buddleia ever makes me an Aunt I will not take after Miss H. I am not going to pine over Edgar. Broken hearts do mend, and anyway, one daughter lost too young is quite enough for Father. It struck me last night as I lay in bed, in profound talks with the ceiling, that Cameo lived life so quickly. Maybe she had a notion she had better grow up double fast. Our lives seem like waves, some that will go the distance of all the oceans, and some that will lap gently two or three times before heading straight for the shore.

Talking of which, I am trying to persuade Father, who is now sixty-four, to come away with me for a day or two's break to the seaside, just to get him out of the house, as he is in such bad shape at the moment. But he said he can't in December, because he has an 'appointment'. 'December's a write-off,' he says. He's a curmudgeon, a hermit, and extremely bad tempered. And I wonder if I live to be old, will I start to shuffle too?

Oh, and Buddleia's won a novelty prize at school. I wonder what it was for!

To Do List
Make Will
Syringe ear

Sue

HAMPSHIRE-BORN WRITER, LIKES CUISINE AND
GROUPS, SEEKS SPARKLING EYES AND TRANSPORT.
CONTACT S. BOWL, EGHAM 69950

IT HAS STRUCK me that finding a rambler in a trespasser trap holds huge
potential for falling in love, so I have put a little notice in each, in case
someone lovely should chance to fall down one. Can you tell I am losing
hope of Icarus? Love is blind; but love is also impatient.

It is the dankest day of the year. All the buckets are out to keep the
rain off the carpets, and I have removed the conservatory furniture, for
the sky is threatening to come in. It is lucky I have had this to distract
me from despair over not finding that key.

We couldn't find it anywhere in the house, so we drove back to
Egham empty-handed. Later I rang Aunt Coral, and she was as confused as me.

'Could your Father have found it?' she asked me.

'I'm sure he didn't know about the floorboard. And Ivana wouldn't
be bothering with the floor because they have a cleaner,' I said.

234 ⸻ CAMPARI FOR BREAKFAST ⸻

'I'm so sorry Sue. Perhaps you'll just have to ask him if he's got it?'

'But what if he hasn't? Mum said that she didn't want him to know.'

'I know. It's a mystery. I'll need to have a think, try not to worry, I'm sure it will turn up,' she said, trying her best to rescue.

She also told me by way of distraction that she has formed a salon in Knightsbridge that is sitting *every* evening. It's clear that she and her entourage are getting very serious about Group. And as the gala is galloping up, Aunt Coral has called an EHG for next Friday, to be held at the flat in London, with all the hirsutists travelling from the four corners of the earth. (Well, Egham, London and Alpen.)

Friday 18 December

Egham Hirsute Group in the Capital

Joe and I took the train together and he kept both our tickets in his wallet like a true gent. Over the tannoy the guard said: 'Please ensure you have all your personal longings with you when you leave the train.' I wonder if he knew just how accurate he was in his little mistake.

It was a much larger Group than expected, with Daphne and Mrs Stock Ferrell and her Labrador Daniel, and the Admirals G and T with their friend Admiral Ranger, and Admiral Little, Joe and me, plus George Buchanan, a dentist. The Admirals sat according to rank, out of respect for Admiral Ranger. Delia was fresh back from the airport, and rather heavier than usual. As a consequence, she'd glued a picture on her pad of a thin woman smiling at some berries. There was a fire going in the hearth, and we each had a Knightsbridge cushion.

'Welcome, welcome, *welcome*, to the Metropolis EHG!' said Aunt Coral, and the Admirals raised their pencils like a row of tiny cannons.

'Let's start with a warm-up,' she said, as the Admiral poured her a Sapphire. 'Now, quick fire, who can tell me another word that means the same as style?'

We all put our hands up.

'Sue,' she said.

'Panache.'

'Excellent, yes, and Avery?'

'Flair.'

'Excellent, yes, and George?'

'Chic.'

'Excellent, Admiral Ranger?'

'Fence,' he said.

'Jolly good, yes, it also means a type of fence,' she said, moving quickly to the next exercise in her notepad. 'Now, could I have someone to kick off with a sentence from their story? And if you haven't written a story, don't worry, you'll still be able to follow the exercise.'

We all put our hands up.

'Sue,' said Aunt Coral, and I read aloud from 'Brackencliffe', hoping I hadn't shown how much I had wanted to read.

'"My name is Knight Van Day," he said, "and I come from wither and yonder."'

'Thank you, Sue. And who'd like to have a go at expressing what Knight Van Day says in a different way? Avery?'

'"I am Knight Van Day," said the Admiral, "and I get around."'

'Excellent, Avery, yes. And George?'

'"My name is Knight Van Day and I'm not telling you where I live."'

'Good George, well done – a completely different take on the same edit. Excellent, and Admiral Ranger?'

'"My name is Knight Van Day, that's my house over there."'

'Thank you Admiral Ranger, very good.'

Aunt C definitely has her ways of making the gentlemen feel very special about themselves. George, Admiral Little and Admiral Ranger were what I can only describe as glowing, even if their edits of my line were completely off of the mark. She seemed oblivious to the ladies, other than myself, who had their hands up too. It's like she has a sort of lady blindness, or at least a dominant eye for the gents!

'Now, it seems to me,' she said, moving Group forward, 'that the majority of us are of an age where childhood wasn't yesterday. I only mention this because I want us to think about time. If I might use my own life as an example,' she said, reading aloud from her notepad:

'The air looks different in the past. When I watch back my old reel-to-reels it's as though the air is thicker, mellower, sweeter, the sky is pale and warm. Or is it that I imbue the past with a misty significance? A honey haze that didn't exist at the time? For I'm sure the air was exactly the same then, perhaps, but for less deodorant.'

She paused to allow Group to laugh and appreciate her wit.

'I expect all of us would like to be able to take what has happened in the past and change it to make something different happen. But we can write ourselves a *future*, and we can even try and make it happen. So, I'd like you to write a short piece and mess around with your time frame. You might wish to write about the past, or you might set yourselves in the future, and if you do, what will you be doing, and who will you be?'

The assembled heads tilted in contemplation over the exercise. Before I had even finished writing, Delia stood up to read.

'The girl I was in childhood is unrecognisable to me now; she has become the child of others, existing in other people's memories. And the house that I didn't want to leave, is now just a building in a photograph. Time changes everything, even who we are.'

'Excellent Delia, well done. Goodness me,' said Aunt Coral, clipping open her handbag to take out a hanky. She polished off the dregs of her Sapphire as a car turned round in the road outside, momentarily lighting her hair with an evening lamplight halo.

Some of the Group's spirits had clearly become melancholic, so she swiftly moved to the youth of the group to try and deliver a mood swing.

'And so . . . have we a future, Sue?'

I began in an old voice:

'As I look back over my life, favourite moments come to mind. Sitting in my play pen; school days; hey days; arriving at Green Place; my husband, who for many months didn't even know I was there. Funny to think of it now, following the birth of our dear children: George, Hattie, Henrique, Jason, Claudius, Cordelia, and Annabelle.

Alas, though my mind is still sharp, I'm old and can't walk very far, and so I live more and more for my writing.

Tomorrow I am going on a talk show to tell them about my books, and whenever anyone asks me how it all began, I will give them the same answer: it began for me with Aunt Coral and The Egham Hirsute Group.'

A silence fell on the hirsutists, and some were visibly moved. Aunt Coral, Delia, Daphne and Meriel all had to leave the room. I was terribly flattered to have had such a profound effect on them. And I still feel a bit high now.

Coral's Commonplace: Volume 4
Green Place, April 5 1968
(Age 46 but pass for 37)

Local News:

Braeburn Grange at the bottom of Clockhouse Lane has been bought by aspirational new owners. It formerly belonged to Marigold who was a Cheltenham lady and who was happy to call it Braeburn. But as Places, Lodges, Manors, Halls and Parks are the great hierarchy of housing, the new owners have found the need to upgrade themselves to a Grange.

I still think of the botanist sometimes, pottering around in Hampshire. He has a child now, Frederick Alun. All the things I loved about him still call to me over the miles. I wish he had been a hundred per cent horrid and not fifty per cent nice.

Daphne is coming to dinner later on. At the shops I indulged in some luxury loo roll which triggered an outrage in Father. He doesn't much care for Daphne.

'You should give her British number three,' he said.

British number three was the toilet paper we got in the war, when there wasn't enough money to import large amounts of timber.

'Like sandpaper,' said Father baring his teeth, although I would have said it was like tracing paper.

I have a lady arriving shortly from the Cooks directory, her name is Mrs Bunion. She is coming to cook us a meal. Father says he will not come out of his room until she is gone. But needs must; I did not get the cooking gene. I would live on biscuits if I couldn't have a cook.

Buddleia rang to say she got the job with BOAC (British Overseas Airways Corporation).

'Somebody up there cares!' (That's the BOAC slogan!)

To Do:

1) Get estimate for the Turner. (The drawing room has got so damp that the pink summer sky in the painting – a painting that has survived two world wars – has gone green.) However I don't think I could bear to sell.

2) Get gardener. (The garden is a mine of tunnels.)

3) Get bat boxes to try and coax them into the woods. (We have three different species of bat that I'm aware of: *soprano pipistrelle*, *roof void barbastelle*, and the *greater horseshoe*. Their babies are born in June and can end up in peculiar places, such as my handbag. I have started a policy of bat patrol, to move them on.)

4) Get plumber. (The tank above the great hall leaks and when it rains we have Niagara on the stairs. God but it's beautiful, who wants a boring old staircase?)

5) Syringe ear.

6) Make Will.

7) Insulate letter box.

Sue

TODAY WAS THE shortest day of the year, which means tonight will be the longest night. The sky has been hanging round a weak stump of moon and the stars are too misty to shine. In fact this whole month has had a mist over it, because of Dad's wedding, and they were all out earlier: black cats, magpies, everywhere I looked there were omens.

At dinner time I sat and had an absent-minded sandwich, before I checked the house on bat patrol. I was half oblivious to what I might find, because the burning question of tomorrow is: 'Do you, Ivana Schwartz, take Nicholas Bowl to be your husband?'

In my head, I saw the priest blessing them at the altar. Ivana was in her car shoes. Imagination is the nasty little comic of the mind. And when the sun rises, if it does, they will begin their coupledom just like Mum had never been born.

I completed the bat patrol, and was plumping the cushions in the drawing room, when a blast of cold air surprised me rushing in under the door. Then I heard fast steps, eventually stopping in what I hazarded might be the conservatory. I froze for a time before I summoned up the courage to go into the hall to have a look. But I found no man with a gun or chainsaw there, or a ghost or a ghoul or a spirit, only a bouquet of flowers with a note which read:

> For Miss Susan Olivia Bowl.

It blew my evening away! He couldn't have been from the other world; not if he had been to the florist! It was a shock that was big enough to take my mind off the wedding. So, I decided to leave him some fruit cake as a thank you, with a welcome note beside it.

> *Dear Visitor*
>
> *Thank you very much for the flowers, I hope you have every-thing that you need.*
>
> *With all best wishes from,*
>
> *Sue*

I preferred to use the phrase, 'Dear Visitor,' as it is much more polite than saying, 'Dear Tramp,' and there was no way I wanted to cause offence whilst I'm extending the hand of friendship. Perhaps also somewhere in my unconscious, the word 'Visitor' is also less scary than 'tramp'.

Now I am sitting up in bed in the attic. The wind outside is powering itself into a frenzy of banging and tapping. It makes me think of far-away storms raging in other lands, called sweet things like Hurricane Enid. And it is peculiar, and yet strangely reassuring, knowing that the tramp must be somewhere on site. But I'm certain that the storm, and the tramp, and the wedding, will thieve me of a deep, unknowledgeable sleep.

Tuesday 22 December

This morning my card and the cake were unchanged, so I left them out just in case, picking up the paper and letters from the mat to read on the bus.

Sometimes a day can be salvaged by forcing the mind to other things. It can also be swept along by the madness that is Mrs Fry's Toastie. It struck me that people die at the same time as breakfasts are served and eaten, and shouldn't everything stop or close each time out of respect? But if everything stopped each time somebody died, the economy would fall. Things can't stop, and neither can I.

My morning at the 'Bistro' coincided with Dad and Ivana's nuptials, and a heavy day lay ahead. We were parading a sample menu, for the purpose of market research: soup de la rue, saucisses de la mer and camembert served with a juice.

The Mayor and a local celebrity came, and they had their photos with Mrs Fry, which she clipped to the till for posterity and future bouts of showing off.

La Toastie was hung with tinsel and a presumptuous amount of mistletoe, and Mrs Fry conducted herself completely in French. Her hair had been treated to repeated visits so that its sheen could not be outclassed by any of the other ladies.

'Bien venu a la Toast,' she said, speaking through a crowd pleaser. 'Et aussi, j'espere que vous avez le meme que bon appetite!'

'Are you OK, Sue?' said Joe. He gave me a killer smile, stolen straight from Icarus.

'I'm OK.'

And I was. In fact the build up to the wedding was much worse than the day itself, when I was so busy with Mrs Fry's ambition. Aunt Coral rang through to the Toastie twice to check if I was OK. When the chips are down, you certainly find out who your friends are.

Later on Joe offered to cook me a meal, so we returned to Green Place after a wipe down. It was already dark when we walked up the drive, lit by a sharp half moon and a sprinkling of lights in the windows.

'Do you leave all those on?' said Joe.

'It's the wiring,' I said, 'or it might be the tramp. But there's no need to be alarmed.'

'No need to be alarmed?'

As we entered the hall I showed him my flowers. The card and the cake were also still there.

'See, he must be a goodie,' I said. 'He's even left me some flowers.'

Joe looked a little in flabberghast.

'I know it's surprising isn't it?' I said.

It was a lot for Joe to take in, but finally he managed to speak. 'I think you're jumping to conclusions Sue. You don't know what sort of a man he is; he might be a lunatic.'

He strode over to the staircase with masterful steps I had not noticed before.

'He's been here for weeks. He keeps himself to himself,' I said.

'Well when did you ever hear of a murderer who was gregarious?' he said. 'Do the police know?'

'They know, and I have a police radio for security.'

'Does Aunt Coral know?'

'She knows, but she thinks he might be a ghoul.'

'A *ghoul*?'

We checked upstairs, patrolling and switching off the lights.

'You're so brave,' he said when we eventually got to the kitchen.

'Mum dying makes me more fearless.'

'It also might have made you more foolish,' he said.

We had a campfire dinner of jackets with beans and listened to a play on the radio, in which a Welsh shepherd was in a lot of trouble with some of the sheep on his farm. Then we heard a late night news, and after, the hours disappeared in a conversation. At about four o'clock in the morning, when the subject of my being alone came up again, Joe offered to stay.

'I can't leave you alone here, Aunt Coral would never forgive me,' he said.

I didn't agree straight away but decided to pour us nightcaps from the bar, a cognac for him and I had a Campari, both on ice in their proper glasses. I wanted Joe to carry on telling me I was brave and such things like that.

'So how many ghosts have you got?' he said, taking his shoes off and swishing his drink.

'I've never actually seen anything, but theoretically there's Nana Cameo, the lady, the whisperers . . .'

'The whisperers?' said Joe, in his growing tradition of repeating me.

'When the shower's running upstairs, the pipes sing and it sounds like someone in the kitchen is whispering.'

'When I was ten I saw the ghost of my father a few days after he died,' said Joe. 'I woke up and he was lying next to me.'

'Were you dreaming?'

'I was wide awake, but nobody believed me.'

'I'd be happy to wake up next to my dead mother,' I said.

'I understand that,' he said.

'Sue,' he said, after a long silence broken only by the noise of ice tinkling in our nightcaps, 'I'd feel better if I stayed here. Honestly.'

With perfect timing a singing began, coming from upstairs.

'It's an air lock,' I said.

'How can you be so sure?'

He put his arm round me quite naturally, as though he had done it before. I didn't move it away. I wanted it to be there. I never had Campari for breakfast before; it's the sort of thing people do on desolation holidays. And the drink and the hour and the quiet led to the first real kiss of my life.

It lasted for many exceptional minutes and then it turned to an embrace that fell amongst cushions and we passed a magnificent hour. No one has ever kissed me in the way that Joe did. He kissed me as though it was urgent, as though, if he didn't kiss me for a good long time, he might have to have a cold bath. And, for the time that he was kissing me, all anxiety ceased.

All this time I have waited, wondered what it would be like, *who* would it be, *where* we would be, and *what* I might be wearing . . . A white dress, in the long grass, on a beach, or a hammock by a river? But I haven't been able to see the face of the man kissing me until now. I want to go back and tell the child dreaming in the Titford bedroom, that it will be Joe Fry, in a pinafore, in the drawing room at Green Place.

'I love being with you,' said Joe, when we eventually paused what felt like very much later on.

'The best things in life are worth waiting for.'

The wind outside dropped and as it did the climbers tapped softly on the windows.

'We must make up for lost time,' he said, which led to a temperature tremble in my body.

There were no bells or birds as had been forecast, but the sense of being desirable and treasured and feminine. It was like all the money in the universe flew to my account at the love bank, and I had gone from an account in deficit, to a gold account with cards.

The morning moon was so bright and clear it looked like it had been cut in two with a scalpel. I thought it could make a good book title, *December Moon* by Susan Bowl. It would be about a gypsy.

I was amazed that I still had room for creativity in the presence of love. But these sorts of things are not as linear as I thought, but flatter each other enormously.

The remaining moments of the night sped by carried on shooting stars, showering me in a dawn of ice diamonds, shimmering in the early light. The frost in the air was frostier and the sky a ridiculous blue. Those hours will be forever lodged safe inside my memory, and if I live to be a Nana, they will flash into my mind, like welcome visitors from that winter in my youth.

I wonder if anyone will be able to notice anything different about me tomorrow?

Brackencliffe

By Sue Bowl

And in the fine fields of Sage and Parsley, Cara had many fold admirers, chief among whom was a simple peasant called Philip. When Philip first kissed her, her girlhood finally came to fruition, exploding into radiant womanhood at the touch of his workaday hand. From the date of that kiss Cara's loveliness knew no bounds, and even the men in the field sang a song of her, with her skin as fresh as the snowdrops, and her voice as soft as the day, and her love as sweet as the cider to wash a man's care away!

With such an admirer as Philip, Van Day fell from a top his high horse, and Cara looked back on her childhood and thought in her maiden's way, that if her life were a tree with bare branches, who wanted for interesting landings, 'twas in looking back that she realised, her branches weren't bare very long.

Wednesday 23 December

At about 6.54am I woke from a fleeting dream where I was a southern belle running down a staircase, and a swooney beau was waiting at the bottom to meet me. I should say for the record that it definitely wasn't Icarus!

When we got into work at the Toastie, Mrs Fry didn't twig me and Joe. Her antenna must've been rusty, for we each had terrible helmet rings, which can take a couple of hours to plump out. And I felt euphoric about the silliest thing, such as the light bouncing on a teaspoon.

But Michael rumbled me in the toilets while we were both brushing our hair. She'd changed hers to packet dye chocolate-brown, because she was seeing someone new.

Back in the canteen Mrs Fry was busy making up new names for the coffees when we joined her. Her bracelets jangled over her jotter.

'Café La La, Café Clever, Café Scrumptious . . .'

'Café Amore?' said Michael, with a wink.

Joe dropped me back at Green Place later on. A storm was gathering its disciples, but Joe couldn't stay as he had a family dinner.

'I'm so sorry I've got to leave you here alone. I'd be much happier if you had company,' he said.

'But I have got company; there's my visitor.'

Joe had to concede he'd been out-clevered.

There'd been communication from the tramp, in that the card that I'd left him had vanished. Upstairs the locked-room light was switched on again.

I was just about to baton down the hatches for one of my famous nights in, as daggers of sleet started to rage warfare over the holidays, when I looked out of the window and saw someone in the distance flickering a powerful torch. Its bright shaft shone out over hills and the roads, picking up rain in its tunnel of light like fine just-visible pins, illuminating the tarmac with a vicious sheen of water. The plumes of buddleia caught in its beam were still hanging just as they had been in the summer, exactly the same shape, but now brown, as if they'd been smoked. And their scent was no longer of lilac but of tobacco. I opened the window so I could smell them.

But what a sight awaited me: the light flashing up the drive appeared to be Joe on his way back. And there was someone on the back of his bike, sitting side saddle in a skirt. The sight of her bird legs dandling off the edge – I know I will never forget it. Her cold, thin face was full of concern and urgency when they stepped inside.

'What are you doing here?' I said.

'I was unable to get a taxi,' said Aunt Coral.

'I was passing the station and I spotted her waiting in the rain,' Joe said.

'Yes, it was blessed, thank you Joe,' said Aunt C.

'But where are all your things. Delia, and the Admiral?' I asked her.

'I needed to come back without delay. There's something we need to look at. I don't mean to be cryptic; it'll be easier if I show you.'

And without taking her coat off she went into the drawing room.

'The house looks good,' she said absent-mindedly, dripping rain all over the floor.

She looked through her important papers, which I had been keeping under heavy covers for her, and drew out the log book of Mrs Morris, the old housekeeper. She turned over a few pages before presenting it to me.

'I don't know why I didn't think of it until this evening,' she said. 'I'm so sorry I've been so slow. But better late than never. I wanted to get here as soon as I possibly could.'

FAMILY ROOMS, 1947

Trout Suite (West Wing) – Mr Garden
Pearl's Room (East) – Mrs Garden
Bluebell Left (East) – Ms Coral
Bluebell Right (East) – Ms Cameo
Grey Room (West) – Ms Buddleia

We ran up to the Grey Room like two crazed surveyors. There *was* a loose floorboard, and there *was* a key underneath it. I'd always thought it was odd she should leave it in Titford, right in Red Indian Territory.

I took it up in my hands, as if it were her precious ashes. Here lay the answer surely, in the shape of a small brass key.

'When did she last come here?' I asked, with the growing awareness that this must have meant she had planned her death for some time.

'She came for the funeral, and once more in September,' said Aunt C.

'Didn't you ask her why she'd come?' I said.

'I wasn't here,' she said.

'I feel sick.'

When I returned from the loo, Aunt Coral was on the telephone calling through to the Egham Fleet. It took twenty minutes for a taxi to come because it was busy season; I was going to start walking had it taken a moment longer.

The lockers at Titford station are par-owned by the leisure centre, impersonal metal boxes, used mostly for sweaty clothes. Our car drew up into the warm clouds of exhaust that hang at the side of the concourse, filling our noses with the fumes. There were doors clunking, warmth inside cars, and people heading home for Christmas.

But once we were inside the station, I doubted if ever the platform had been walked for such a grim purpose. The ground was polished and cream under foot, and Aunt Coral held my hand. It was the same floor that Aileen and I used to slide along in our socks if we happened to be taken out with a grown-up to meet friends coming in on the train.

Dread and excitement filled my heart when we stopped at 402. It was almost like going to see her. The door was black as a coffin, and the little white number was chipped. We hesitated for a moment, uncertain if it was the right one.

Aunt C looked at me and gently tried to take the key from my fingers.

'No, I want to,' I said.

With a shaking hand, I opened the door, to be met with the sight of two quite plain shoeboxes. I don't know what I was expecting – guns, perhaps, or a sawn-off head – but the contents seemed much too ordinary in relation to my expectations. I'd imagined stolen money, or drugs, or bloodstained clothes, something fantastic, but not inanimate boxes.

I drew them out, and we returned to the Titford rank. The sound of our steps on the platform was like a solemn military band. I carried my grave treasure tight in my arms like a baby. Aunt Coral had brought her shopping basket, in case we should need a container, but I didn't put the shoeboxes in, so she carried it along quite empty.

Unfortunately, the next cabbie was a chatterer. Aunt C made valiant conversation, the effort of which she signalled to me via secret squeezes. He went on about the road works on the bypass, and told her he was a Santa in the department store but they wouldn't give him a grotto.

'They only provide an elf,' he said.

Even at such moments as these, it seems there is no time for silence. Although, God bless him, how was he to know?

The moon broke through the night sky like a torch suddenly illuminating the floor of the car, searching the top of my boxes with sad, silver light. The same moon that shone for me and Joe, the same moon that silently watches everything.

Back at Green Place, I went straight into the drawing room, with my hat and coat still on, and Aunt Coral sat in the window. I tipped the contents of the boxes out on the floor. I was shot with adrenalin head to toe; the blood of courage.

She had left me a savings account with her rainy day fund, ten thousand pounds in all. And there were old birthday cards and baby photos, and the things from her empty 'Blue' folder. Some snippets she'd made into a collage, with some pictures she liked, her eyelashes from the sixties, and ribbons from her bouquets. A life can boil down to two shoeboxes it seems; to remembered birthdays and holidays. Her life was short, but now it also seemed small.

Odd pages from her schooldays lay scattered on the floor like confetti. There were pages from her days at St Hilary's, a rambling kind of poem, and something that was addressed to Aunt Coral.

St Hilary's Freedom Party Manifesto, July 30 1954

Deputy Minister, Buddleia Garden

A Way to Change the World

- Nuns need to relax. Compulsory leisure moments for nuns.

- Compulsory toast for all boarders.

- All children to be given the choice to board at school or not. All parents to comply.

- Shorter terms.

- Baths not compulsory.

- Lessons not compulsory.

- School not compulsory (to be discussed).

Kitchen Novelty competition, St Hilary's 1962
Buddleia Garden's Entry:

ROSE PETAL WINE

Here is a family recipe, inadvertently discovered by my sister.

For the infusion:
Sugar
Champagne yeast (never use bread yeast, it tastes foul)
Cooled boiled water

Method:

1 Activate the yeast by adding sugar and warm water in a bowl. Let it sit for ten minutes.

2 Mix together with the rose petals, add more water to taste.

3 Pour into bottle with scrunched sock in the top.

NB this must allow AIR as fermentation can cause EXPLOSION.

'My father' (A poem by BG)
July 15 1986

Who are you?

An emperor, or a king? If I saw you in a café, would I know you?

Would I have the nerve to tap you on the shoulder and ask,

'Are you my Dad?'

To Coral,

The truth has finally made sense of why I have always felt like an outsider, of why I was sent away to school, of all that has been missing.

But I'm actually very grateful that they protected me from the stigma of illegitimacy. They were still my parents because they behaved as such, so in that sense it wasn't a lie.

But I wish I had known my Father. And my poor Mother. I know so little about her. It is as I say, a gap.

Dearest Coral, I do see that you were an unwilling witness to this, but I wish that there had been truth between us. Love and lies; fascinating misfits, like the terribly uncoordinated little girl next door who is so in love with dancing. As I was once.

I wish things had been quite different. But I don't blame you at all.

With my love to you always,

Your sister, your niece,

Buddleia

Aunt C did not speak for a while, but just shook her head.

'It's too late now,' she said, 'to say I didn't know, *I didn't know.*'

Her sobs won their bid to be free, and I held her together for some moments.

Then we continued on through the remnants, sewn all over the floor. There was a bill from the film 'Now, Voyager'. The man on the bill was lighting two cigarettes and giving one to Bette Davis. It was in black and white and lay next to a bundle of letters which were written on intelligent-looking paper and did not have any stamps.

On the back of one of the older envelopes was the first verse of a poem by W. B. Yeats that began, 'Had I the heaven's embroidered cloths,' and ended, 'Tread carefully for you tread on my dreams.' At the bottom, in the hand of the letter writer, there was a tender line which read:

'I would give you all Heaven.'

I recognised the handwriting but could not place it at first. The letters dated back years, and were marked 'private' in Biro, which is a red rag to a bull, certainly at times like those.

Aunt Coral was looking at something else at that moment, and so quietly and with some strange guidance from my sixth sense I read the last letter first.

Darling
This is the last I can send you. We must cease all contact.

I shall always be grateful to you for the happiness you have brought me at a time in my life when there were shadows. I do love you, you know I do, but J would not be able to cope.

I'm only sorry it's taken me so long to be certain I can't go ahead.

Please understand me. I can't get rid of my conscience, and I will never be free till I do.

I wish you everything good.

Mick X

The letter was dated September 17, 1986. A week later she was gone.

'Aunt Coral,' I said, handing her the letter, 'I think this is what we've been looking for.'

She read it slowly, her hand trembling.

'Who is Mick?' she asked, her tone was very cautious.

'It's Mr Edgeley . . . It can't have been for a *man*, it can't have been,' I said.

My shocked tears were not of sorrow but plummeting tears of rage. 'I HATE HER. How could she do this to me?'

'But this man was just the tip of it. *She didn't know who she was,*' said Aunt C.

'I should have been able to stop her. I should have known,' I said.

'There's nothing you could have done, she must have been too unhappy.'

'But other people get divorced and lose loved ones and they don't *kill themselves.*'

'But she wasn't other people; so much is a question of character. Just think of all the poets who cannot bear to be alive. Or imagine a spider whose vision extends into the ultraviolet range, they are bound to feel things more keenly, so keenly it hurts so much you will do anything to stop it. You know she was—'

'Born serious. I know.'

She was trying so hard to make sense of it for me in her own way. She now held me up by my shoulders, for I had become a limp rag, and she looked into my face directly with the kindness of all her days.

'You made her happy Sue. She said as much in her note. YOU MADE HER FEEL HAPPY. You hold on to that.'

'I don't hate her, please don't think that I do,' I said, giving all that I had inside me to the expression of undying love.

'Of course you don't,' she said, shivering in her silly little blouse and cardigan.

I laid my head on her shoulder for a long time in the silence, and we sat still amongst the scraps and remembered her. The clock on the mantelpiece, oblivious, carried on with its Westminster chimes.

24 December (Christmas Eve)

This morning there was a letter in the post from life:

Dear Miss Bowl

Please accept my apologies for the delay in replying to you; I have been overwhelmed by letters.

In answer to your question about whether it is better to write from experience or from the imagination, I would say that in the majority of cases, it is better to write from the imagination, most particularly in affairs of the heart.

Although we may not actually know a love in real life, I think it is true to say that the heart knows, and this is because of its close bond with the imagination. The imagination is the best friend of the lover, whether in real or in imagined courtships. You can be your own author in imagination, whereas in real life others have a say.

I'm sorry to hear you've known heartbreak, but even a bad experience is copy.

May I take this opportunity to thank you very much for your letter and to wish you every success.

Yours truly

Benjamin O'Carroll
MBA Hons.

They are back! And Green Place is once again buzzing. Admiral Gordon returned from a trip into town this morning saying that a consignment of rabbits is heading for Egham. And he's ordered one for Delia, to help her to come to terms with the loss of Bertie, who was never successfully identified.

Admiral Ted spent his first few hours home chiselling the front door free from ice, and then sanding it down where it had warped with the rain so it was possible to get in and out normally.

It is just like they have never been away, although I must say, the house looks very different. Gone are the acres of wallpaper, and instead pink plaster glistens, giving off an odour of ointment like Green Place has been sent to the clinic.

I overheard Aunt Coral and Glenn Miller discussing his invoice for works when he popped in today. He was agreeing to wait until she gives him the green flag to present it, which she says will be in the New Year. She told me she has come to the conclusion that it is time to sell off her shares, and what good is rainy day money, if you don't use it on rainy days?

So without further ado, so she doesn't have to do that, I have hatched my own plan with Glenn, and I'm going to transfer my ten thousand straight to him after Christmas, so that Aunt Coral won't have to worry. It is the least I can do for her, and I'm certain Mum would have approved. What a surprise it will be for Aunt C to find she's in credit for once! I'm not going to tell her until after the transfer's gone through, and I've asked Glenn to keep it under his hat for now too.

Every time I think of my father it is accompanied by a strong feeling of guilt. Aunt Coral keeps on saying I shouldn't blame myself for not knowing there was a whole other story. The revelation of Mum's secret relationship has changed everything. I do wish it was all for a more stomachable reason. She has fallen off the pedestal that death had put her on. She is human again, and herself, not the saint I mourned. As soon as they get back from their trip I will arrange to see Dad.

*

Aunt C hasn't had time as she normally would to prepare anything much for Christmas, because of the building work. And now that the greater anxiety had been addressed, she has become consumed with making sure we are on time for the Gala. We had a special Christmas Group after lunch, where our stories were handed in. The judges now have one week to read and make their choice.

I worked right up until the final minute, but it was difficult to concentrate on 'Brackencliffe'. The house was busy, and I felt raw inside. How could Mum's revenge on Mr Edgeley not feel like revenge on me? As a mother, she had always tried to protect me from fire, drowning, cruelty or fear. So it's ironic that the one thing she couldn't save me from was the force of her own despair.

But as there was no more time left for reflection, I had to find an end to my story. I worked in the attic until the deadline, interrupted only by Delia wondering where to teach her Italian to Admiral G. She had changed into a skirt for the benefit of the lesson.

Loudolle got back about twelve, just in time to hand hers in. I heard her taxi pull up through my skylight, but I had nothing to do with anyone until we assembled for Group after lunch.

Egham Hirsute Group
Pre Gala Christmas Special

'Some days it seems to me,' said Aunt Coral, 'that everything sounds like a book title. I was saying to Pat earlier, "I am too short for this chair," and realised that it sounded like a title. She replied, "It's not like you to sit down in the afternoons," and I thought that sounded like a title too, but I think it's just that I am so excited that we have finally come to this hour. I wish you all the best of luck. Now, why don't we share a little flavour from our entries?'

We all put our hands up.

'Sue,' said Aunt Coral, with a tear in her eye.

Brackencliffe

Yet Pretafer Gibbon was not satisfied, and stole unto the Pasture of Sage and Parsley. Here she placed a knife at the tender throat of Cara, knowing that Keeper was gone for a gamble, and Fiona was in haste to the market. How beautiful she looked in the icy dawn, with her blooms about to burst out.

Pretafer toyed at Cara's milky throat with a ravaged and shaking hand, when suddenly her death wish was halted by the footsteps of a stranger.

'Happiness is like a distant cousin I hardly ever see,' cried Pretafer Gibbon, thwarted.

'Then you must make happiness your bed socks,' said Nurse Chopin, who was in full conspiracy with the evil. And they scurried away.

But happiness attends on the good, and in all those in its bosom.

Keeper came home safe, and Fiona, with a basket, and then suddenly, clear from the woodsmoke, the maker of footsteps was made plain. And if Cara had ne'r gone to Brackencliffe, she would n'er have known his dear step.

'Twas Philip, and he held out his man arms and betook a diamond from out of his horsecoat.

'Marry me, Cara,' he said.

'Keeper, my Knight is come home.'

The End

The Group members gave me a small round of applause. Joe and Aunt Coral were beaming like they were my parents.

'And Loudolle?' said Aunt Coral.

The Polo Player

By Loudolle Shoot

Argentinean Allain D'Angelo had won more matches than Kitty had even bet on, but he thought she was hot enough for an invite to a private pool party for two.

'You give the love, I give the booze,' he growled, knowing the effect this would have on Kitty.

'Oh Allain D'Angelo!' said Kitty, 'I . . . Yes! Yes! Ye—'

'Why don't you come over here and let me show you how to play polo?' he said, pulling her on to a sun bed.

'What? Here?' she said.

'Yes here, you hussy, I want to show you my rod.'

'Thank you, Loudolle,' said Aunt Coral, cutting her off to save the Admiral having to excuse himself. There was again polite applause, though her clip was absolutely awful.

'And Avery?'

Controversially, the Admiral *still* hadn't quite finished writing, but paused to read some out.

'We are all trains arriving at the station, and some arrive sooner than others,' said Aunt Coral in his defence.

The Socialites

By Admiral Avery John Little

There was a vast array of dresses, so many pretty things. In the fast-moving world of fashion, they had to keep up with the looks.

Debs was late to the catwalk because she had got into a dispute; she was going to take it up with the council very first thing the next day. Apparently, her car had been contravening a white line, and she'd had a heated exchange with a warden, before being issued with a paper ticket which he said she would have twenty-eight days to appeal.

'Writing about our favourite things. Well tried Avery!' said Aunt Coral on full beam. After his applause died down she resumed. 'And Joe?'

Roger Mead

By Josef Fry

Roger Mead may have had the wool over Vienna's eyes, but he never had it over Hawley's. Had Hawley the money or a plane, he would have taken Vienna far away. Instead he returned to the office, where she was photocopying the letter.

'I still don't believe you. You've made it all up, where's Roger?' said Vienna.

'Does it matter?' said Hawley.

'It matters to me.'

'Vienna, please, Roger's gone. He's gone and he's not coming back,' said Hawley, thumping his wrist in frustration against the idiotic machine.

Again we applauded; there was a strong atmosphere of support, although this would end soon because at the gala we'd be pitted against each other.

'Goodness me, a thriller! I literally can't wait,' said Aunt Coral. 'Thank you Joe. Admiral Gordon?'

At Forty Knots

By Rear Admiral William Percival Gordon

He was only a lad, and it was only his first year at sea. He was like a duck on the bathroom floor. Yet when the wind got up and they opened the sails, something happened; it was like he hadn't existed until they were moving at full speed.

'I've seen many bright lads like this,' said Cap'n John, 'and they usually end up as Officers.'

'Or overboard,' said the deckie, whose own brother had been claimed by the sea.

'Goodness, thank you Admiral Gordon, what a variety we're offering!' said Aunt Coral. 'Thank you. And Delia?'

Don't Wait

D Shoot

Would there come a day when he felt at peace,
when he could forget the thorns in his side?

'You'll be seventy and you'll still not
have let go,' said Imogen, prancing round
doing her drama.

It was all right for her; nothing bad had
happened to her yet, she hadn't been alive
long enough. But Ray was old and round with
a goatee beard and a temper.

'Thank you Delia, how mournful. And finally, Admiral Ted?'

An Excellent Hand

By Vice Admiral Edward Anthony

The smoke-filled parlour played host for the
last time before they left. Language was no
barrier; they knew the language of the game.
He shook the pot and the die was cast. Iris
shook off her shawl.

'Thank you, Admiral Ted, well done. Goodness, another cliff-hanger.
Well, we shall all have to wait and see!'

We handed our stories in to Aunt Coral in proud A4 envelopes, and she
placed them in a pile with significance.

'I hope one day this will become a ritual,' she said. 'Well done everybody.'

At which point Glenn and Mrs Bunion came in with a Christmas cake, hats and sparklers. Pat stayed on and Glenn Miller tuned in while he planered one of the walls.

'I'm just listening in, but I do keep a diary at home,' he said.

One of the things I love most about Group is the totalitarian mix of people; there were the high-ranking Admirals sitting beside Pat Bunion, both equals in aspiration.

'Now,' said Aunt C, looking as though she had been up all night inventing things. 'This is our penultimate exercise of the year, inspired by the Egham Hirsute Group itself which takes its name from a mis-understanding of language. And so, I would like us all to think of words which we have misunderstood. Hands up please if you can think of one. Sue?'

'Dumb waiter,' I said.

'Excellent Sue . . . and Avery?'

'Antimacassar; I thought it meant against Scotland.'

'That's wonderful Avery! And Admiral Gordon?'

'Scruples; I thought it meant a kind of eczema.'

'Oh dear! Admiral Gordon. And Admiral Ted?'

'Uxorious doesn't mean fragrant,' he said.

'What does it mean?' she said.

'It means wife-loving.'

'Good, really excellent, that is a *very* good one. That little exercise shows us that words can mean anything which we *want* them to.

'And now for some fun final questions! Quick fire, who can tell me what "N" is another word for something a lady might wear to bed?'

We all put our hands up.

'Avery?' said Aunt Coral.

'Nightie?' he said.

'Well I'll give you it, but I was actually looking for negligee.' I couldn't help suspect a plan. She was on full beam again, which he didn't notice because he was so busy hoping to guess the next word.

'Now, who can tell me, what word covers sprouts, carrots, parsnips, peas etc.?'

We all put our hands up.

'Admiral Gordon?' said Aunt Coral.

'Gravy,' he said.

'Well I'll give you it, but I was actually looking for vegetables.'

She was finally beginning to show signs of judgement on what was certain stupidity.

'OK, let's go again. Who can tell me what "P" is another word for bucket?'

'Sue?' she said.

'Pisspot,' I said.

'Right. Perhaps we should crack open some champagne, and go out into the drawing room?' I think she had realised we were all brain-dead from our stories.

The Admiral popped open the bubbles while Aunt Coral carried on. 'What "L" is another word for affection?'

'Like?' said the Admiral.

'Well I'll give you it, but I was actually looking for love . . .'

Later

It has turned out to be an exciting Christmas Eve.

After champagne the Ad went out to do his shopping, leaving the rest of us to sit down to a hot broth of cheery tomatoes. We were just about to start, when we had a call from Egham Police to say that the Bentley had smashed into a parked car at high speed, in reverse, across two areas of grass, before driving off in front of a bus, taking out four bollards and an ornamental gnome. They were looking for the Admiral to get him to surrender his licence.

'Avery's at the club,' said Admiral Ted. 'What the blazers is going on?'

Then the Admiral telephoned from the station, having been arrested at his club, wondering in his innocence if Aunt Coral had been the one driving. Her alibis were quickly established, as were his, so he was set free.

Admiral Gordon took the Rover to go and fetch the Admiral while the rest of us checked for witnesses along Clockhouse Lane. Mrs Bunion stayed to answer the phone, and Loudolle went to unpack, being the only person not to be bothered at all by any of the fewrory. By the time we returned home after about an hour or so, the police had a sighting of the Bentley being driven by a male with long hair, 'aka the Green Place Tramp, over', said Papa X-ray on the radio.

'Probably borrowed it to go to the hairdressers,' said Aunt Coral, flippant as ever in misadventure.

The car was only insured for a thousand miles per year, being mainly used just for Egham, so Aunt Coral went upstairs to look at the policy. We were planning to go to 'Carols By Candlelight' after dinner, and there were still all the presents and bits to do, so the rest of us got on with our preparations.

I managed to find time this morning, before any of this had happened, to update one of my pinafores into a racey little dress – and although it shows my knees, it still had a devastating effect on Joe. I have never fully understood until now, the minx one can find in one's wardrobe! Or maybe it's because Joe sees me in this way, and so in a strange way I will become it, like he is the creator of a hitherto unknown croquette.

He had to go home for dinner before joining us at carols, but first he helped me set the table, handling Aunt Coral's dishes with the care of museum pieces.

'I'll see you at the gala, if I don't see you before,' he said.

'Thanks for everything, Joe,' I said.

He didn't speak but looked overwhelmed. I know he was feeling sad about leaving me again and returning to the madness of his mother. She is very strict with him over Christmas; I think he is her stand-in husband. I watched him ride down the drive, and as soon as he'd gone, I wished he'd come back. He has the power to make setting the table feel like jazz.

Mrs Bunion rang the dinner gong on her way out; she was heading to the village hall with our stories.

'See you soon Mrs B, have a nice break,' said Admiral Ted as he opened the front door for her forlornly.

'I've put you a mousse in the bottom of the fridge. Just one, just for you,' said Mrs Bunion.

Every chef needs someone to love what they make. Without that, life has no meaning.

Apart from the missing Bentley, there was an upbeat glow to the eve. The Admirals doused themselves with fragrance and all the bathrooms were singing. There was vanilla in the air, and butter and herbs and musk and chicory. I felt so under-scented that I went upstairs to put a dot behind my ears before we left. And then I went to the carols with the oldies who, hirsute, *did* know how to have a good time. (I'm using hirsute here deliberately – maybe it will become a convention.)

Christmas Day

The Bentley was found this morning on the drive with a few bumps and bruises. None of us heard a thing. There must be at least twenty tramps in Egham, and more than seven with long hair – although I'm not convinced that the tramp took the car at all. But PC Pacey believes that it must be the same tramp who broke into Green Place, as he would have had access to the car keys to make copies. He wants to come and see if the prints from the car match those in the house, but because it is Christmas, these things are bound to take time.

I hope it wasn't my visitor. He is my strange friend, just mine, and he never once tried to hurt me.

When I came downstairs this morning, I stopped myself outside the drawing room, listening to my housemates' snippets, neither being with them, nor being alone, in the no man's land of the Hall. Bing Crosby was playing and they had begun to open their presents. Aunt C is a black belt shopper and was reaping the rewards of her trips.

'Beryl's a little belter,' said Delia. She was talking about her new rabbit, which has been given complete run of its own suite in the East Wing.

'Another G and T?' asked Aunt Coral.

'Oh, yes please. In fact make it a double, and save your legs,' said Delia.

'P. D. James,' said Admiral Ted, in reply to some question or other.

'If they don't find any prints, then it means they've got the wrong man,' said the Admiral.

'Or that he was never here,' said Aunt Coral. 'Sue has quite an imagination . . .'

'Ted, where are you?' shouted Admiral Gordon. He was calling from the kitchen.

'I'm fine,' said Admiral Ted, on account of his tittinus.

It must be how we sounded to the tramp. Loudolle passed me on her way out. I pretended to be cleaning the door frame, so I don't think she suspected. She was dressed till the nines and was on the way to a luncheon, having already generously given her mother a couple of hours of her time. She eyed me somewhat nervously in the hall. We hadn't actually spoken since the Toastie.

'See you at the gala,' she said, elongating her vowels as though she was having difficulty sounding authentic.

'See you at the gala,' I said, knowing that, if there was any justice in this life, by the New Year she would be conkered.

'There were so many birds on the feeder this morning, you just missed a starling,' said Delia, coming to say goodbye to Loudolle.

'Great,' said Loudolle. 'See you later.'

Delia believes that no matter what she does, her progeny walks on water. But both she and Loudolle have been very altered by their experience of life. Delia is a cynic who thinks men just want women to waft about, when back in girlhood she was an irrepressible optimist, and

Loudolle has reinvented herself to the point where she is no longer even English. When Loudolle shut the front door, Delia went into the kitchen to write up her pretend calendar. There are dark shadows for each of us even in the Christmas light.

'From the moment they are born, they are leaving you,' she said in a moment of close confiding.

'Indeed,' I said, and it stung. I can't remember why I ever preferred to sit at the bus stop with Aileen rather than watch Christmas TV with Mum.

After lunch, while Aunt Coral and her tenants were playing Beggar-My-Neighbour, I decided to go for a walk. I was feeling restless.

There was nothing open in Egham but a shop selling things like tins of peaches, and it was one of those days where the sky can't be bothered to get properly light. I could hear a brass band in the distance and watched a paper bag blow down the road in time to the oom-pah-pah. And suddenly, like we were magnets, I found myself at Joe's.

The Frys' flat is in a conversation area, in keeping with them being part of the chattering classes. It was Mrs Fry who answered the intercom, surprised to hear my voice, and after a minute Joe came down in a private dressing gown with airplanes on it.

'Sue!' he said.

'Hello.'

'Sue.'

It was as though he had only one word in his vocabulary.

We weren't allowed to fraternise at the flat, so we floated on his bike till teatime, stopping at a viewing point on the edge of Egham where he played me a tune on his Walkman. He confessed he had been playing it over and over to himself since we kissed. It's called 'Classic' and the lyrics say something like 'I wanna to write a classic, I want to write it in an attic . . . Yeah!' I liked the idea of Joe going into an attic and writing me a love song. I wondered if that was what he was going to do after I'd gone, but he told me he had to go with his mother to visit relatives in Staines.

On the way home the streets were lit up by winter displays of lights. I looked in the windows of houses. I always think strange lives look nice in the evenings.

I have realised that I feel good with Joe. He appreciates the things I'd rather overlook: my turned-in foot that bends all my shoes out of shape; the way I pronounce a French starter. The time goes so quickly when I'm with him that I have to relive it at half-speed in my memory afterwards to get all the good out of it. I'm a sweet in a wrapper to the others, but Joe is able to unwrap me. It's like the difference between sitting downstairs at a dinner, in uncomfortable tight trousers, hot and bored and tense, and then going up to lie on your bed with your trousers off, cool and interested and relaxed. My heart breaks at the thought that one day Joe will die.

When I returned, Aunt C and Delia were very emotional about my going to see Joe. We hadn't been to the coast and written each other's names in the sand or anything like that, but try telling that to two old ladies who can't conceive of anything but altars. I had a little talk with Aunt Coral about it, because I knew she was dying to know things.

'It seems a part of me died the moment that Joe kissed me.'

'That's very dramatic.'

'I mean it was the part that had wanted it to happen for so long, and I do not mourn the loss of it.'

She looked into the middle distance, which is where she generally finds her wisdom.

'One day you might yearn the other way – for the time when you were a girl.' Then she scooted back to her tenants.

'I don't think I will,' I said.

I went with Aunt Coral and the Admiral for a meal in his private club this evening. They don't ordinarily let in ladies, but make an annual allowance. The waiters were very pompous and served my food like I didn't deserve it, sweeping my crumbs between courses as though I'd made a terrible mess.

After the main course Aunt C left the table to go and powder her nose. She never says she's going to the toilet. It's because she was a young woman of the 1950s, and they had no shiny noses and no weeing.

While she was gone I was left alone with the Admiral, and his manner was a little strained. I think that he felt ill at ease because he's been persuaded that I made up the tramp. He's heavily influenced by Aunt Coral, and this is her own opinion, because it's more comfortable for her to think I imagined him, than that he was actually there. It's her Carolinian nature, (it can be a little annoying).

'I'm trying to talk myself out of the sticky toffee pudding,' he said, with great relief when Aunt C returned from the toilet.

'And what are you trying to talk yourself into?'

They both decided on the sorbet.

In the pocket between Christmas and New Year, a time that sometimes really drags, it is exciting to know that somewhere in Egham, a judge is reading 'Brackencliffe'.

Thursday 31 Dec, New Year's Eve

Aunt Coral hadn't told anyone she'd asked Mr O'Carroll to attend the Ramblers' Association Gala.

'I don't know how I managed to keep it a secret,' she said, twinkling at me.

'It's a first,' said Delia, who was, hirsute, blown away.

The entire salon from Knightsbridge had turned up to the event at Grossacre Hall, which is the Ramblers' Association HQ on the edge of the Egham borders. There was also Nigel from the *Herald*, plus the Nanas, Badger, Tornegus, Mrs Fry and team Toastie, including Sandy, Icarus and Mary-Margaret. There was Pest Control – Derek and Pigpen – and the regulars from the tyre place too, and finally Glenn Miller and Dean Martin. The Admiral joked that if his friend Gary Cooper had come that would have made it a hat trick.

The attendees were handed the writers' biogs as they filed into the hall, and I noticed a gentleman reading mine. Joe had written it up, and done a great job in bigging me up, when the terrible truth was that until that year I'd spent most of my life in a bedroom that was eight by eight. We were sitting together on a row of chairs marked 'EHG' on the back.

There were *two hundred* overall in attendance, on top of which was the panel. To say I was nervous was to undersell it. And I'd made a fashion error, in that the playsuit I'd worn was too fiddly to go to the toilet.

Mr O'Carroll stood up to give an opening address. He had a nice face that looked as though it spent a lot of its time in thought.

'My thanks go to Ms Garden for inviting me to come this afternoon,' he said, 'and to the judges who have given me the privilege of awarding the winning prizes, but I think to begin with we are going to hear from . . . Arthur Dunn,' he said, referring to his prompt sheet, and taking his glasses on and off often from his two sharp eyes.

There was a big round of applause and then a boy in maroon corduroy came on stage.

'He's the warm-up,' said Delia. She was in one of her own designs, which wasn't suitable unless you were a flamboyant.

'Why do we tell stories?' said the boy. 'Why do we want to write them? The Celts never wrote down anything but handed fables by word of mouth. But storytelling is an ancient art form, and I would like to sing you a song about it. Strike up please,' he said, and Joyce from the church got up to play the piano.

The Admiral swung his foot at a jaunty angle to the music and

Loudolle was yawning. I felt every second build in anticipation and I urgently wanted a poo.

Arthur finally finished and there was a polite round of applause, and then there were *four* other acts that followed. I don't know how I managed to sit through it, my stomach was in taters.

'So, just like a beauty pageant,' said Mr O'Carroll at long last, 'I won't keep you waiting any longer. I will announce the individual winners, in reverse order. In third place . . .'

My stomach erupted.

'With her story, "The Stunt", is . . . Lady Jillet from the Egham Remnants,' he said.

A lady with wispy hair got up from amongst her members who were patting her. She went up to collect a voucher, looking surprised and a bit disappointed, then returned to the Remnants where they all wanted to see her prize.

'In second place is . . .' said Mr O'Carroll. My inner drums were rolling.

'"Roger Mead", by Josef Fry of the Egham Hirsute Group.'

We shot to our feet to applaud Joe. It was so thrilling and un-expected, and Joe looked at me with his mouth open, silently saying he couldn't believe it. If it's possible to be happy for somebody at the same time as wanting it so badly yourself that it hurts, then I was.

'And now,' said Mr O'Carroll, 'the moment we've all been waiting for . . .'

The drums of my heart beat nearer. I thought of all the Groups and all the hours of toil in my room. Of all my days alone at Green Place, when I could eat prawn cocktail for breakfast if I liked and go to 'Brackencliffe' all afternoon. Of Cara and Keeper and Fiona, each a part of my consciousness. I thought of Aunt C and her gift of encouragement, and I thought of Mum throwing out an embroidered cloth to decorate Heaven's table.

'The winner of the 1987 Ramblers' Association Gala, is . . .'

My drums beat louder.

'Loudolle Shoot from the Egham Hirsute Group with her story, "The Polo Player".'

The applause began, but not from the EHG. We were too surprised to move. As Loudolle got up to accept her prize, every disappointment I'd ever felt rushed to join in with this one and lumps assembled in my throat.

She was handed a cheque for £250 plus an electric voucher. She looked like she'd been rehearsing shaking her hair while looking shocked. How I wanted to step up to her. I bet she bribed the judges. I bet she gave them special coffees. But how? We didn't know who they were until today. They can't have had any taste.

She was just about to leave the stage and return to a Group in shock when Mr O'Carroll stopped her. 'One moment, Miss Shoot, I'm sure we'd all like to hear the winning story,' he said, 'I know I would, having not had the opportunity to read it.'

The crowd thought this was a good idea.

'So if you wouldn't mind reading aloud . . .' he said, gently showing her where to stand.

'I'm too shy, I couldn't,' she said, wriggling like a kitten.

Too shy? She seemed to have undergone a complete metamorphosis.

The audience started cheering, egging her on, but suddenly Loudolle dropped her pages and ran back stage. Delia went straight after her to find out what was the matter, immediately followed by Icarus, immediately followed by Mrs Fry.

'Ah,' said Mr O'Carroll, 'I was shy once too.' He looked at the judges, who seemed equally baffled. 'Perhaps another member of her group would like to come up and do the honours?'

The Admirals all looked at me, but I was too distressed, so that just left Aunt C and Joe, who decided between them that Joe would do it. He was completely out of his comfort blanket, but Aunt Coral was too upset to do the job herself. So Joe went on stage for the second time, picking up the scattered pages and putting them back together. The audience was going mad by this point with the drama and anticipation, clapping profusely for him to start, so much that he had to quell them.

'"The Polo Player", by Loudolle Shoot,' he said, and finally everyone fell silent. "She awoke on the course ground, as it sprung back to life beneath the shimmering frost. Calling Keeper to her, they set off together on foot. High, high she climbed, her skirts full of wind and Keeper gambling after, to yonder on the edge of the cliffs . . ." I'm sorry,' said Joe, 'but this isn't right.'

There was a silence in which nobody knew what to say. I was struggling to understand.

'The boy is correct,' said Mr Lucas who was head of the panel, 'the story he's started reading *is* the one we have chosen – the seventeenth century satire – but,' he broke off to refer to his notes, 'Ah, I thought so, the *title* page seems incorrect, the *title* of the winning story, is . . .' He referred to his notes once more. "Brackencliffe!"'

'And it's by Sue Bowl,' said Joe, pointing to me.

'A satire?' I said to Aunt Coral, who by this time had started sobbing.

There was a moment of bewilderment while the audience put it all together, then there was a smattering of applause, which grew into a full-bodied round, and then the full-bodied round grew into stamping and shouting, before finally they exploded, chanting, 'Author! Author! Author!'

I stood up, though I couldn't feel my legs. Joe shook my hand and then supported me to the lectern, before handing me my pages and returning to his seat. A hush fell in the village hall as if I were making a war speech. I began to read aloud in a voice too thin to hear. But mercifully the voice of emergency came to the rescue, which is what tends to happen when I'm shaken.

As I neared the end I looked out into the faces of people old and new. They seemed to find it more entertaining than I would have guessed in a million years.

"'Keeper, my Knight is come home,'" I finished.

There was silence.

"'The *End*,'" I said. They exploded again and Aunt Coral was on her feet.

At least no one can look at my life and say that it's beige.

Coral's Commonplace: Volume 5

Copy of a letter received 30 December 1987:

> 10 Charter Lane
> Derbyshire

Dear Ms Garden

Please accept my sincere apologies for the delay in contacting you. Owing to the highly sensitive nature of this matter, I have deliberated for a long time.

For many years I have wondered if I might hear from you, and when I saw your ad in the paper on my visit to see Mrs Viller, I knew the day had come.

You need not have been concerned about my not knowing about Jack and Cameo. Jack confessed it all to me after it happened, and somehow our marriage contained it. But your Father urged our silence, which we were quite happy to agree to, save only for Jack's terrible feelings of guilt about the child. But then we discovered something which totally altered our position.

What I have to tell you now is going to come as a shock, but after such a tragedy as this I feel compelled to set things straight. Jack suffered for years because of your sister's claims. And I suffered too because I believed I couldn't have children. But finally after years of trying we decided to investigate, and found as a result of medical tests, that it was *Jack* who couldn't have children. I have the paperwork to back this up should you wish to see it. It proves without any doubt that he cannot have been your niece's father.

I know this must be very hard for you, but I hope it means you can move on with your search. I send my very best wishes and hope that you find who you are looking for.

Yours sincerely

Emily Marian Laine

Sue

Dec 31, Later

AFTER THE GALA Aunt Coral threw a spontaneous party, to celebrate our win and also the brand New Year. But before the party got started she took me aside for a moment. I thought she wanted to congratulate me privately, but actually she wanted to talk to me about quite a different matter.

'I'm sorry I didn't tell you earlier today, I didn't want to stress you before the gala,' she started, and then she showed me a letter she had received that morning which I read with some concern.

'So you see, we are back to the drawing board with the search for Buddleia's father.'

It was a great let-down to find that the trail had gone cold, and that Major Laine, God rest his soul, had been a red herring.

'But why would Cameo have named him on the birth certificate? Unless Emily Laine is not telling the truth?' I said.

'But she says she has medical proof,' said Aunt C. 'It appears that one mystery leads straight to another.'

Before we could talk any more, the doorbell went and there were lots of visitors in want of a host.

'We'll have to talk more in the morning,' said Aunt C. 'It is all somewhat bewildering.'

But it was the cusp of 1987, and a New Year was heading our way.

The candles were flickering, the glasses shone, and Mrs Bunion was back in the kitchen.

'You know my Group,' said Aunt C, showing off Mr O'Carroll, who she'd successfully convinced to come along.

'And this is George Buchanan, Meriel Stock Ferrell, Daphne Podger, Mr and Mrs Rodriguez . . .'

'How do you do,' said Mr O'Carroll, taking the best chair, which had been left out specially for him.

Outside, though it was dark, Delia had lit one of her bonfires. She'd been up in her room writing letters to herself while Admiral Gordon tried to persuade her down. It seems to be the way she manages when she is stressed these days.

She took me aside in the kitchen earlier in a profusion of apologies.

'I am so sorry Sue. Loudolle's very sorry about the Gala and fully intends to apologise to you. I don't know what got into her. But in the meantime, I just wanted to say I'm so sorry – and well done.'

Aunt C took the seat next to Mr O'Carroll, to settle him in. He is a reserved man for someone so successful; he is serious and has a depth.

'Mr O'Carroll would like to speak to you,' she said, when I came over with the voller vongs. 'Let me take those.' Then she moved off to mingle, giving me her chair.

Mr O'Carroll took off his glasses exposing his two small eyes, placing them on his lap. 'Your story was very good, *very* good. It's not everyone who can write comedy.'

'Thank you,' I said, feeling truly disappointed that such a great man could miss my mark.

'I wanted to ask if you might be interested in a place on my next writing course?' he said. 'I'll waive half the fee.'

'Thank you so much, I'd love to. Where will it be held?' (I was hoping he was going to say London.)

'Greece,' he said, 'on the island of Crete.'

'Well thank you so much,' I said, trying to appear normal.

'You'll just need five hundred pounds to cover you. We go through from January to April.'

'It's a long course,' I said, not knowing what else to say.

Then Aunt Coral caught my eye from her position among her guests, and came to join us, overwhelmed.

'Excellent Sue, isn't it excellent?' she said.

'But I can't,' I said, 'I'm so sorry, but I can't afford it.'

'Excuse us, Mr O'Carroll,' she said, quickly pulling me into a private area while making an excuse about the snacks.

'What do you mean you can't afford it? Your mother left you ten thousand pounds!'

'I used that to pay Glenn,' I said. 'I wanted to surprise you.'

'Sue!' she said, in flabberghast. 'I can't let you do that.'

'Of course I'd love to go, but I'd be just as happy to stay here.'

'But there's a world of difference between happiness and joy, and it would give me such joy if you go.'

'But you need the money for the house; it could mean another room for you.'

'I would have lost this house if it weren't for you.'

'It was your shoes that saved you.'

'Let me put it another way. I *insist* you go on that course.' She put her hands on my shoulders, like heroes do in the films when they want to persuade heroines to marry them.

'Imagine I am in bed with a book,' she said, 'I who have read all the greats, twice, and the author of the book I am reading is not Dickens, or Defoe or Austen, it is *my very own* Hampshire-born Sue. Nothing could give me more pleasure, nothing, not even a boyfriend. My darling Sue, if there's one thing I've learnt in this life, it is that we must drink the wine while it's red.'

She kissed me, and it wasn't just a cocktail kiss, but a strong kiss of devotion. There was just no arguing with that.

We walked back to tell Mr O'Carroll.

'Thank you Mr O'Carroll, I would love to,' I said.

The rain made a noise like strings of pearls falling on the parquet. Perhaps it was a shower of fortune.

'You shall go,' Aunt C mouthed from across the room amongst the elite of her salon, nearly stumbling into the Ad with an excitement that made her tipsy much quicker than anyone else.

Loudolle had gone to Mrs Fry's with Icarus after the gala, but halfway through the evening I turned and saw the three of them coming into the drawing room. It was as though the saloon doors had swung open, and the baddies had come in.

'Ah, Loudolle,' said Aunt Coral. 'How nice of you to come.'

Then she ushered Loudolle and Icarus into the conservatory and called the entire EHG in too.

'Won't be a moment, Mr O'Carroll,' she said, leaving him with Mrs Fry.

Loudolle looked the picture of innocence, sitting in the conservatory window, Icarus beside her.

'When did you swap the pages?' said Aunt Coral, getting straight to the point.

'Straight after Group,' said Loudolle.

'But we were all at home,' said Aunt Coral.

'You were out looking for the Bentley,' said Loudolle.

'So you seized the opportunity to swap titles. It's too fantastic!' said the Admiral.

'Yes, I know,' she said. 'Sorry . . . will that be all?'

'Not quite,' said Aunt Coral. 'I want to talk to Icarus.'

Icarus looked to his side to make sure there was no one else called Icarus sitting there.

'Tell me, Icarus, have you passed your driving test?' said Aunt Coral.

'For my bike, but not for a car,' said Icarus.

'But you managed to drive the Bentley?' said Aunt Coral.

Loudolle coughed unserenely and Icarus sat still for a moment of struggle as Loudolle tried to guide his reply with her eyes.

'Sorry,' he said finally, 'I was only going to take it for a spin.'

'Voila! The thief of the Bentley!' said Aunt Coral.

'Twirling moustaches!' said the Admiral.

It is staggering. So Icarus created a diversion to get us out of Green Place, giving Loudolle a chance to swap the title page of my short story with hers. But she didn't bank on being asked to read aloud, something a mind with some brains would have thought of.

Icarus and Loudolle were mortified and made their escape through the conservatory doors, offering up hasty excuses as to the reason they had to be anywhere else. Delia was cringing, because she'd invited Nigel from the *Herald* and it was too late to stop him from hearing. What a scoop.

Once we got back to the drawing room, the party began to get going. A complete stranger – well, a friend of Aunt C's called Poseidon – congratulated me on 'Brackencliffe' and said that she was a fan. The Nanas raised their glasses of special fruit cocktail, resolved to wait until midnight to have 'just a drip of champagne'. George Buchanan the dentist and Daphne were in discussion about fillings. The Ad was talking to Aunt C about the latest legislation on parking in the town centre. In spite of this she looked happy.

After a while Mrs Bunion came in with a gold trolley, laden with shimmering drinks and we did the countdown with a Scots man on the news. 'Ten, nine, eight, seven, six, five, four, three, two, one . . .'

'Happy New Year!' said Aunt Coral, with great rhythm.

'Happy New Year!' said Joe.

But I was still thinking about the gauling behaviour of Loudolle.

'I was just wondering if it might have also been Icarus who left me those flowers,' I said, 'all as part of their plan?'

'Could be,' said Joe, 'Green Place is very easy to get into.'

'I think they wanted to add to my belief that there was a tramp here, so I would believe it was a tramp that stole the Bentley. I'm starting to believe that there was never a tramp here at all.'

'Maybe you might have been . . . *Sue*ifying things,' said Joe with great compassion and a small rakish grin.

I looked at him and the goosebumps on my forearm indicated I had undergone a transfusion of love.

1st January 1988

'Please come quickly Aunt Coral,' I said, 'and bring your key.'

It was two this morning and the locked room light was turned on again. Aunt C was still on a high from the soiree, so I didn't have to drag her.

'There's somebody in there,' I said.

'I think it's the wiring,' she said.

But this time I was determined. The gala and Joe and the scholarship, all had played their part.

'Hello, it's just Sue,' I said, knocking. 'Happy New Year.'

All was quiet, and then the light went off. There was definitely somebody there.

'Please don't be alarmed,' I said. 'I just want to know who you are.'

The light went on and then off again, and shadows played under the door.

'Give me your key,' I said to Aunt Coral, and she went to the keyhole in the *dividing* door on the landing.

'It's not there,' she said. All along she'd kept the key just there in the keyhole of the other door! But I didn't have time to interrogate her on the matter.

'Hello,' I said and knocked again. 'It's just Sue Bowl.'

Then, very slowly, the lock clicked and the handle began to turn. Then the door swung open and there stood an old man with long hair lit by the moonbeams.

'Good God,' said Aunt Coral, collecting herself as though she had seen a ghost.

'Johnny?'

She had to summon all of her senses before the following conversation took place.

'I'm sure that you'll understand if I come straight to the point. What I'm wondering is, what on earth you are doing here?'

The man looked from Aunt Coral to me. He must have been in his sixties, but he still had a frolic in his eyes.

'My wife died, I was down on my luck, so I got a place in the Egham . . .' He was hesitant in his approach and spoke with emotional difficulty.

'Go on,' said Aunt Coral.

'I remembered my days at the house, and I wondered if you were still here. I wanted to come back to see it all again, they were happy days.'

'How long have you been staying here?' I asked, my mental calendar was spinning.

'On and off since June,' he said, vindicating Joe's theory that a family of six could live in Green Place and you wouldn't know they were there.

So there before me stood the likely explanation for the sausages, lights, shower, and ceilings.

'But why should you stay here so long? Didn't you have anywhere else to go?' said Aunt C.

He seemed reluctant to answer, but with a small struggle he continued.

'You see I dreamt there was some evidence of me in this room and that someone was waiting. But my dreams are not what they were, and they're not always so clear. But it kept on coming back to me, there was something – somebody waiting. Please forgive me, I wasn't intending to stay.'

'I don't deny you're a prophet,' said Aunt C, 'I remember that well. But what I'd really like to know is, *how did you know where the key was kept to get into Cameo's room?*'

'Yes, I'd like to know that too,' I said.

And then his expression went into a small anxious frown covering one half of his forehead. It appeared that Aunt Coral's question had gone straight to the heart.

'Please forgive me,' he said forlornly, 'I know that I was unsuitable.'

Aunt C reacted calmly, though I sensed that her feet were paddling madly under the surface of troubled waters.

'On the contrary, a man with the soul of a poet is totally suitable to Cameo,' she said.

She was already level with his revelation, although I had yet to quite catch up.

'But did you find what your dream meant?' I asked. 'Was there something – or someone?'

I was imagining ghosts of sad ladies in linen nighties crying in the locked room. But he pointed at a black smudge on the bed cover, as though *that* was the evidence he sought.

'It is forty-year-old coal,' he said. 'Please forgive me.'

'Forty-year-old,' said Aunt Coral. She was looking at me in the code way she has when she hopes I will catch on to her drift. Something was too hard for her to say and so she had to say it with her expression. And we stood in silence for some time, while nine months of maths crossed three generations of untold things.

'My mother would have been forty,' I said.

The man's face was a picture.

'And I think what Aunt Coral is trying to tell you, if I'm correct, is that you are my Grandfather.'

'I think that's right,' said Aunt C.

He reeled and swayed with the shock of it. He held on to himself for support. I don't know who was the more astounded, Aunt Coral and myself for discovering him, or he, for the drop of the bombshell that was telling him who he was.

And then as his frown became more serious, I recognised Mum's expression in his. It was there in his eyes, like a glimpse of her, and

I found it was not inappropriate for me to rush into his arms, even though he was in a poor state of repair and smelt like old turnips. He cried too, in fact words failed us both and tears took over; not only tears of joy and sorrow, but tears of awe. It was unique and overwhelming to embrace a stranger who was my blood.

'You're the key to my dream,' he said.

He cupped his hand gently to my cheek and almost fell under the weight of old sorrows and profound surprises. 'You look like me!' he said, in flabberghast, though he was half blind from sobbing.

'I do!' I said, and I do. It was like what I imagine to be the moment when a Doctor holds up a new-born baby.

'She looks just like the Father,' the Doctor might say, only here there was a missed generation.

'But where is she? Where is Cameo's baby?' he said.

'I think we could do with a drink,' said Aunt Coral.

We went downstairs to talk, for there was life and death itself to catch up on. It was very hard for him to discover the baby, the girl, and the woman that he had missed. In just one brief moment he celebrated the birth and mourned the loss of a daughter he never knew.

'It feels as though she's been with me all this time, in the embodiment of you,' I said. 'She sent you to tell me the truth, even though you didn't know it.'

'Too much secrecy is never a good thing,' said Aunt Coral.

Then she opened up a bottle of her purest medicinal whisky to help ease all the pain. I won't ever forget the way she looked at me and my new Grandfather so fondly, though I think she felt quite a little outsider in such a great twist of life.

Weds January 6 1988

It's now just a few days before I leave for Greece, and a bitterly cold day.

CAMPARI FOR BREAKFAST

I went to hand in my notice at the Toastie on Monday, and Mrs Fry asked me to come in for a coffee. The café was still closed for the holidays, but Icarus was at work doing the community service of duties – the dishes – as penance for his lies.

Mrs Fry apologised for having been severe in the past and said I should ask for a job again if ever I wanted one in the future. I felt like a company girl, part of her team, a lifer, and she said I was a first-class waitress. And then, as though they'd rehearsed it, Icarus sat beside me and she was 'called away'.

'I'm sorry,' he said, 'I didn't mean you any harm. Loudolle made me do it.'

'I understand,' I said, and I did, because she had probably put a spell on him. 'There's no harm done, we can still be friends.'

'In fact I was wondering if you'd like to go out for a drink before you go?' said Icarus.

If he had said that one month earlier, my heart would have tangoed out of the Toastie. But the landscape is very different now. The mountains are topped with Joe.

'Thanks,' I said, 'that would have been lovely, but I'm going away and I'm not back till April.'

'In April then.'

As Aunt C sometimes says, doesn't everyone love a winner? But I have different loyalties now and looking at it on paper, I have a definite preference!

'I'm really sorry, Icarus, but I just don't think we're on the same wavelength.'

'What's a wavelength?' he said.

Loudolle couldn't face me, but instead left a designer notecard on my bed before going back to Alpen. I felt smirched that she'd been in my bedroom, but softened when I read its disclosures. The picture it bore was of a vintage perfume bottle designed by Yves Sean Laurent, and inside it read:

Hey clever you,

I just wanted to say I'm so sorry I lost my head. I just think that you're so amazing, and I wanted to write just like you. I hope you can find it in your heart to forgive me. Let's go get lunch or something next time I'm back in the country.

I hope we will always be friends.

Love, love, love

From

Loudolle X

As *if* we would go and get lunch! Just like we were Aunt C and D on the brink of being lifelong friends! It was going to take more than the sending of an insecure card for me. Forgiveness isn't instantaneous, but I will try for the sake of Delia.

Speaking of which, Delia went into a little decline after the gala, and Aunt C said we had to look out for her. Not that I think that everyone who has a bad hour is going to commit suicide, but once it has happened you worry. I found one of her letters to herself outside, mashed almost to a pulp but still just legible. In it she said she felt she 'existed to reassure happily marrieds it was possible to survive being alone'.

But there is a silver lining for Delia, because she has found Admiral Gordon. It turns out that their love has been growing through all that time spent on the Italian. I'm not sure if they have been off to bed together or anything yet, but they have plans. He is taking her to visit his nanny, who is ninety and lives in a hall.

We ordered a plaque for Mum with bright-gold lettering and put it next to Cameo's dolls' plaques as she asked, where the wind could sweep over it and the sun could beat down on her name.

> ## IN MEMORY OF BUDDLEIA ROSE
> ### May 15 1947 – Sept 23 1986
>
> ❧
>
> Had I the heavens' embroidered cloths,
> Enwrought with golden and silver light
> The blue and the dim and the dark cloths
> Of night and light and the half-light,
> I would spread the cloths under your feet:
> But I, being poor, have only my dreams;
> I have spread my dreams under your feet;
> Tread softly because you tread on my dreams.
>
> *W. B. Yeats*

We stood and paid our respects when it was set, sombre under the mizzle. Our coats and cheeks were covered in rain so fine it barely wet us. Johnny Look-at-the-Moon came too. He wore his best suit. We must have made a strange picture as we bowed our heads to remember her name. Daughter, Aunt, and Father, I am sure she would have been astonished.

And in years to come, when we have all passed away, there may come a jogger who'll think they have stumbled on graves of family pets. Mitzi, Mae, Cameo, Buddleia. Sadly missed.

'Let's go in,' said Aunt Coral after a short time. She always has a cut-off point for such sorrow, and I think I understand why now.

We had to say goodbye to Johnny, as he needed to be on his way. I watched him walk down the drive, as I had the first time I ever saw him. He headed towards Clockhouse Lane, and disappeared once again, like magic.

'I hope he'll be back,' I said.

'So do I,' said Aunt C.

We spent the next few hours making cakes, thawing in the warmth from the oven, and found ourselves with a rare opportunity for one of our satisfying 'chats'.

'Why do you think that Cameo pointed the finger at Major Laine?' I said. 'It seems quite awful when she knew she'd been to bed with Johnny.'

'Maybe she thought Laine could be the father. Maybe she was hurt and angry, maybe she was protecting Johnny, maybe she got her dates muddled. Maybe it was all of the above; we have the rest of our lives to speculate.' This she said with an air of weary sophistication, cracking an egg into a bowl with a terrible lack of skill.

'You think she'd been to bed with both of them?' I said.

She gave me a peculiar smile that contained something looking like sympathy.

'But a married Major and a lowly coal boy,' she said. 'Father would have bust a nut.'

'I still don't understand,' I said, piping up with further questions, 'why she didn't tell you about Johnny. You wouldn't have told anyone, would you?'

'Because she loved me,' said Aunt C. 'Look in my Commonplace.'

'But I've read your Commonplace, there's nothing in there to tell me.'

'Go back and look at the letter I wrote to Johnny when he was sent to the front.'

'I've read that too, it's a nice letter, very newsy.'

'I wrote it at the time of censors and snoopers and spies,' she continued. 'I felt unsafe in many ways, to expose my true feelings, so I decided to write it in a code. That way I could be certain I could say what I wanted without Johnny understanding my message. It was just something I wanted to express without the consequences of *anyone* knowing, just my own little secret to treasure in the privacy of my thoughts. Father and Doctor John used to communicate with each other in a code, so I just borrowed their idea. I decided that the first word of every fourth sentence should spell out another sentence. I *think* you'll find it on Aug 12 1944, if I'm not mistaken . . .'

*

Some time later after old flames had been recollected, we were sitting down to eat the cake, when suddenly Aunt C bellowed, 'Stop! No, wait!' she said. 'We never take them alive.'

For the Admiral had forgotten himself and was about to hoover a spider. I think, compared to the mystical Johnny, that the Admiral is somewhat an unlikely possibility for Aunt Coral. But a possibility in itself is obviously no bad thing. And Aunt Coral thrives on possibilities, almost more than on realities. Maybe if she grows to be fascinated about parking spots, and the Admiral becomes more romantic and learns some respect for spiders – maybe then they'll be one of those couples who've been friends for years and then suddenly marry. Whereas someone like Admiral Ted did it the other way round, and was married for centuries before spending the rest of his days with the cricket. And someone like my mother had what they call a clandestine relationship, which means hidden, and someone like Nana Cameo had only the briefest passions, and before any of these things happened, they were all just possibilities, and I think I agree with Aunt C, that possibilities can be preferable to outcomes.

Coral's Commonplace: Volume 5
Green Place, Jan 6 1988
(Age 65 but look older!)

A new year, a new illness. My ear has erupted with a savage gunge, and there is no doctor unless it's an emergency. During a fitful sleep I dreamt Green Place was a college, of Romance, Literature and Chivalry; Father wouldn't approve. Nor would he have approved had I kept Sue's inheritance. Talking of which – there's something I need to do. I will star it on my list.

I have spent many hours crying over the past week, as I have not cried for years. Johnny unlocked all my lost ones.

Sue asked me once: 'Why do you think we have a memory? Is it so we can remember who we are and how to get home, or is it so we can live on after we've died, in the memories of the people who love us?'

Dear me, she's too young for this sort of thing.

Still, it is a New Year and I shall not give into black dogs. The sun is burning like a giant strawberry in the sky, crimson as of 7am, and I have a date with the Admiral this afternoon, to walk into town for the band.

I wish I had known him longer, wish that when he looked at me, he recognised all these lines as visitors, remembering the radiant twenty-five-year-old I was, and always having that in mind when he sees me. I litter the place with snapshots of myself in my heyday, to display the full gallery of Corals he has not been acquainted with, but it doesn't have the same impact as long-term knowledge, or remembering. Perhaps Johnny might see me this way? But it seems his eyes were always for Cameo.

The difference between us has taken forty years to merge. If anything he looks the elder now. A woman of sixty-five and a man of sixty-three is nothing, but a girl of sixteen and a boy of fourteen, not so. And the difference between coal boy and Green Place girl is also not what it once was. Though we were not 'born equal', we have become equal through the small battles and triumphs of our own lives.

There goes Sue, she just walked down the drive in a peachy little outfit, her limbs full of bounce and vigour, and I find myself thinking that it will only take a few good nights' sleep, and the skipping of dinner, followed by a brisk run down the drive before I will look like that again too. But even if that were actually possible at sixty-five, I still want to eat and drink till I'm full and stay up late drinking cocktails. I remember I asked Father on his eightieth birthday, how it felt to be eighty, and he replied, 'I don't know.'

But I'm so glad Sue's been with me this past year. It's wonderful to live with the hope of youth, even though she has been to a dark place already. Her innocence, and her way of seeing the world as if she were an alien just landed. She makes me remember to wonder and to look.

'Each friend represents a world in us, a world possibly not born until they arrive, and it is only by this meeting that a new world is born.' (Anaïs Nin)

MOSCOW SLAMMER
(for the Common Cold with Ear Infection)

1 Boil: Fennel seeds, Methi seeds (from Indian shop), 6 lemons, chunk of ginger
2 Steep
3 Add honey

Drink at least 3 cups

After a few hours the patient shall feel much friskier and be able to get stuck into life.

A snapshot of the Egham borders

Early moon in the afternoon sky, ping pong in a distant garage. Fern fronds uncurling, carpets of snowdrops. Patches of bracken flanked by yesteryear hazel. I once pressed a switch from that hedgerow. I keep it in the back of my book and it often falls out when I open it, a little bit of 1930 in 1988, like the whisper of distant voices in this building, never to be forgotten.

To Do List
Make Will*
Pump tyres
Clear bat box
Sort briefs

Sue

I WENT TO Titford today to make amends. The town was basking in a morning of unseasonal sunshine which would no doubt be the subject of many a resident's diary. Dad said he thought it was because Ivana had brought it out; I had to hold myself back. I felt sad for them after the grandiosity of Green Place, with their little dishes and papery doors.

I didn't tell them anything about what I found in the locker – I expect they just thought I'd come round – but Dad was relieved and delighted we were speaking again, that was for certain. He kept on and on embracing me, as if I were a long-lost collie who'd been found at a neighbouring farm. He even seemed interested in my scholarship, and asked if I would read them my story.

Remembering Ivana's comments on my previous efforts I prefaced it: 'Please don't interrupt.'

'I will not,' Ivana said. 'I will listen and then I will say something.'

I read them 'Brackencliffe', from start to finish, glad that I'd decided to take it – I nearly didn't, because I didn't want to be disappointed if Dad hadn't wanted to know.

'The End,' I said as I reached it, and in unison they both decided to clap.

'That's wonderful darling!' said Dad. 'Why don't you ring up the bookshop?'

'What for?'

'To ask if they want to sell it.'

Sometimes I think that he has *no* idea how the world works.

'And I have cousin in Denmark,' said Ivana, 'who has poem in print in a book.'

I do believe they were trying, but somehow they always manage to put out my fire.

After an eternity Ivana left Dad and me alone and we did some hard talking and fast, assuming she would not be away very long. I said I was sorry for missing the wedding and for rifling through his correspondence. Then he revealed something that completely blew all of my preconceptions out of the water: he had known about Mr Edgeley – but Mum hadn't *known* that he knew.

How can husbands and wives not know such glaring enormous things about each other? Yet they share the same bed, the same fridge, the same table. Aunt Coral is right that you never really know a person.

'Does Aileen know?' I said, jumping ahead into the ripples in the pond.

'I don't—'

He mimed zipping up his mouth as Ivana returned with some snacks. It was something Danish on specialist un-bread which Dad found dangerously nice.

We resumed our conversation again later, when Ivana had taken the plates to the kitchen.

'Why didn't you tell me?' I asked.

'I wanted to, but you wouldn't talk to me. I did try.'

'Why did Mrs Edgeley give you that birthday card?'

'I think perhaps she found out and thought she should let me know. And Sue, there's something else. Ivana's having a baby.'

Ivana's having a baby. It was like being concussed by four little words.

'She's having a baby? Are you sure it's yours?'

'Of course it's mine! Come on darling, you're going to have a sibling!'

'Congratulations!' I said, but I didn't feel like celebrating.

One is expected in such instances to take these things in one's stride, behave in a grown-up way, at the same time as your whole world turns upside down and you have to re-identify yourself.

'Congratulations,' I said when Ivana came back. 'Dad's just told me your news.'

'Thank you. I was worried, you know, because in the last chance salon you must act.'

Their news made me think. It is odd the way that families develop traditions such as age gaps. I'd always wanted a sibling, but of course, one that was born of my Mum.

Aileen rang, very late after I got back to Green Place, and we talked about her father and my mother. Of course Aileen had guessed.

'Your Mum did that over my Dad. I'm so sorry,' she said.

'No, it was a build-up, there were many reasons,' I said. 'I've accepted as much. And with all the limitations of her seriousness, I know that she did her best.'

'Yes, of course she did,' she said, like she was talking about someone who'd just popped out to pick up the milk. I'm almost certain she hadn't understood what I meant.

Then I told her about Johnny Look-at-the-Moon, and she couldn't believe it! I have to agree that it's not often you find your vagabond Grandpa hiding in your dead Nana's room.

Aileen had her own revelations to tell me about in her love life. She has found a new love, who is, of all things, a bricklayer. (It must have brought back memories.)

I still don't know why out of all the people on earth Mum would have chosen Mr Edgeley. But Aunt Coral says that one can never really know the secret place that is a relationship.

Everything is new, everything old has gone. Different mother, new sibling, new Grandpa – I feel as though I am walking backwards with my socks on back to front.

Aunt C and I had a tussle about mum's money. She wasn't very comfortable that I had paid Glenn, and straight after the gala night she apologised to him and asked him to put it all back in my bank account. She insisted she couldn't keep it. I insisted she must. So, we have now come to an agreement that it is a *loan*, and I am keeping just one kay up front so that I can go on the course. The rest of the money has now been transferred full circle back to Glenn for the works. He is a little confused and bamboozled, and only had two words to say, which were: 'Blimey!' and 'Women!'

Aunt C has since been a whirlwind, planning the reappointments to five of six target bedrooms. If Green Place is going to support itself she will need to use the good suites, and with the nine kay left from mum, which is now officially a loan, she should be able to do it – if she doesn't paint the walls in gold leaf.

She has yet to do up Cameo's room, but the door was officially opened as of New Year's Day. When I went in I realised that there was nothing so mournful behind that door, beyond the usual spots of grumbling plaster and a tan patch of damp here and there. It just looks dingy and tired and smells of sad old dust. A two-seater bench with soft cushions stands empty in the window. It has a bird's eye view of the buddleia.

My eye rolled round the room, like a camera over the past. The bed-cover was bleached thin from the sun, and the coal smudge was as clear as day, which, if you think of it soulfully, heralds the beginning of my creation. Cameo's dollies were still on the bed and I swear that one of them was looking at me, afraid I might take it to the garden and bury it.

'You can only shut the door for so long,' I said.

'There's a lot of truth in that,' said Aunt Coral.

But I think she was actually meaning that while there was a lot of truth in it, there was also a bit of a lie – it could have easily stayed shut for ever, because forgetfulness can be blissful.

'You're never going to become one of those ladies who resents sharing her home with strangers are you?' I asked her.

'Not even with visitors I didn't know were here!' she said.

'I wonder if Johnny has ever realised what your letter truly says?'

'He might do some day,' she said, merrily.

'I admire your joy de vivre, I don't think I'd ever be as carefree about Icarus finding out I had a thing with his eye,' I said.

'Or Joe,' she said, flashing me a cheeky wink. 'Anyway,' she continued, reversing back to the earlier subject, 'I like having people around the place, it's a big empty house without them. We have a Mr Hart from Texas arriving today, a colleague of Mr Tsunawa, and a Hugh from Chertsey has telephoned to say he has recently been divorced.'

'They all seem to be men,' I said.

'Do they?' said Aunt Coral.

I woke up this morning with a speck of carrier bag on my face, though how it got there is yet another question.

For leaving presents I bought Aunt C an unnecessary handbag, pink leather with charms. I nearly didn't give it to her; it would have looked so good on my course, but she loves it because it has multiple pockets to fissel in.

The EHG had a whip-round so that I have some money for unnecessaries.

'You must do it for Group!' they said in their card.

Aunt C laid out some things on my bed to pack: lotions, bikini, sarong and some exercises she had designed especially for the Greek climate and written down for me.

There were also some openers for me to finish which I am already eager to start:

```
She unpacked put on a clean white shirt and
fresh lipstick . . .
```

```
'I always buy my wedding dresses here,' said
Margo Chinnery. . . .
```

Joe arrived a few hours ago carrying Mrs Fry's sponge bag with his toothbrush and overnight things, looking for all the world like Atlas, who carried the earth on his shoulders. He is going to take me to the airport early tomorrow morning.

'Three months is no time,' he said. 'It'll be gone in the twinkling of an eye.'

It was a brotherly thing to say but he is much, much more than a brother.

'Thank you Joe, go lightly,' I said. I don't really know what I meant, but I think I was trying to stop myself spilling the beans on my heart.

Joe put a note in my pyjamas, which I found when I got here. It was written on the unused side of an already written card:

> *Glad you liked these Sue, it was my pleasure. Joe X*

And on the used side it said:

> *Dear Visitor,*
>
> *Thank you very much for the flowers. I hope you have everything that you need.*
>
> *With all best wishes,*
>
> *Sue*

They were from Joe all along! Ho! I'm so gullible. I am struck by the unknown effect a person can have on someone's life, maybe I have effected Joe.

It's easy to see Aunt Coral's effect on mine; who knows what would have happened without her. One thing leads to another and the consequences are endless. We can be gods to each other and not know it, though I hope that she might guess.

It's turning-in time now at Taverna O'Carroll, on the beach at Shabany Bay. The upstairs windows of my dormitory are dittled and dottled with the droppings of Grecian seagulls. Creamy stars pop outside in a twilight of pacific blue. 'Pacific' is one of my best-loved words, not only because of the colour but because of what it means – a lustrous ocean packed with mermaids, like silk flowing out to paradise, and those words flow out to other words – to briny, white horses and seashore, words you might not be experiencing at the time and so carry a tinge of longing. 'Joe' flows out to dinner, candlelight, man and boy . . . 'Aunt Coral' flows out to home, to cave, shelter, slippers and nightie . . .

But how strange, I thought I just saw mum walking on the sea in the sweep of a ship's searchlight. She was wearing a kaftan made of rainbows and she was giant, like a legend. The sea air plays tricks, I think.

Coral's Commonplace: Volume 4
Green Place, 15 Jan 1970

Received a telegram from Buddleia and Nick!

```
15 JAN 1970. 6AM GMT IN THE CAR! GIRL. SUSAN OLIVIA
7LBS 4. ALL WELL. THE MEANING OF SUSAN IS 'LILY'
WHICH ALSO MEANS 'JOY OF LIFE'.
```

Acknowledgements

Warmest thanks to my literary agent extraordinaire, Charlotte Robertson. And also to my editor Katy Loftus and to Linda Evans and the team at Transworld publishers, for all their wonderful advice and encouragement and for everything that has gone into bringing this book to life.

To my husband, Sean Carson, for the great gift of all his encouragement and inspiration, thank you. To my Dad, Allen Crowe, and to Roddy Maude-Roxby, for sharing stories and memories of World War Two. To Lizzie Knight, for reading so many drafts and for unceasing hospitality, inspiration, and roast potatoes. Also to Janet Crowe, Siobhan McCallum and Sue Holderness, for their patience and generosity in reading early drafts. To Robin, Siobhan, Mia and Guy McCallum, for all their inspiration and, not least, for allowing me to include some of their best and most wonderful coinages. To Mark Gatiss and Ian Hallard for all their encouragement and support. To Tamsin and Rick Leaf and to Nat, Jakob and Roxie Leaf for all the funny things that they say.

And to: Deborah Crowe, Jeni Hayes, Jim and Anne Carson, Ida and Bill Cochrane, Jessie-May Perry, Annie Michael, Liza Goddard, Michael Hobbs, Angela Annesley and the great many friends who have inspired and helped me along the way. For as the old Chinese Proverb says:

> 'When Eating Bamboo shoots, remember the man who planted them'

Last but not least, I acknowledge most of all how much I owe to my Dad, Allen, and to my late Mother, Neta, who told me that as a child she thought scruples were little people who lived under the stairs, and that therefore an unscrupulous person was a person who lived in a flat. I would like to express my deep gratitude that she was such a very special source of help to me, and still is even now in the treasure of my memory.

Books that I read when researching:

England's Lost Houses, by Giles Worsley, (2011; Aurum Press)
The Imperial Russian Dinner Service; a Story of a famous work by Josiah Wedgwood, by Dr. George C. Williamson, (1909; George Bell and Sons)
Folk Wines, Cordials and Brandies, by Moritz A Jagendorf, (1963; Vanguard Press) (the recipe for Brown Bettys)
The Book of Decorative Furniture, by Edwin Foley, (1911; T.C. & E.C. Jack)